Garfield®

SEARCH FOR POOKY

BY JIM DAVIS

ROSS RICHIE CEO & Founder • MATT GAGNON Editor-in-Chief • FILIP SABLIK President of Publishing & Marketing • STEPHEN CHRISTY President of Development • LANCE KREITER VP of Licensing & Merchandising • PHIL BARBARO VP of Finance • ARUNE SINGH VP of Marketing • BRYCE CARLSON Managing Editor • MEL CAYLO Marketing Manager • SCOTT NEWMAN Production Design Manager • KATE HENNING Operations Manager • SIERRA HAHN Senior Editor • DAFNA PLEBAN Editor, Talent Development • SHANNON WATTERS Editor • ERIC HARBURN Editor • WHITNEY LEOPARD Editor • CAMERON CHITTOCK Editor • CHRIS ROSA Associate Editor • MATTHEW LEVINE Associate Editor • SOPHIE PHILIPS-ROBERTS Assistant Editor • AMANDA LaFRANCO Executive Assistant • KATALINA HOLLAND Editorial Administrative Assistant • JILLIAN CRAB Production Designer • MICHELLE ANKLEY Production Designer • KARA LEOPARD Production Designer • MARIE KRUPINA Production Designer • GRACE PARK Production Design Assistant • CHELSEA ROBERTS Production Design Assistant • ELIZABETH LOUGHRIDGE Accounting Coordinator • STEPHANIE HOCUTT Social Media Coordinator • JOSÉ MEZA Event Coordinator • HOLLY AITCHISON Operations Coordinator • MEGAN CHRISTOPHER Operations Assistant • RODRIGO HERNANDEZ Mailroom Assistant • MORGAN PERRY Direct Market Representative • CAT O'GRADY Marketing Assistant • LIZ ALMENDAREZ Accounting Administrative Assistant • CORNELIA TZANA Administrative Assistant

kaboom!™

BOOM! Studios, 5670 Wilshire Boulevard, Suite 400, Los Angeles, CA 90036-5679. Printed in China. First Printing.

ISBN: 978-1-68415-143-1, eISBN: 978-1-61398-882-4

CONTENTS

"LITTLE BEAR LOST"
WRITTEN BY SCOTT NICKEL
ILLUSTRATED BY ANTONIO ALFARO
COLORED BY LISA MOORE

"PRINCESS PRISCILLA"
WRITTEN BY MARK EVANIER
ILLUSTRATED BY ANTONIO ALFARO
COLORED BY LISA MOORE

"FRIENDLY FOE"
WRITTEN & ILLUSTRATED BY ERIN HUNTING

LETTERED BY JIM CAMPBELL

COVER BY ANDY HIRSCH

DESIGNER GRACE PARK
ASSOCIATE EDITOR CHRIS ROSA
EDITOR WHITNEY LEOPARD

GARFIELD CREATED BY
JIM DAVIS

SPECIAL THANKS TO JIM DAVIS AND THE ENTIRE PAWS, INC. TEAM.

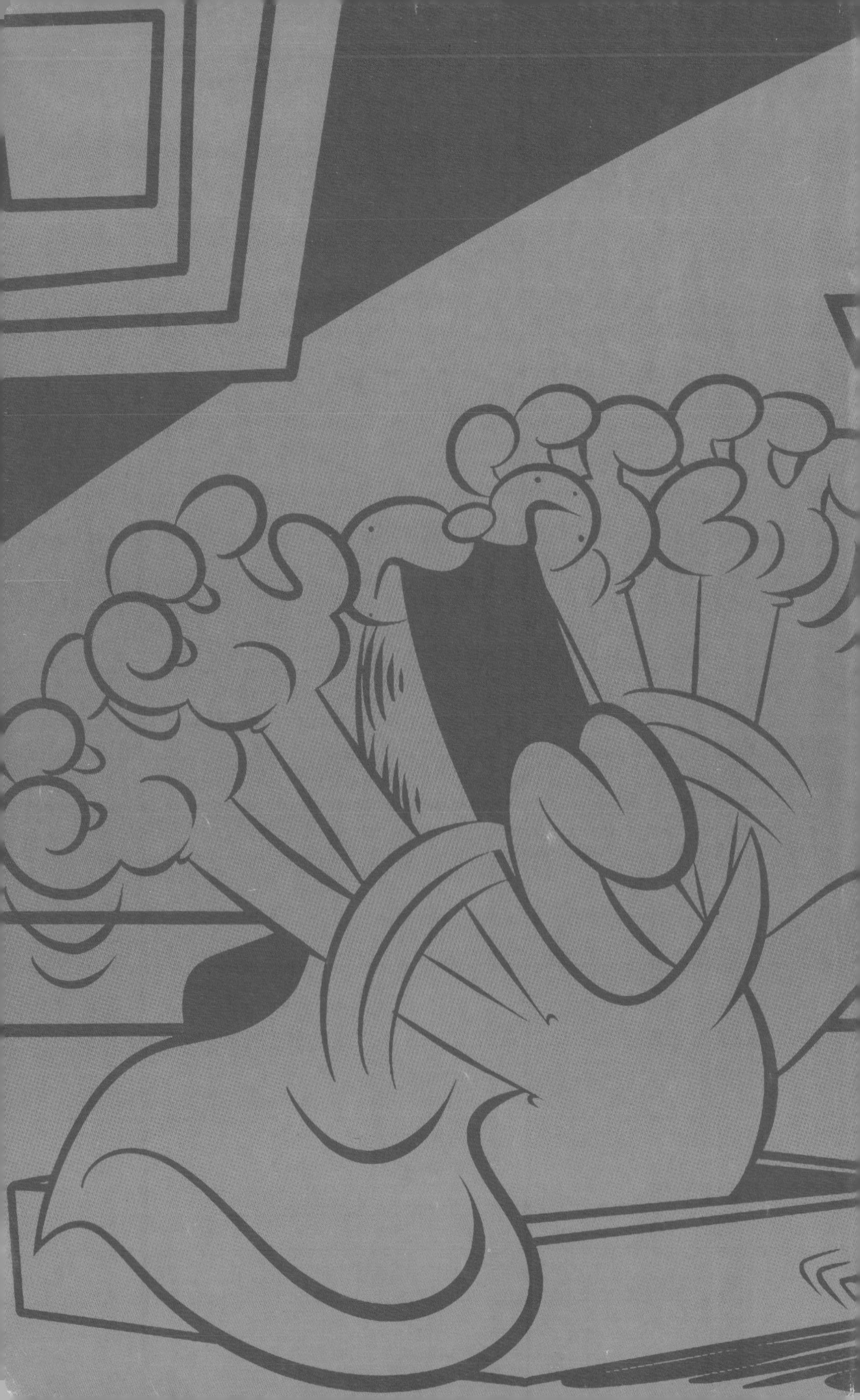

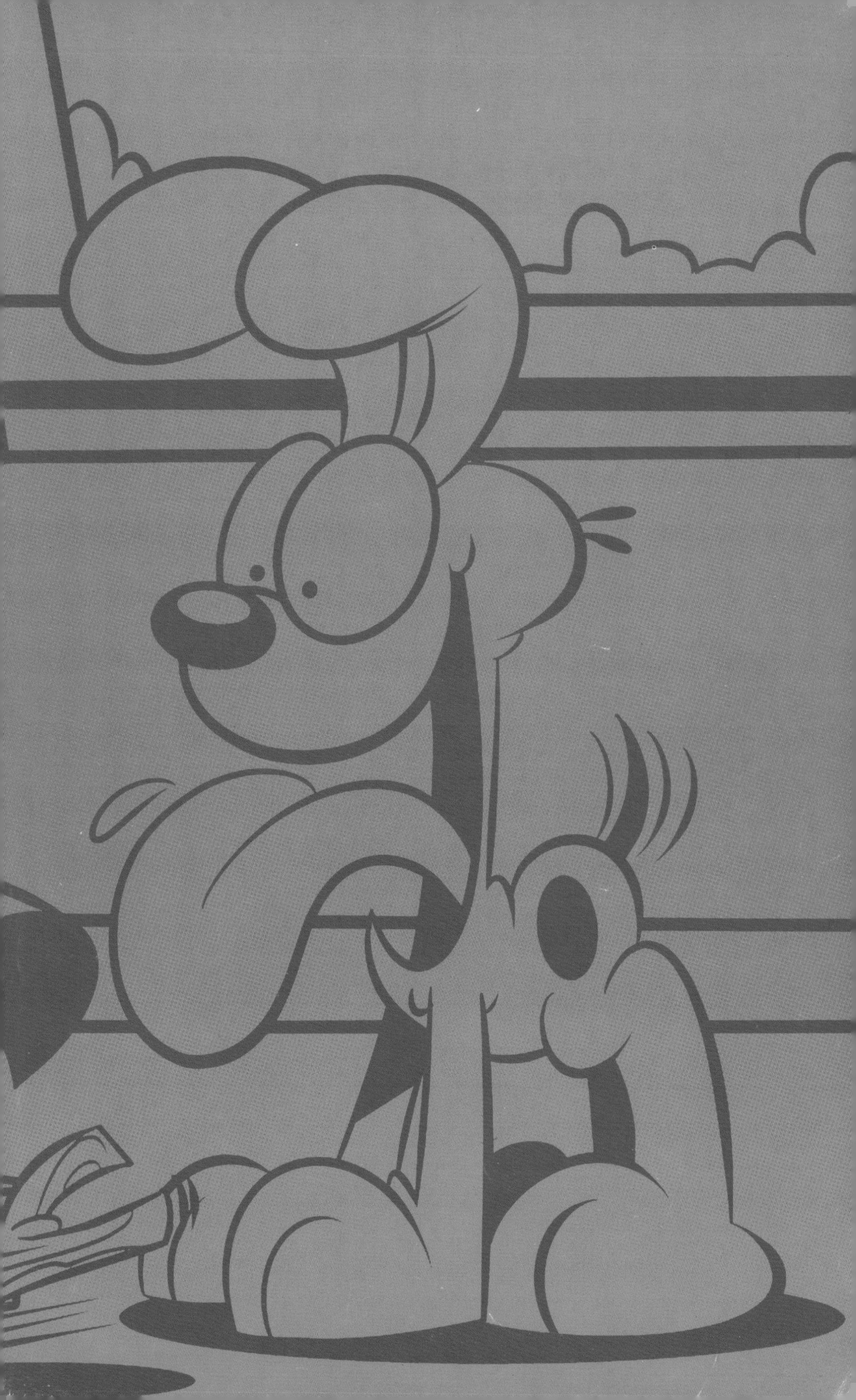

"LITTLE BEAR LOST"

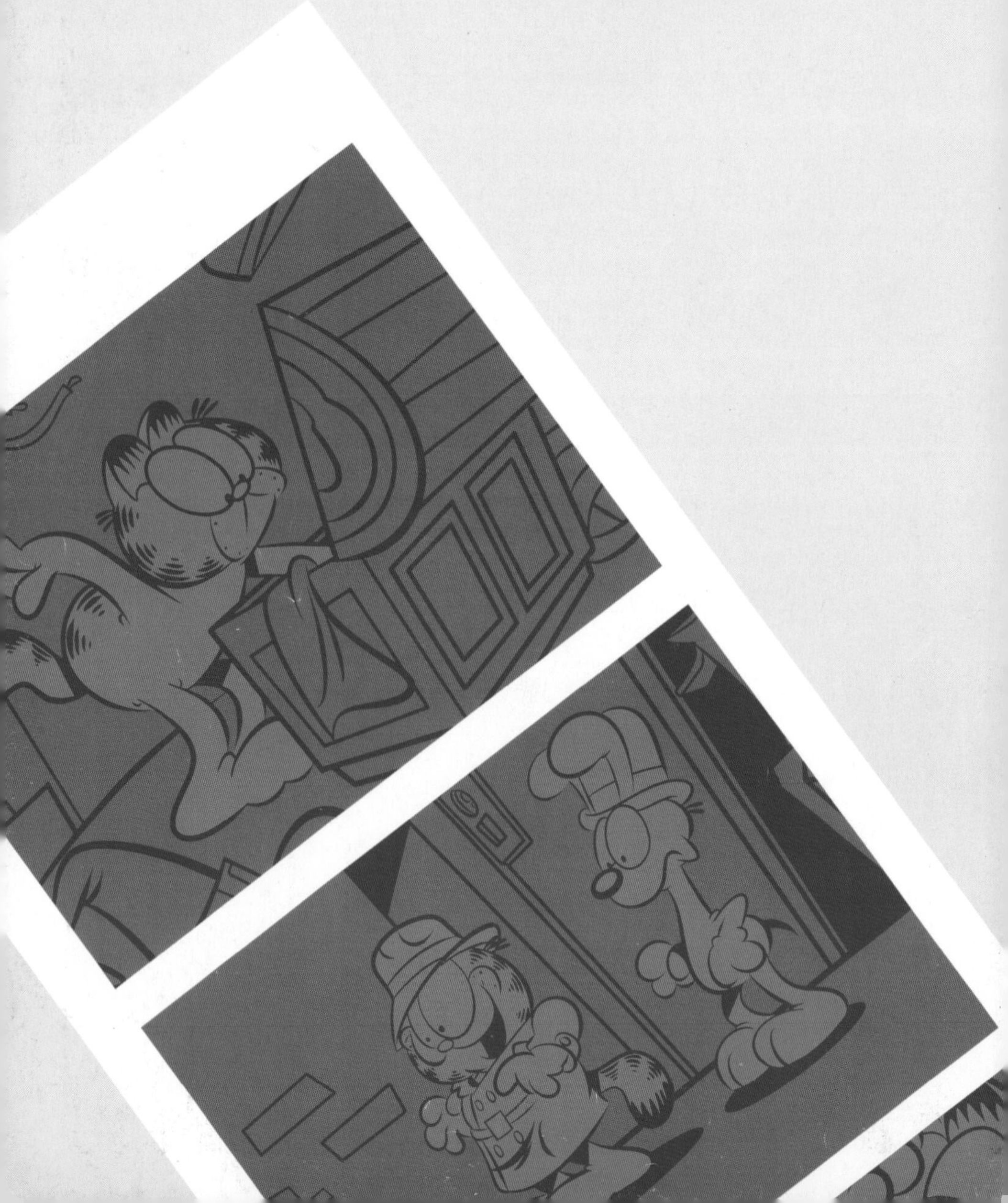

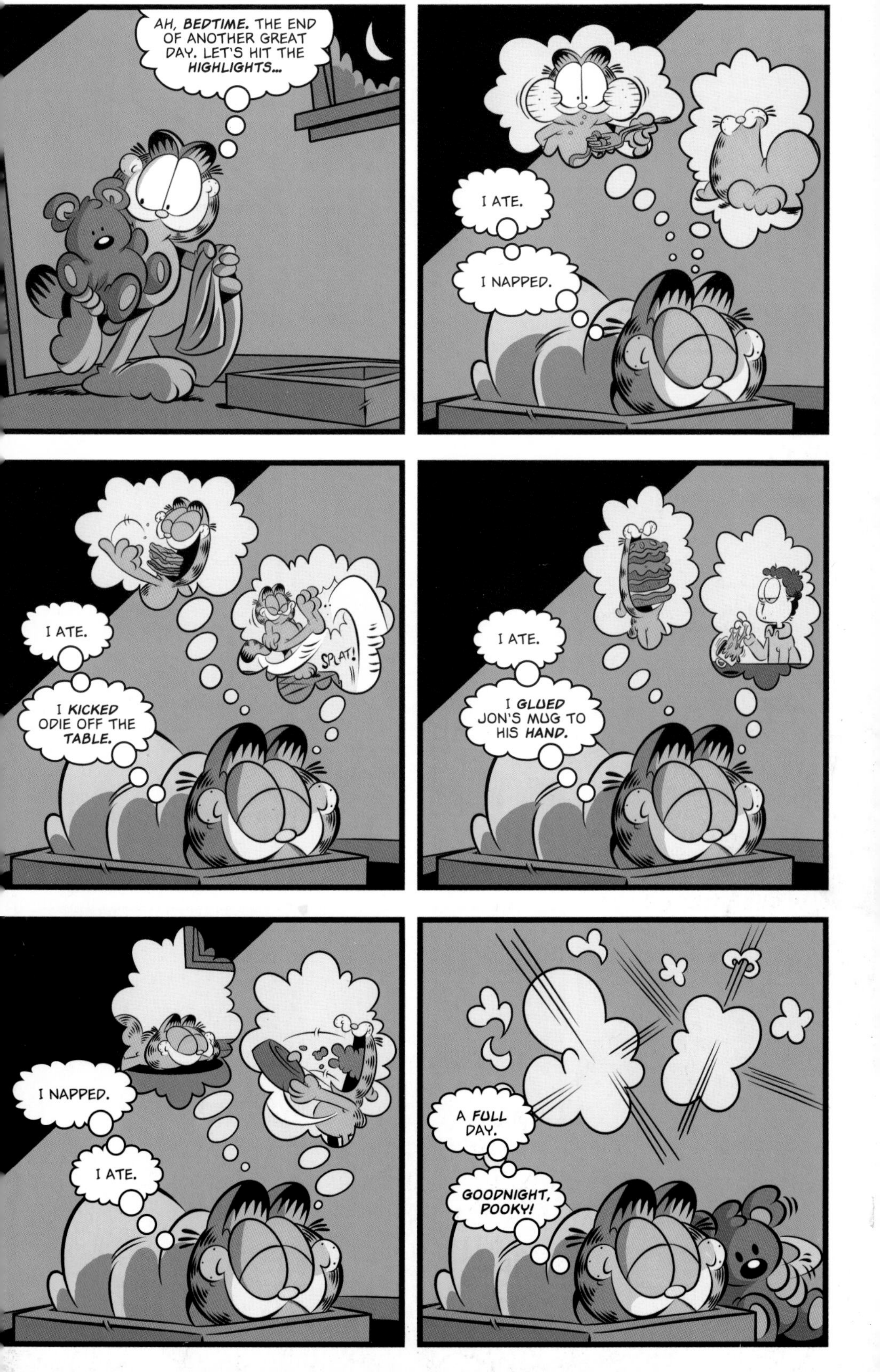
AH, BEDTIME. THE END OF ANOTHER GREAT DAY. LET'S HIT THE HIGHLIGHTS...
I ATE.
I NAPPED.
I ATE.
SPLAT!
I KICKED ODIE OFF THE TABLE.
I ATE.
I GLUED JON'S MUG TO HIS HAND.
I NAPPED.
I ATE.
A FULL DAY.
GOODNIGHT, POOKY!

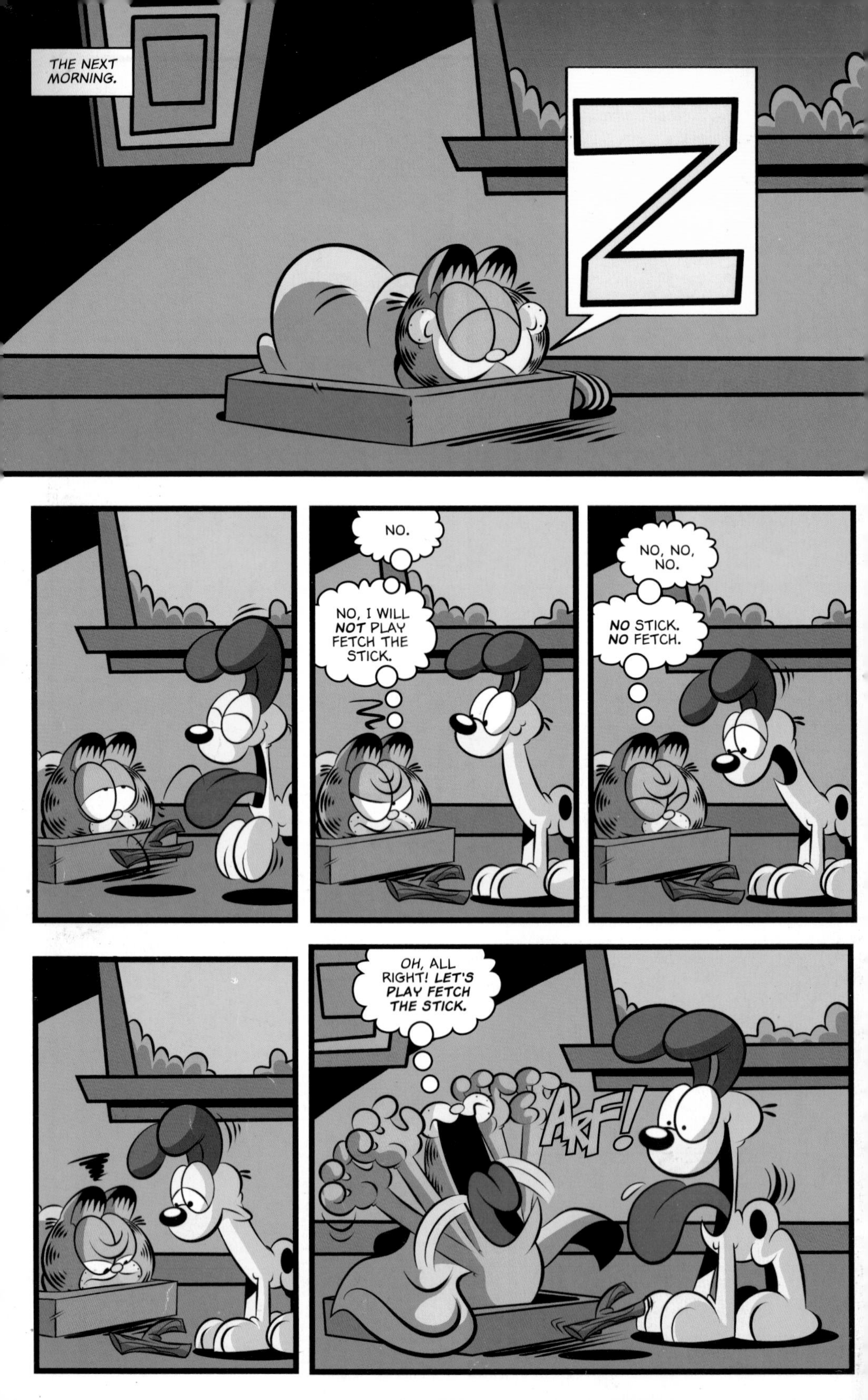
THE NEXT MORNING.
Z
NO.
NO, I WILL NOT PLAY FETCH THE STICK.
NO, NO, NO.
NO STICK. NO FETCH.
OH, ALL RIGHT! LET'S PLAY FETCH THE STICK.
ARF!

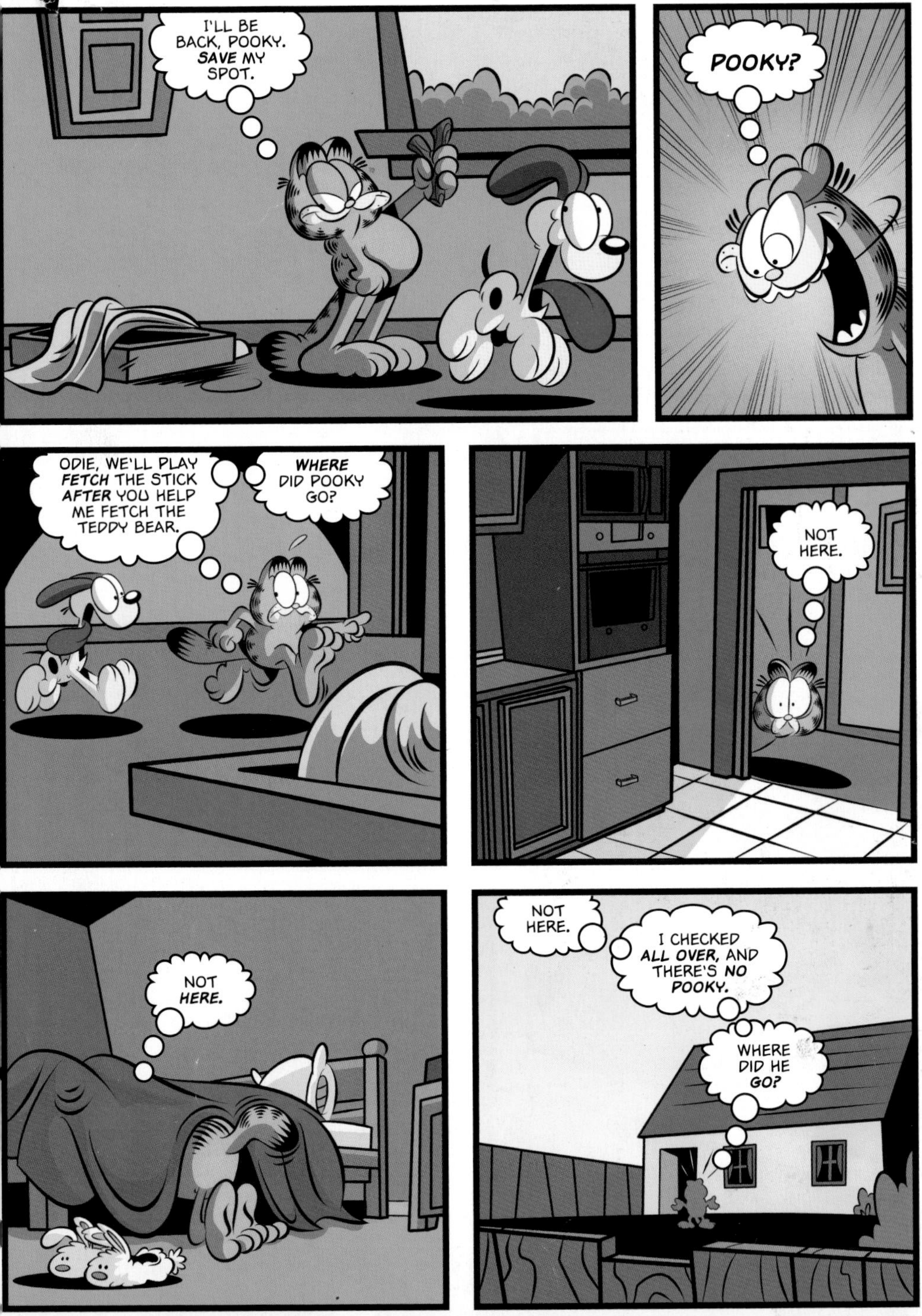
I'LL BE BACK, POOKY. SAVE MY SPOT.
POOKY?
ODIE, WE'LL PLAY FETCH THE STICK AFTER YOU HELP ME FETCH THE TEDDY BEAR.
WHERE DID POOKY GO?
NOT HERE.
NOT HERE.
NOT HERE.
I CHECKED ALL OVER, AND THERE'S NO POOKY.
WHERE DID HE GO?

LITTLE BEAR LOST

EIGHT HOURS EARLIER.

SEND ME TO ABU DHABI, WILL YOU?

WELL, IT'S TIME FOR A LITTLE *PAYBACK*, GARFIELD.

HOW WOULD YOU LIKE TO HAVE YOUR *BELOVED* TEDDY BEAR SENT TO *ABU DHABI*?

TO:

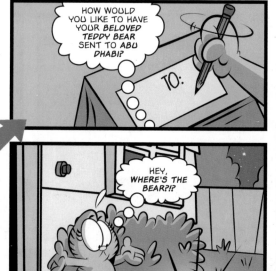

HEY, WHERE'S THE BEAR?!?

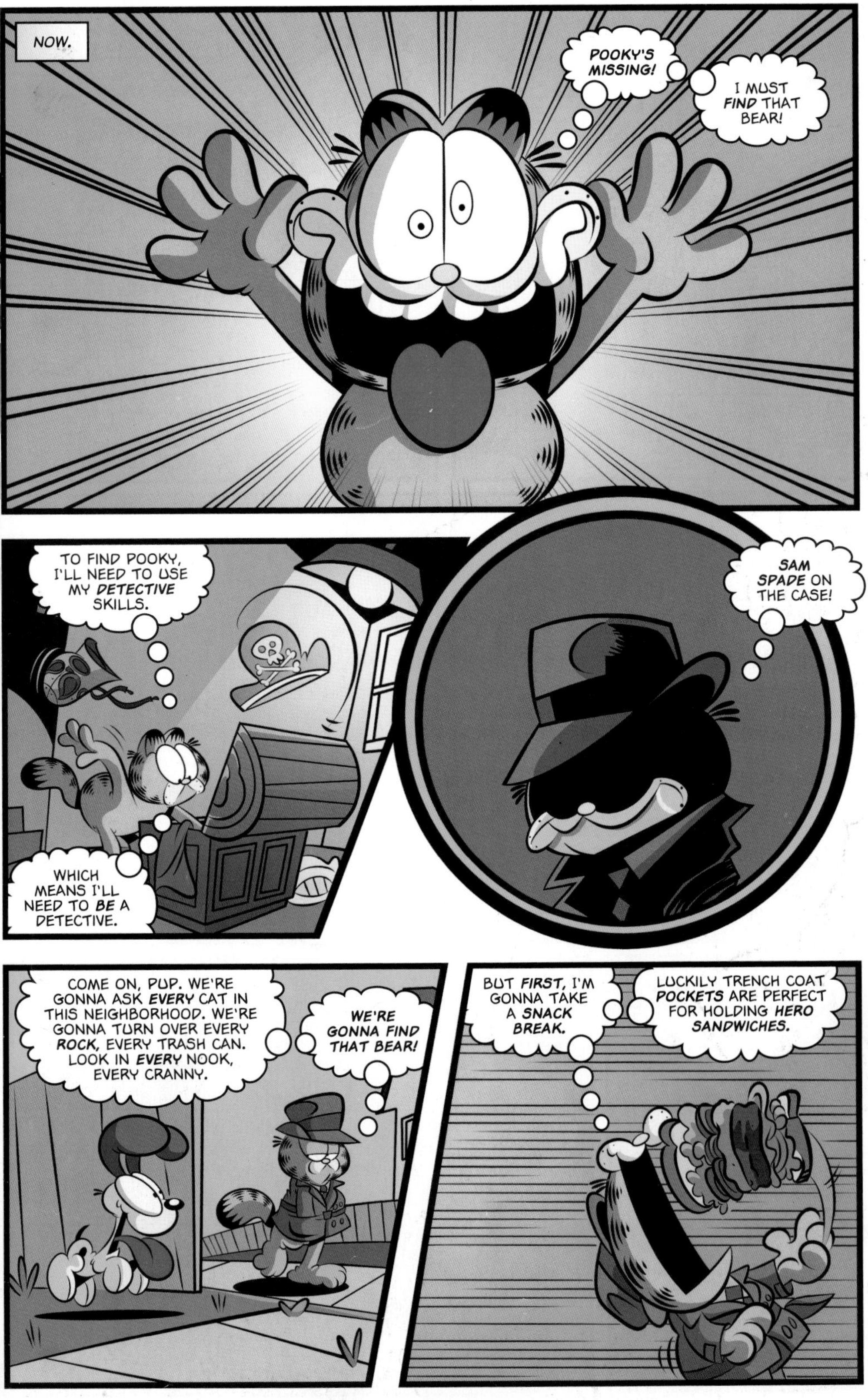
NOW.
POOKY'S MISSING!
I MUST FIND THAT BEAR!
TO FIND POOKY, I'LL NEED TO USE MY DETECTIVE SKILLS.
WHICH MEANS I'LL NEED TO BE A DETECTIVE.
SAM SPADE ON THE CASE!
COME ON, PUP. WE'RE GONNA ASK EVERY CAT IN THIS NEIGHBORHOOD. WE'RE GONNA TURN OVER EVERY ROCK, EVERY TRASH CAN. LOOK IN EVERY NOOK, EVERY CRANNY.
WE'RE GONNA FIND THAT BEAR!
BUT FIRST, I'M GONNA TAKE A SNACK BREAK.
LUCKILY TRENCH COAT POCKETS ARE PERFECT FOR HOLDING HERO SANDWICHES.

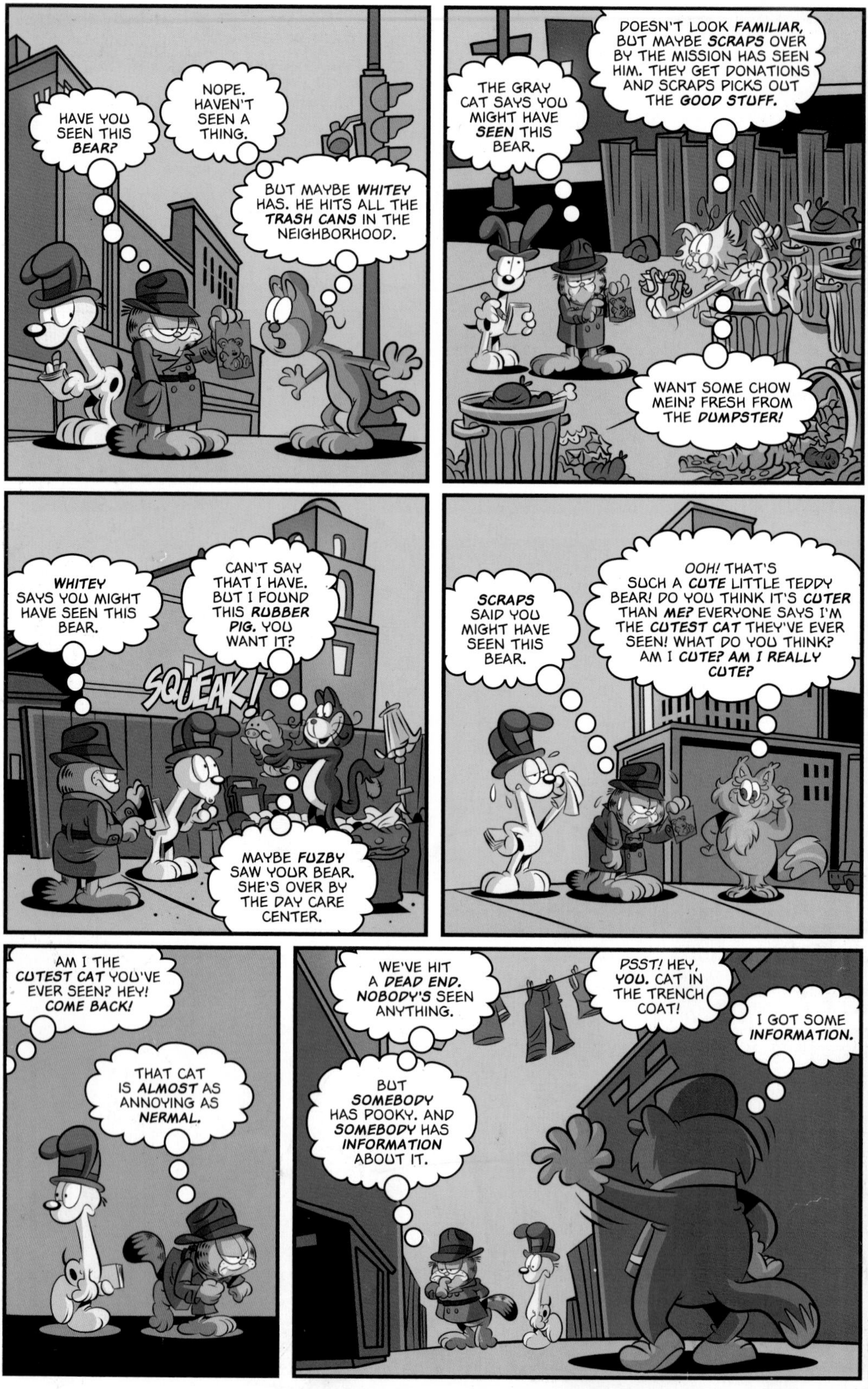
HAVE YOU SEEN THIS BEAR?
NOPE. HAVEN'T SEEN A THING.
BUT MAYBE WHITEY HAS. HE HITS ALL THE TRASH CANS IN THE NEIGHBORHOOD.
THE GRAY CAT SAYS YOU MIGHT HAVE SEEN THIS BEAR.
DOESN'T LOOK FAMILIAR, BUT MAYBE SCRAPS OVER BY THE MISSION HAS SEEN HIM. THEY GET DONATIONS AND SCRAPS PICKS OUT THE GOOD STUFF.
WANT SOME CHOW MEIN? FRESH FROM THE DUMPSTER!
WHITEY SAYS YOU MIGHT HAVE SEEN THIS BEAR.
CAN'T SAY THAT I HAVE. BUT I FOUND THIS RUBBER PIG. YOU WANT IT?
SQUEAK!
MAYBE FUZBY SAW YOUR BEAR. SHE'S OVER BY THE DAY CARE CENTER.
SCRAPS SAID YOU MIGHT HAVE SEEN THIS BEAR.
OOH! THAT'S SUCH A CUTE LITTLE TEDDY BEAR! DO YOU THINK IT'S CUTER THAN ME? EVERYONE SAYS I'M THE CUTEST CAT THEY'VE EVER SEEN! WHAT DO YOU THINK? AM I CUTE? AM I REALLY CUTE?
AM I THE CUTEST CAT YOU'VE EVER SEEN? HEY! COME BACK!
THAT CAT IS ALMOST AS ANNOYING AS NERMAL.
WE'VE HIT A DEAD END. NOBODY'S SEEN ANYTHING.
BUT SOMEBODY HAS POOKY. AND SOMEBODY HAS INFORMATION ABOUT IT.
PSST! HEY, YOU. CAT IN THE TRENCH COAT!
I GOT SOME INFORMATION.

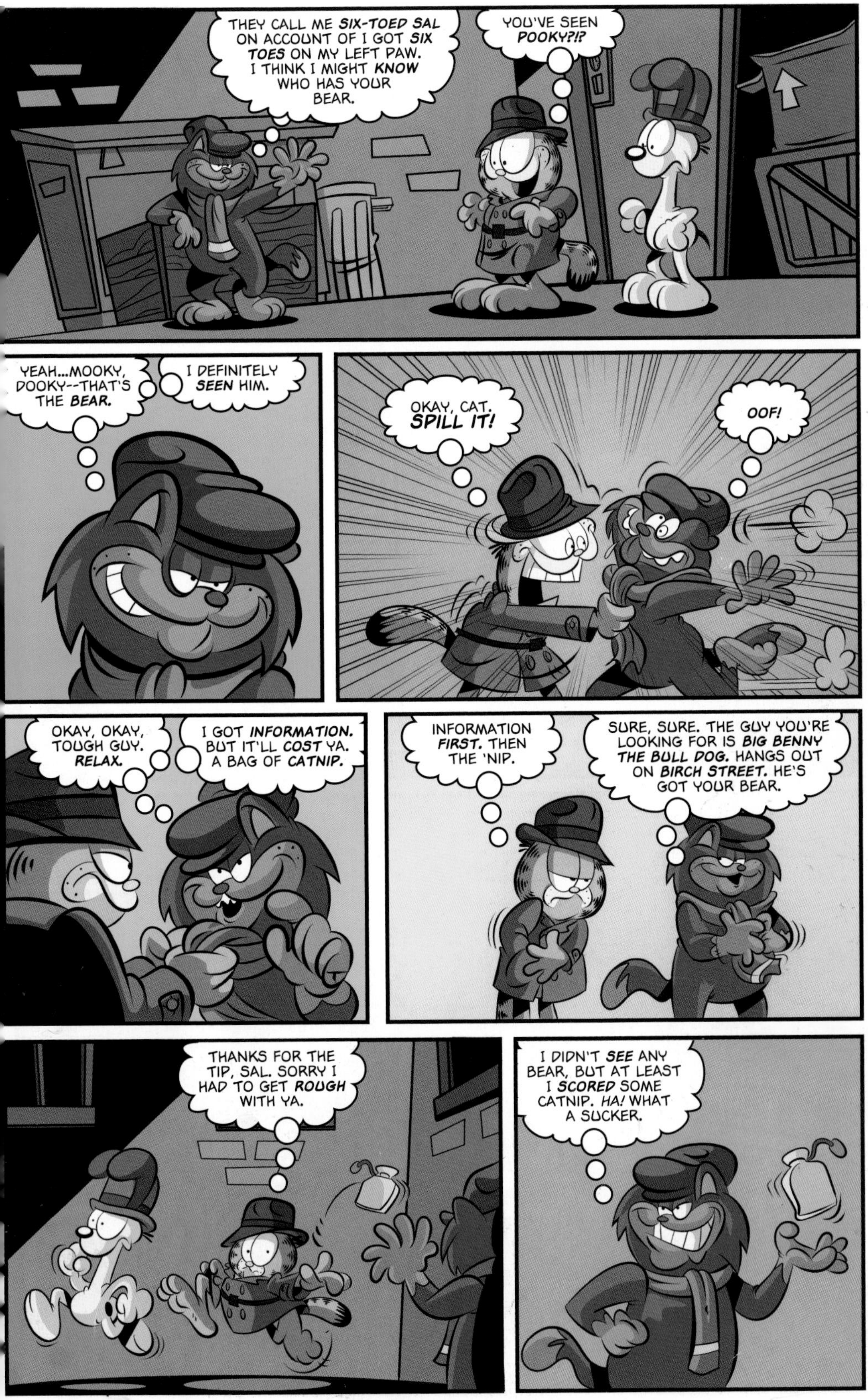
THEY CALL ME SIX-TOED SAL ON ACCOUNT OF I GOT SIX TOES ON MY LEFT PAW. I THINK I MIGHT KNOW WHO HAS YOUR BEAR.
YOU'VE SEEN POOKY?!?
YEAH...MOOKY, DOOKY--THAT'S THE BEAR.
I DEFINITELY SEEN HIM.
OKAY, CAT. SPILL IT!
OOF!
OKAY, OKAY, TOUGH GUY. RELAX.
I GOT INFORMATION. BUT IT'LL COST YA. A BAG OF CATNIP.
INFORMATION FIRST. THEN THE 'NIP.
SURE, SURE. THE GUY YOU'RE LOOKING FOR IS BIG BENNY THE BULL DOG. HANGS OUT ON BIRCH STREET. HE'S GOT YOUR BEAR.
THANKS FOR THE TIP, SAL. SORRY I HAD TO GET ROUGH WITH YA.
I DIDN'T SEE ANY BEAR, BUT AT LEAST I SCORED SOME CATNIP. HA! WHAT A SUCKER.

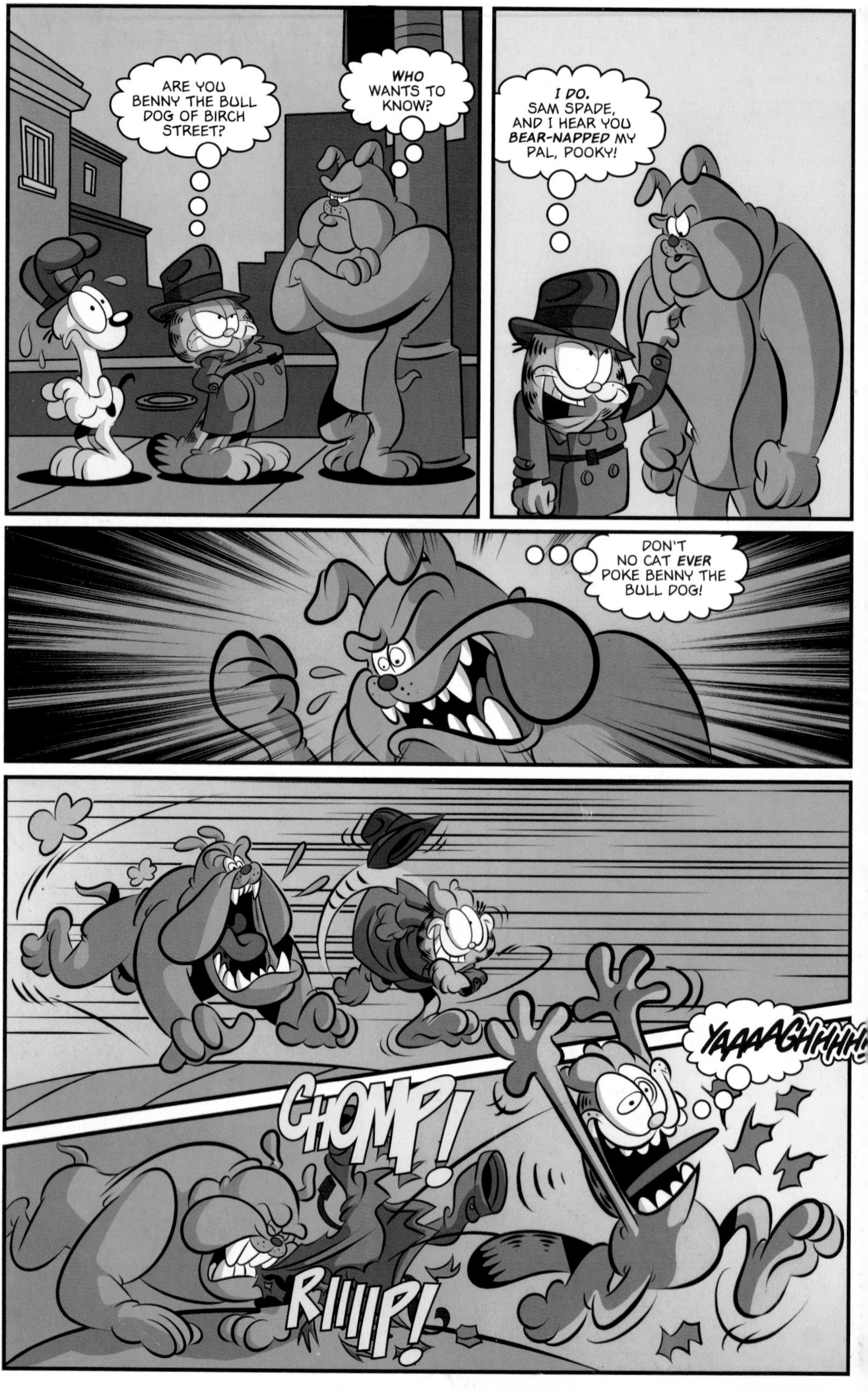
ARE YOU BENNY THE BULL DOG OF BIRCH STREET?
WHO WANTS TO KNOW?
I DO. SAM SPADE, AND I HEAR YOU BEAR-NAPPED MY PAL, POOKY!
DON'T NO CAT EVER POKE BENNY THE BULL DOG!
YAAAAGHHHH!
CHOMP!
RIIIIP!

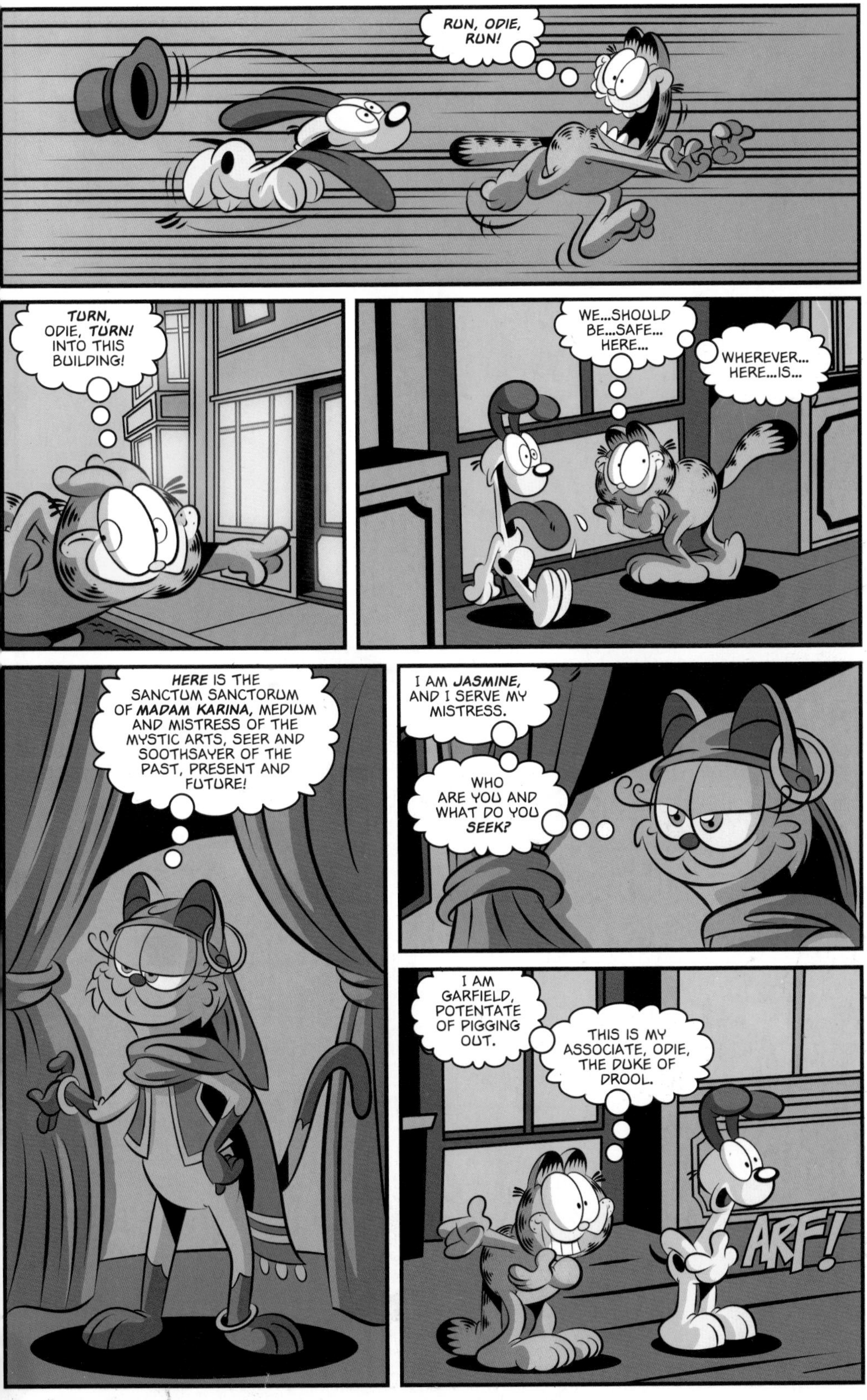
RUN, ODIE, RUN!
TURN, ODIE, TURN! INTO THIS BUILDING!
WE...SHOULD BE...SAFE... HERE...
WHEREVER... HERE...IS...
HERE IS THE SANCTUM SANCTORUM OF MADAM KARINA, MEDIUM AND MISTRESS OF THE MYSTIC ARTS, SEER AND SOOTHSAYER OF THE PAST, PRESENT AND FUTURE!
I AM JASMINE, AND I SERVE MY MISTRESS.
WHO ARE YOU AND WHAT DO YOU SEEK?
I AM GARFIELD, POTENTATE OF PIGGING OUT.
THIS IS MY ASSOCIATE, ODIE, THE DUKE OF DROOL.
ARF!

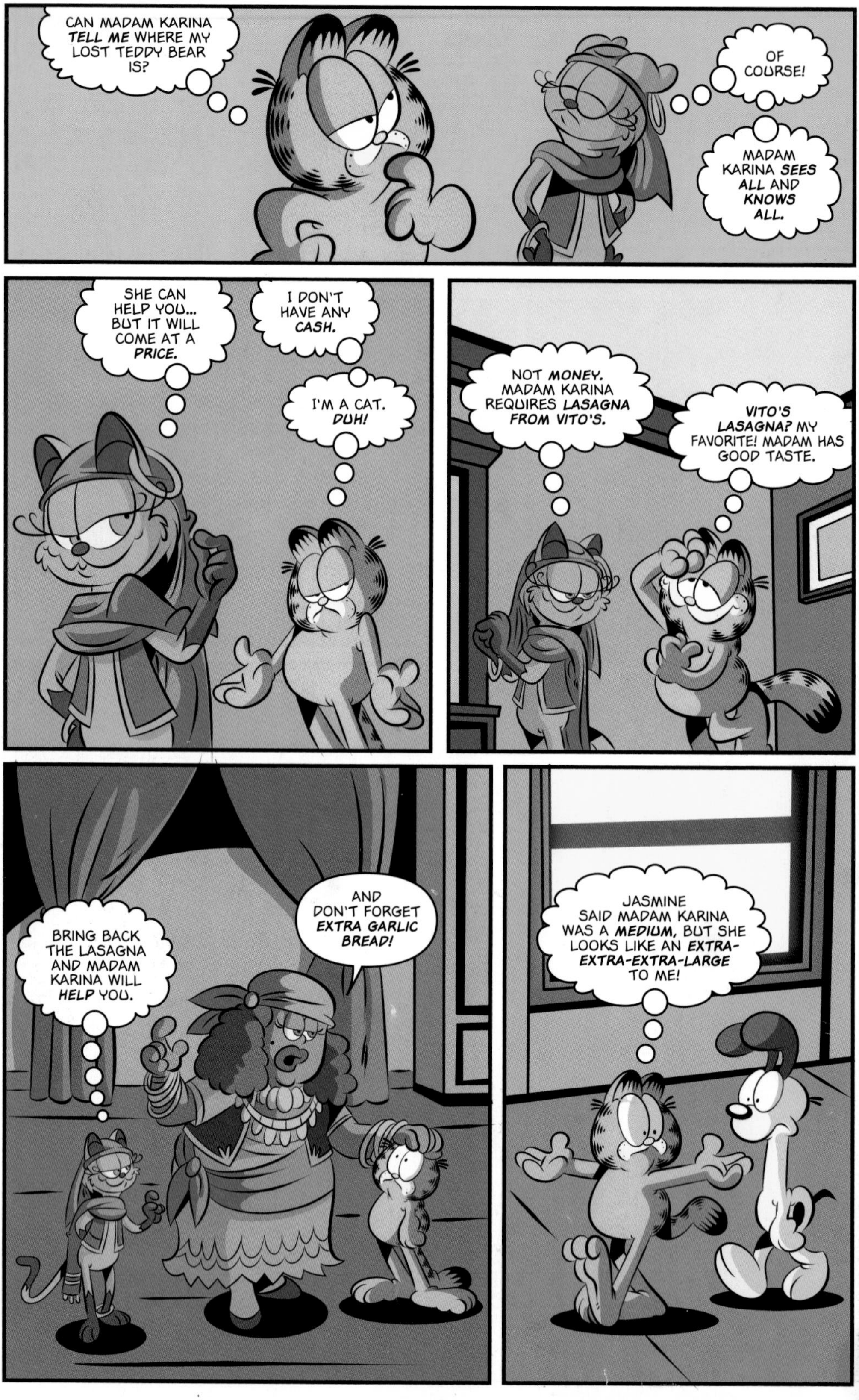
CAN MADAM KARINA TELL ME WHERE MY LOST TEDDY BEAR IS?
OF COURSE!
MADAM KARINA SEES ALL AND KNOWS ALL.
SHE CAN HELP YOU... BUT IT WILL COME AT A PRICE.
I DON'T HAVE ANY CASH.
I'M A CAT. DUH!
NOT MONEY. MADAM KARINA REQUIRES LASAGNA FROM VITO'S.
VITO'S LASAGNA? MY FAVORITE! MADAM HAS GOOD TASTE.
BRING BACK THE LASAGNA AND MADAM KARINA WILL HELP YOU.
AND DON'T FORGET EXTRA GARLIC BREAD!
JASMINE SAID MADAM KARINA WAS A MEDIUM, BUT SHE LOOKS LIKE AN EXTRA-EXTRA-EXTRA-LARGE TO ME!

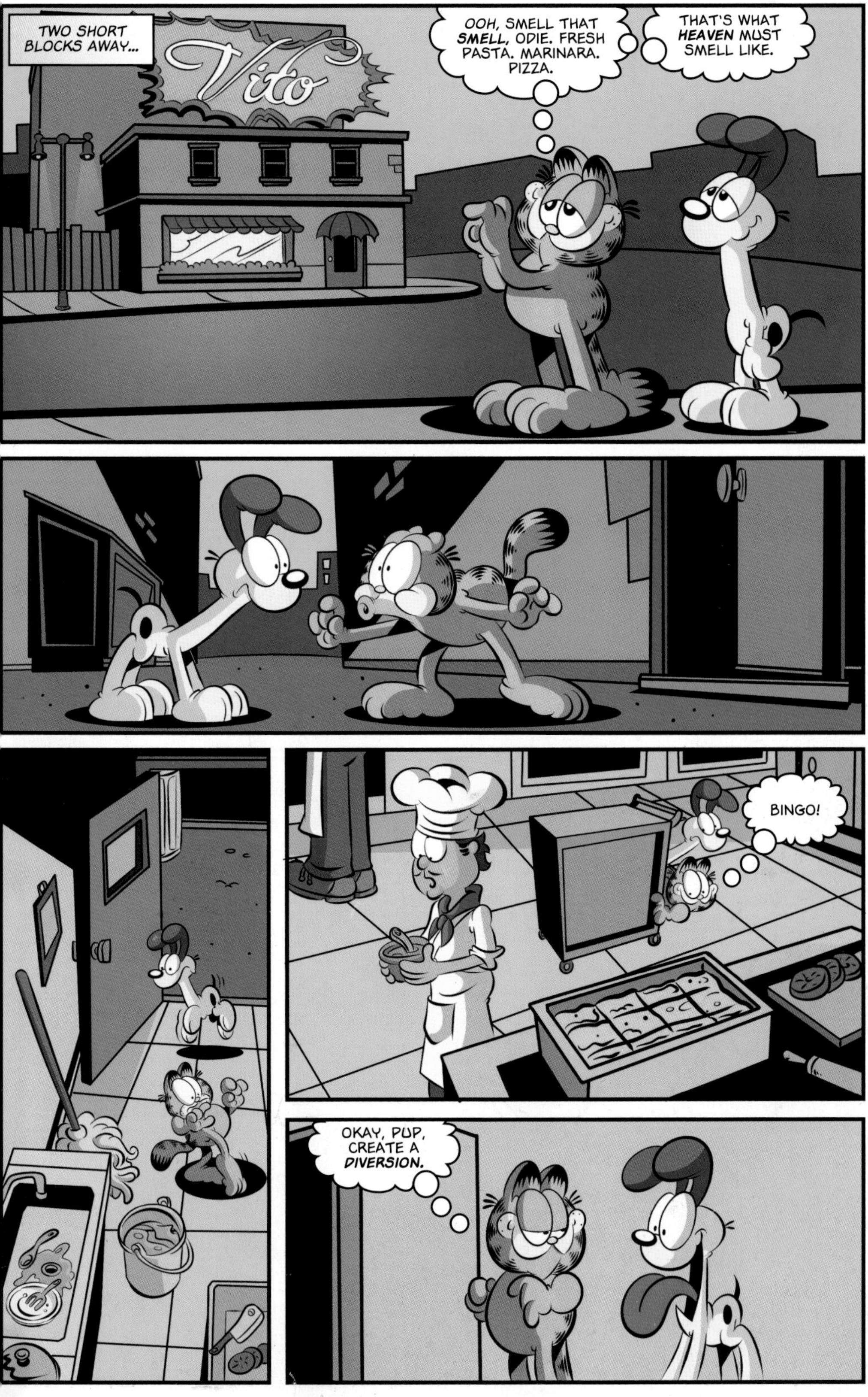
TWO SHORT BLOCKS AWAY...
Vito
OOH, SMELL THAT SMELL, ODIE. FRESH PASTA. MARINARA. PIZZA.
THAT'S WHAT HEAVEN MUST SMELL LIKE.
BINGO!
OKAY, PUP, CREATE A DIVERSION.

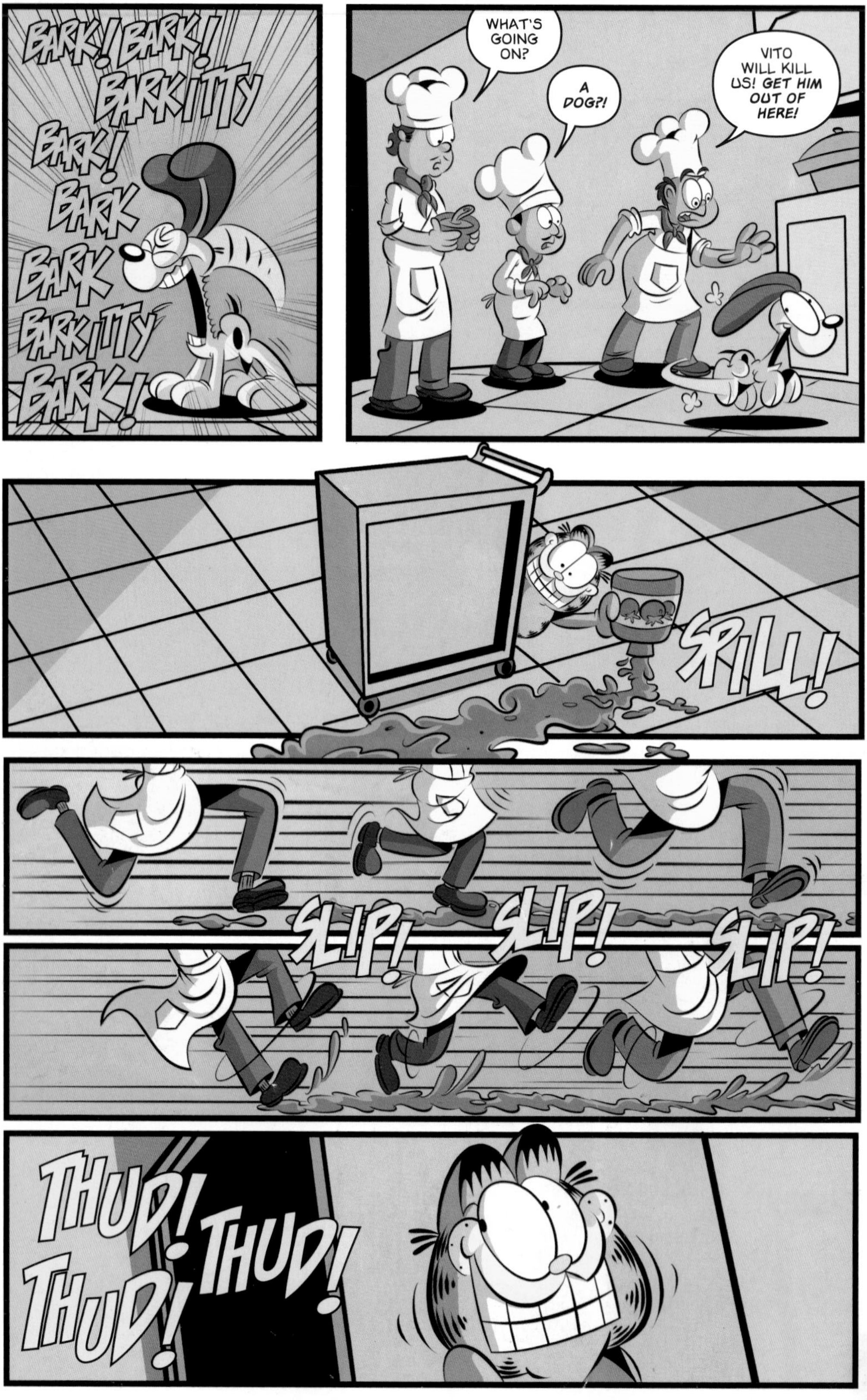
BARK! BARK!
BARKITTY BARK!
BARK
BARK
BARKITTY
BARK!
WHAT'S GOING ON?
A DOG?!
VITO WILL KILL US! GET HIM OUT OF HERE!
SPILL!
SLIP!
SLIP!
SLIP!
THUD!
THUD!
THUD!

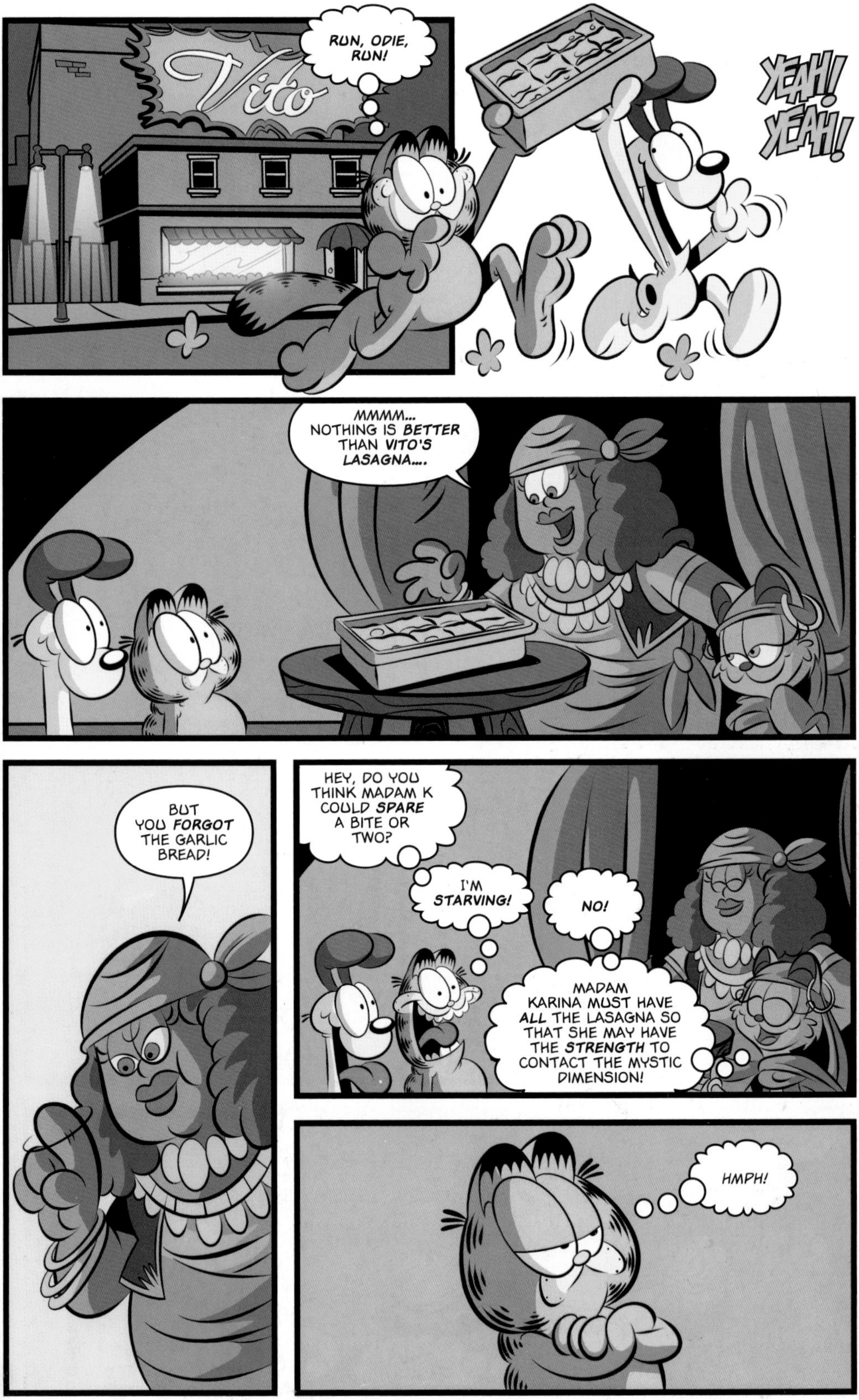
RUN, ODIE, RUN!
YEAH! YEAH!
MMMM... NOTHING IS BETTER THAN VITO'S LASAGNA....
BUT YOU FORGOT THE GARLIC BREAD!
HEY, DO YOU THINK MADAM K COULD SPARE A BITE OR TWO?
I'M STARVING!
NO!
MADAM KARINA MUST HAVE ALL THE LASAGNA SO THAT SHE MAY HAVE THE STRENGTH TO CONTACT THE MYSTIC DIMENSION!
HMPH!

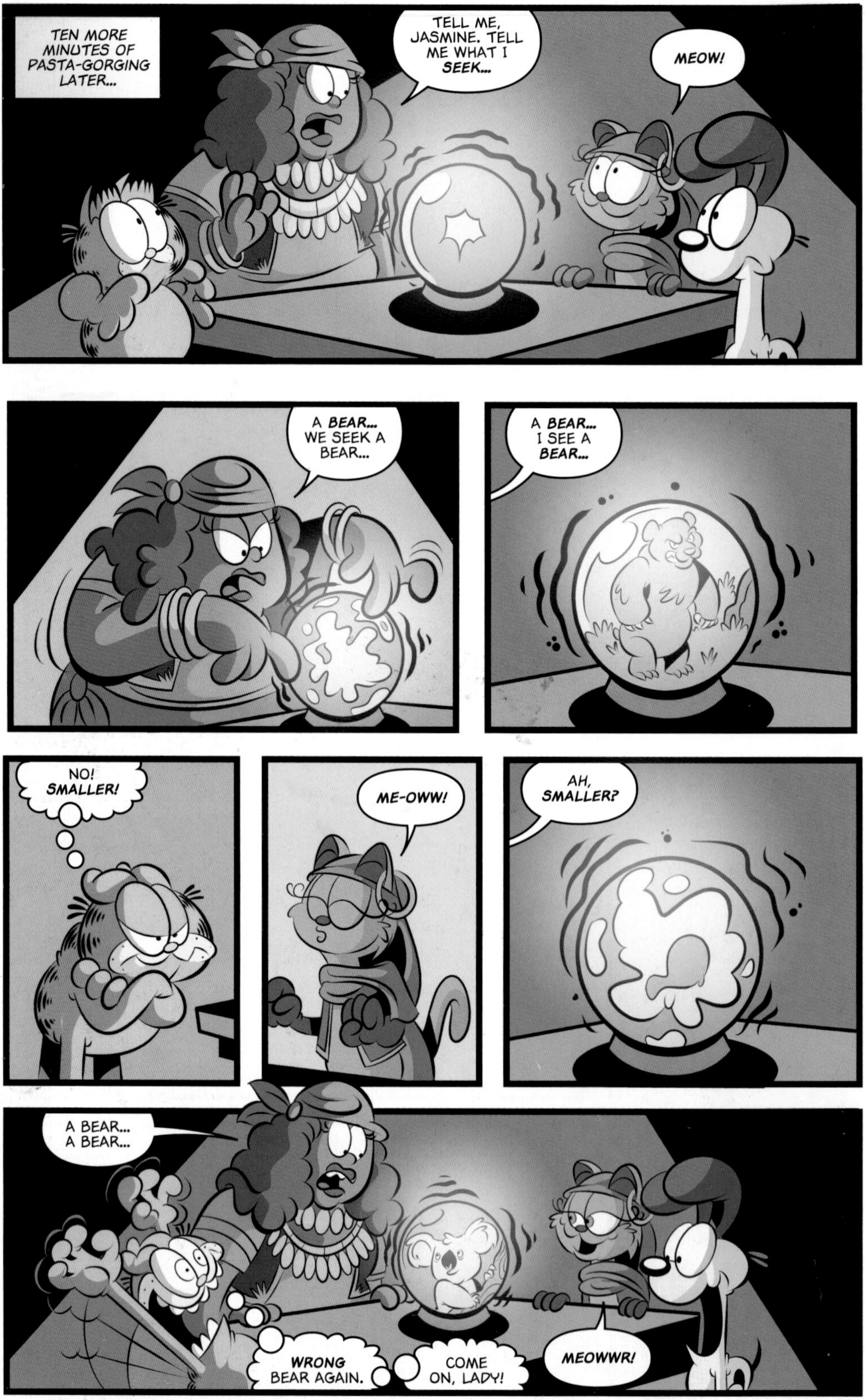
TEN MORE MINUTES OF PASTA-GORGING LATER...
TELL ME, JASMINE. TELL ME WHAT I SEEK...
MEOW!
A BEAR... WE SEEK A BEAR...
A BEAR... I SEE A BEAR...
NO! SMALLER!
ME-OWW!
AH, SMALLER?
A BEAR... A BEAR...
WRONG BEAR AGAIN.
COME ON, LADY!
MEOWWR!

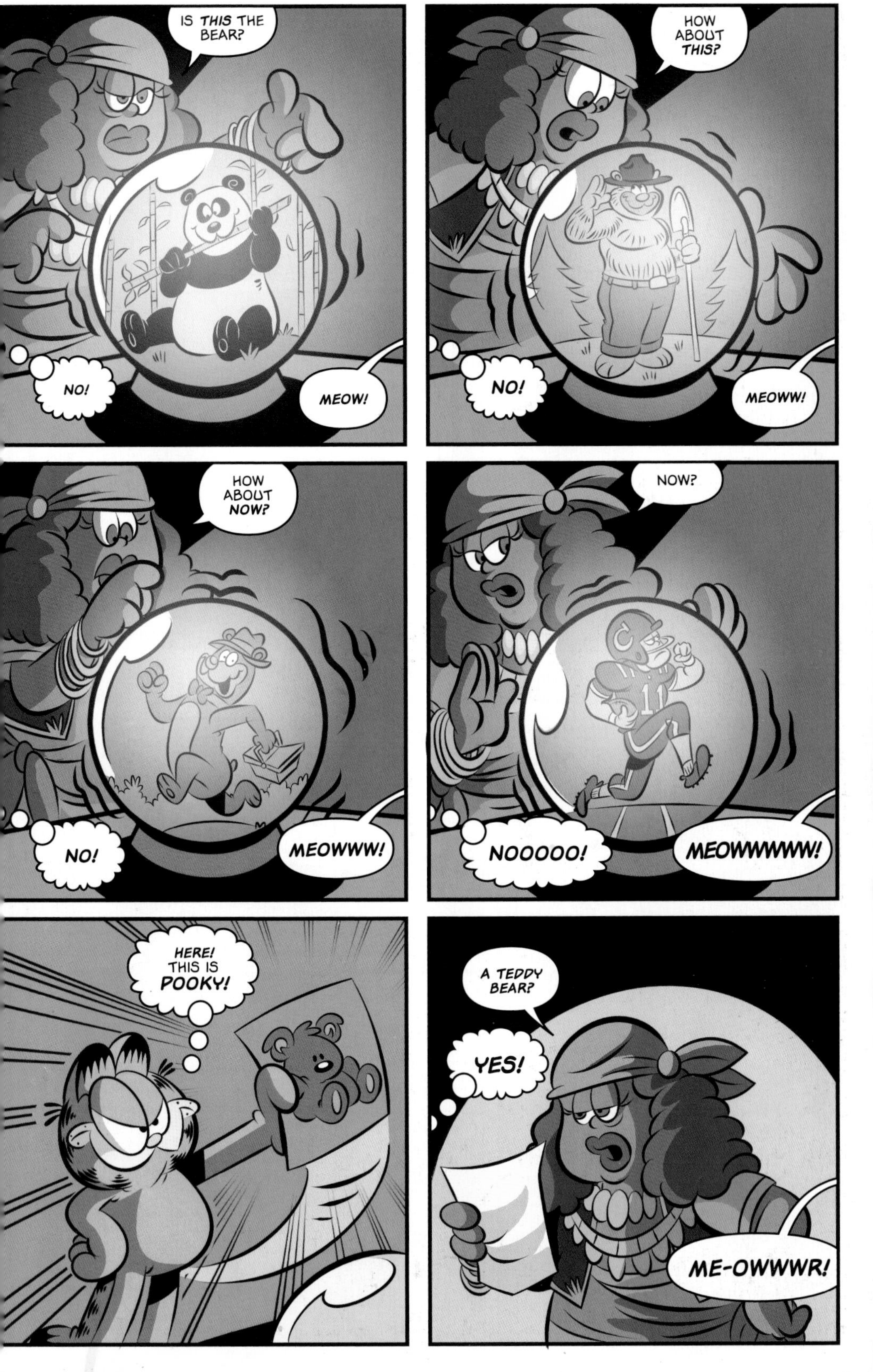
IS THIS THE BEAR?
NO!
MEOW!
HOW ABOUT THIS?
NO!
MEOWW!
HOW ABOUT NOW?
NO!
MEOWWW!
NOW?
NOOOOO!
MEOWWWWW!
HERE! THIS IS POOKY!
A TEDDY BEAR?
YES!
ME-OWWWR!

WHY DIDN'T YOU *SAY* SO? LET ME GAZE *DEEPLY* INTO THE CRYSTAL BALL AND *FIND* THAT WHICH YOU SEEK.

POOKY! *THAT'S POOKY!* WHERE IS HE? IS HE *NEARBY?*

THE IMAGE IS *FADING...* MADAM IS *SLEEPY.*

A BIG PAN OF LASAGNA ALWAYS *DOES* IT. COME BACK LATER. MADAM MUST *SLEEP.*

WAIT, *THAT'S IT?* THAT'S ALL WE GET?

MADAM KARINA CAN ANSWER NO MORE QUESTIONS.

YOU MUST *GO.* GOOD NIGHT!

SLAM!

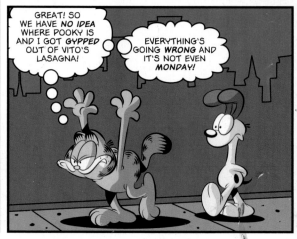

GREAT! SO WE HAVE *NO IDEA* WHERE POOKY IS AND I GOT *GYPPED* OUT OF VITO'S LASAGNA!

EVERYTHING'S GOING *WRONG* AND IT'S NOT EVEN *MONDAY!*

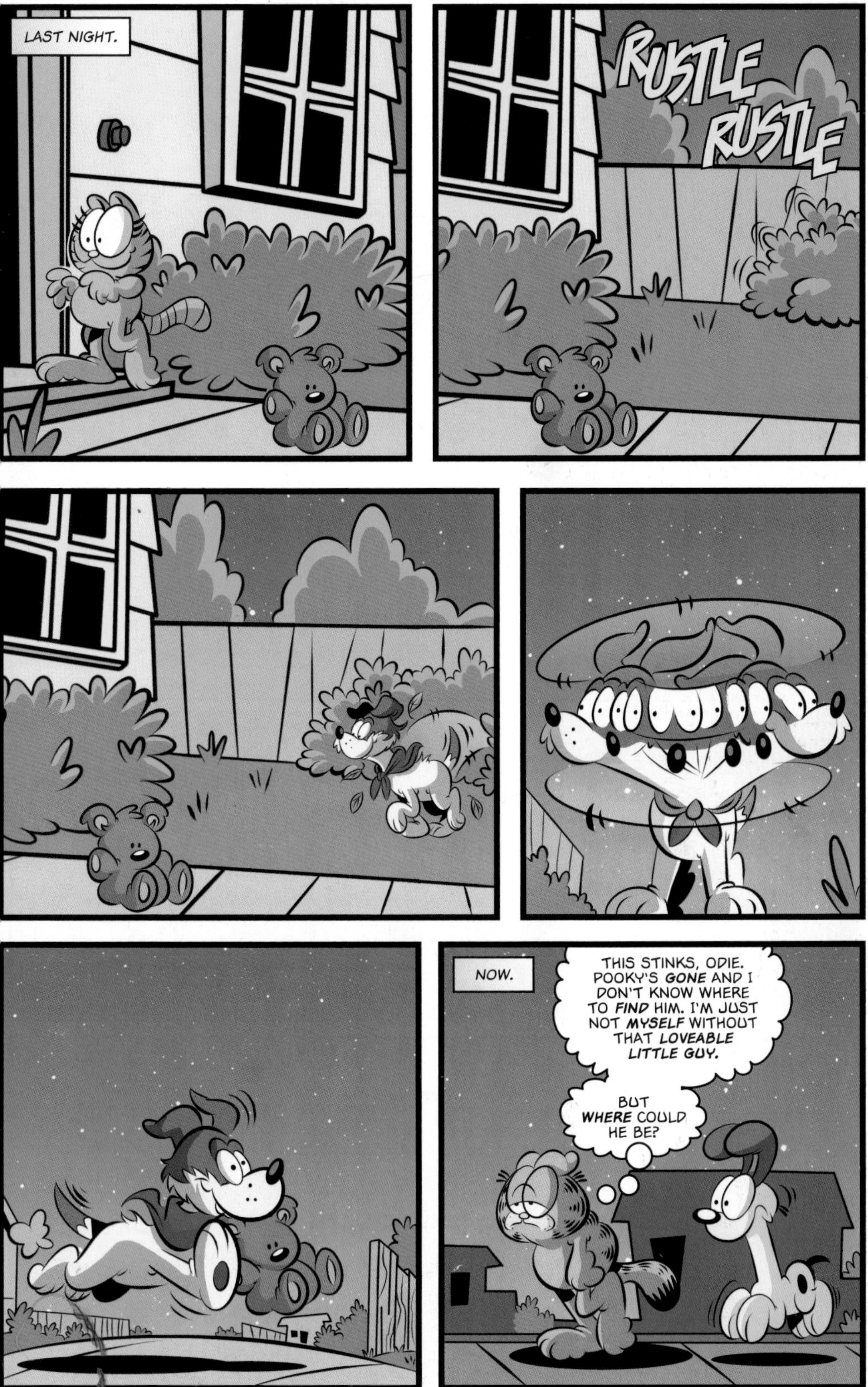
LAST NIGHT.
RUSTLE RUSTLE
NOW.
THIS STINKS, ODIE. POOKY'S GONE AND I DON'T KNOW WHERE TO FIND HIM. I'M JUST NOT MYSELF WITHOUT THAT LOVEABLE LITTLE GUY.
BUT WHERE COULD HE BE?

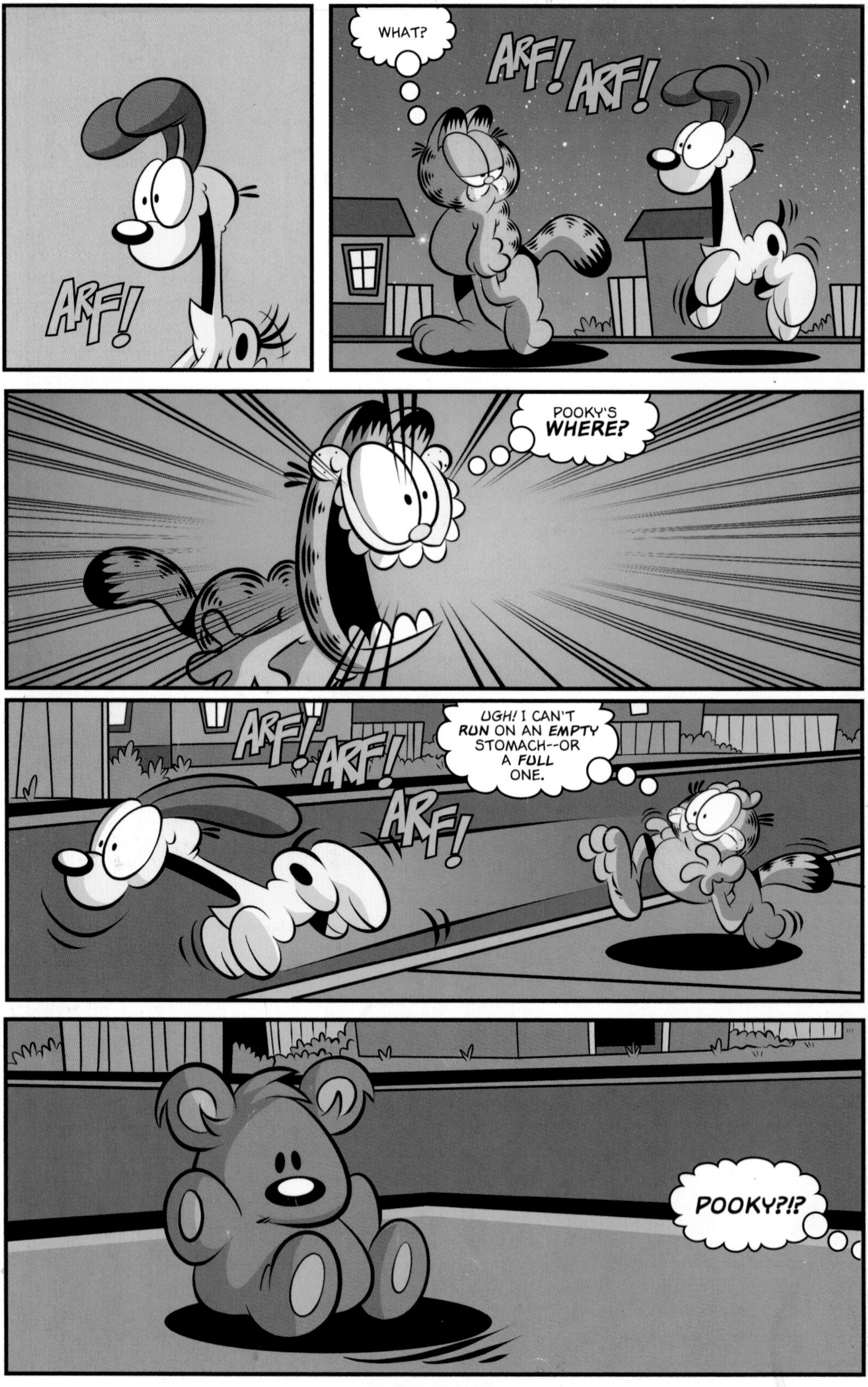

ARF!
WHAT?
ARF! ARF!
POOKY'S **WHERE?**
ARF! ARF!
ARF!
UGH! I CAN'T *RUN* ON AN *EMPTY* STOMACH--OR A *FULL* ONE.
POOKY?!?

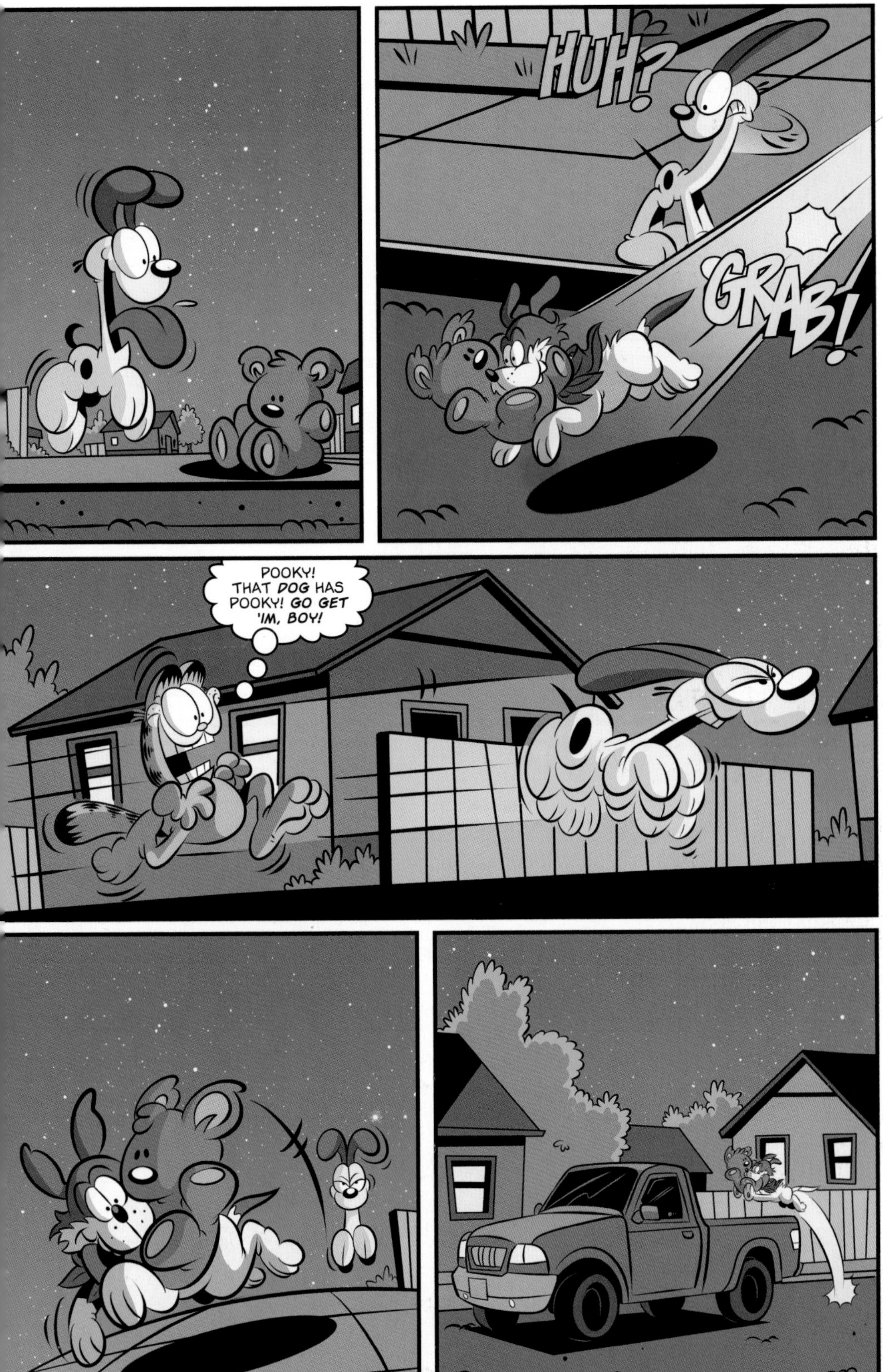
HUH?
GRAB!
POOKY! THAT DOG HAS POOKY! GO GET 'IM, BOY!

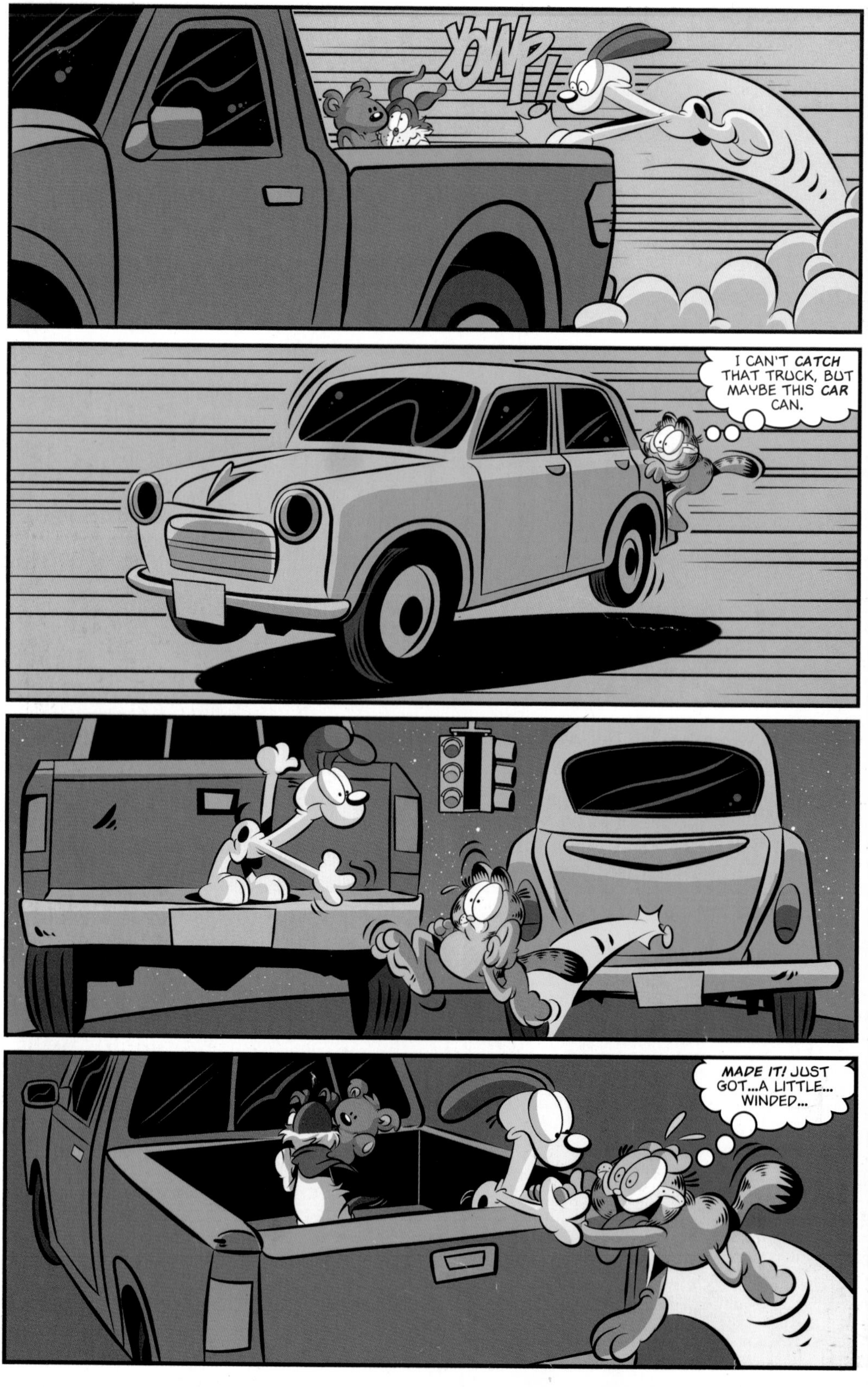
YOWP!
I CAN'T CATCH THAT TRUCK, BUT MAYBE THIS CAR CAN.
MADE IT! JUST GOT...A LITTLE... WINDED...

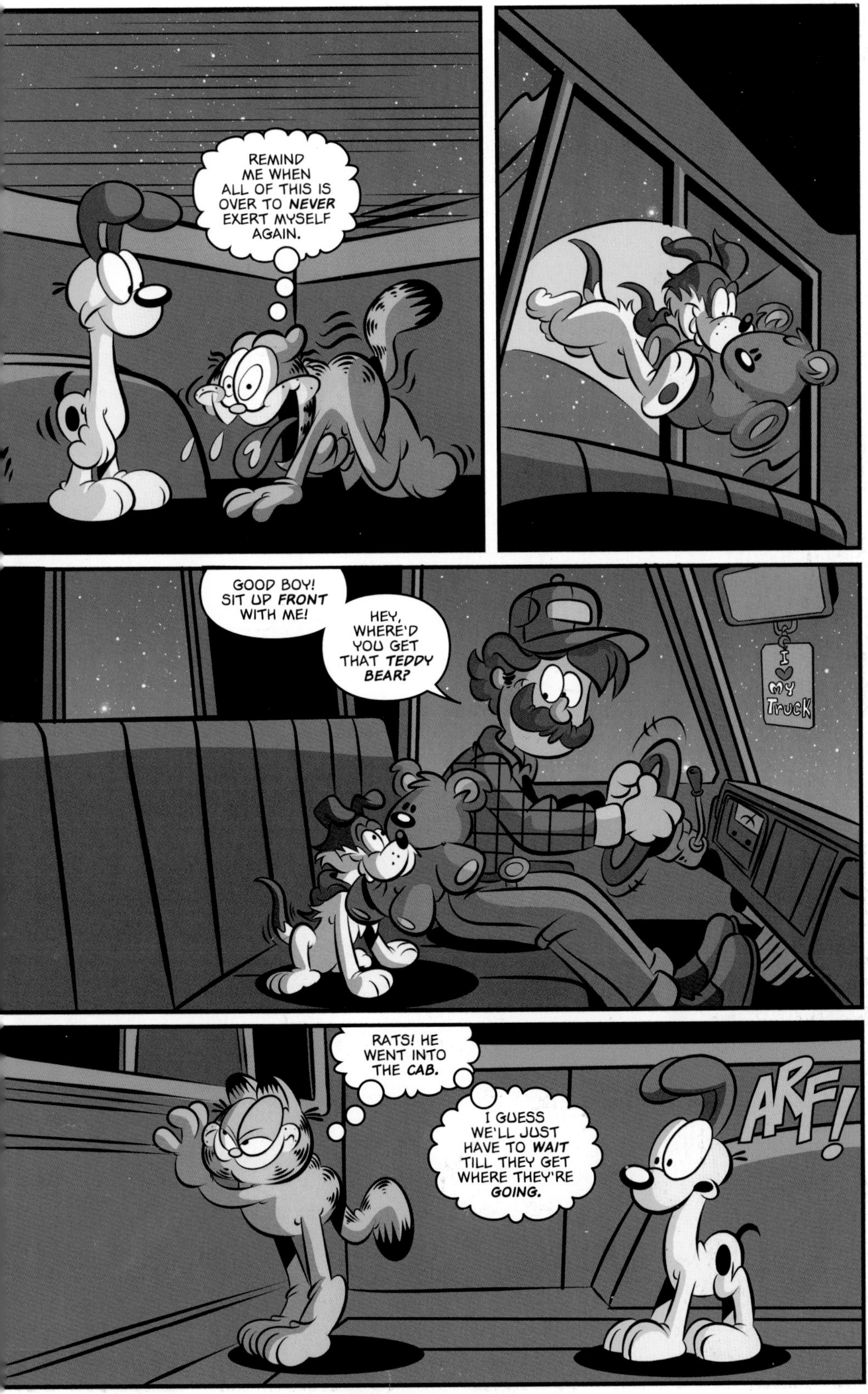
REMIND ME WHEN ALL OF THIS IS OVER TO NEVER EXERT MYSELF AGAIN.
GOOD BOY! SIT UP FRONT WITH ME!
HEY, WHERE'D YOU GET THAT TEDDY BEAR?
I ♥ MY TRUCK
RATS! HE WENT INTO THE CAB.
I GUESS WE'LL JUST HAVE TO WAIT TILL THEY GET WHERE THEY'RE GOING.
ARF!

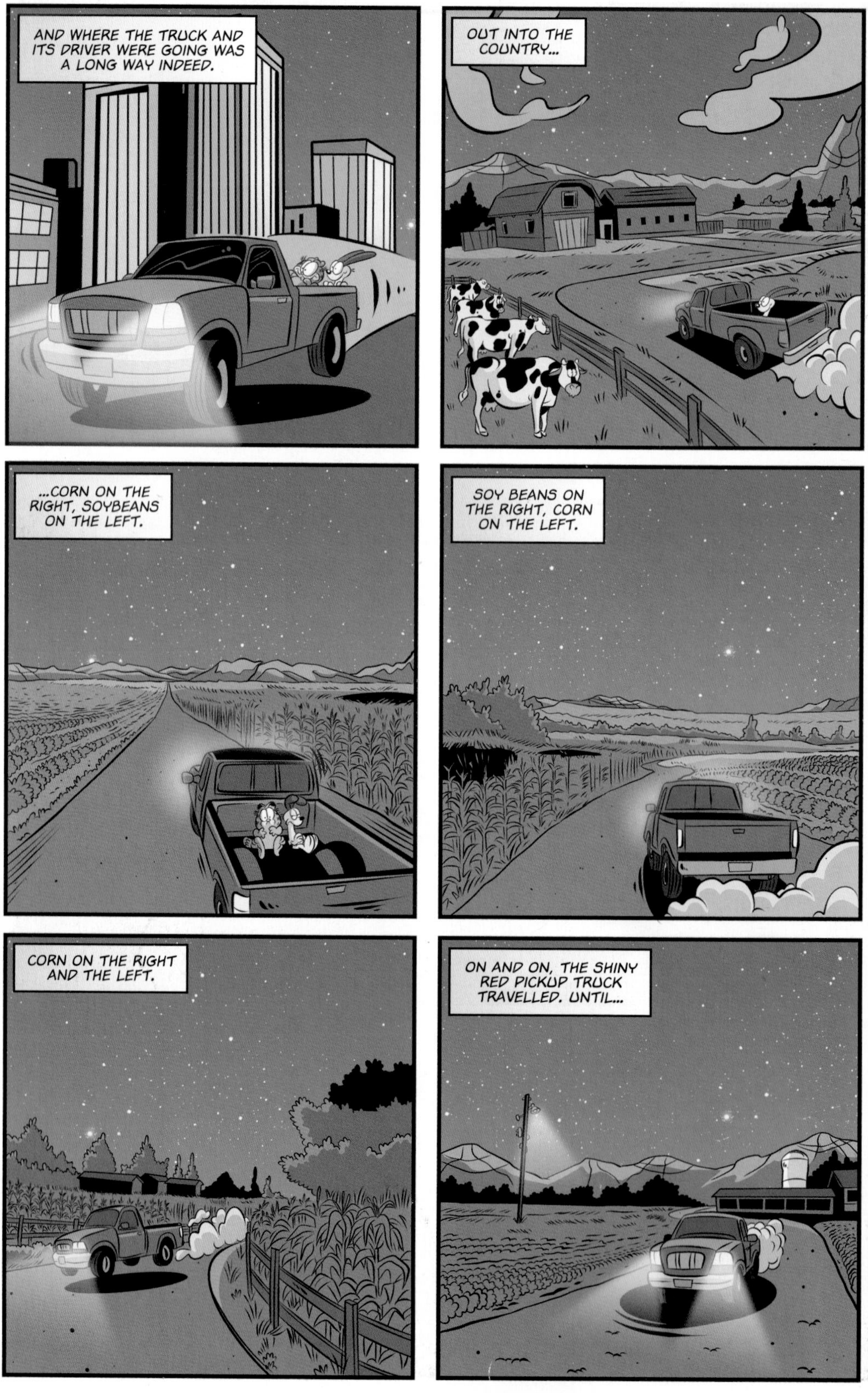
AND WHERE THE TRUCK AND ITS DRIVER WERE GOING WAS A LONG WAY INDEED.
OUT INTO THE COUNTRY...
...CORN ON THE RIGHT, SOYBEANS ON THE LEFT.
SOY BEANS ON THE RIGHT, CORN ON THE LEFT.
CORN ON THE RIGHT AND THE LEFT.
ON AND ON, THE SHINY RED PICKUP TRUCK TRAVELLED. UNTIL...

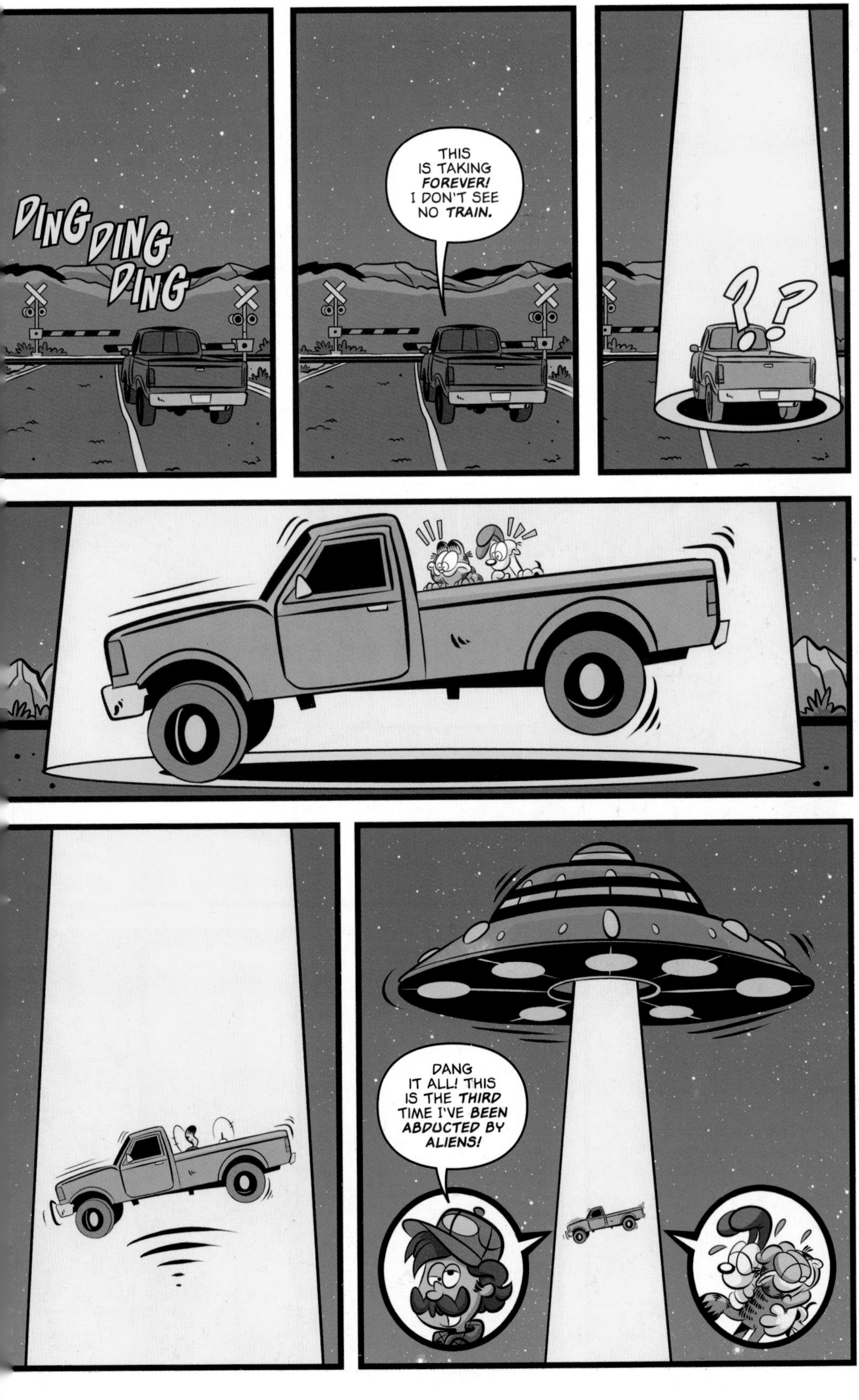
DING DING DING
THIS IS TAKING FOREVER! I DON'T SEE NO TRAIN.
? ?
DANG IT ALL! THIS IS THE THIRD TIME I'VE BEEN ABDUCTED BY ALIENS!

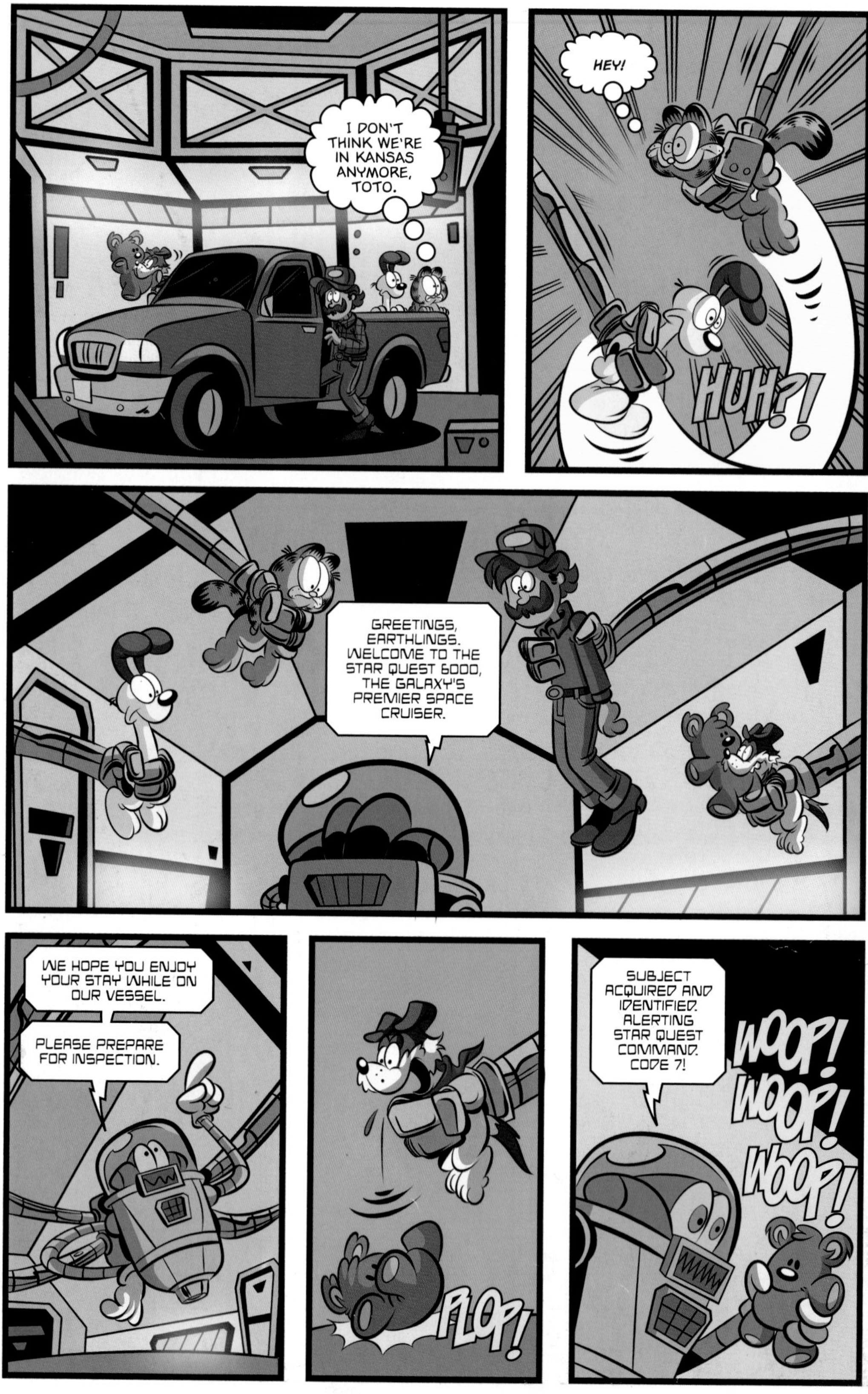
I DON'T THINK WE'RE IN KANSAS ANYMORE, TOTO.
HEY!
HUH?!
GREETINGS, EARTHLINGS. WELCOME TO THE STAR QUEST 6000, THE GALAXY'S PREMIER SPACE CRUISER.
WE HOPE YOU ENJOY YOUR STAY WHILE ON OUR VESSEL.
PLEASE PREPARE FOR INSPECTION.
PLOP!
SUBJECT ACQUIRED AND IDENTIFIED. ALERTING STAR QUEST COMMAND. CODE 7!
WOOP! WOOP! WOOP!

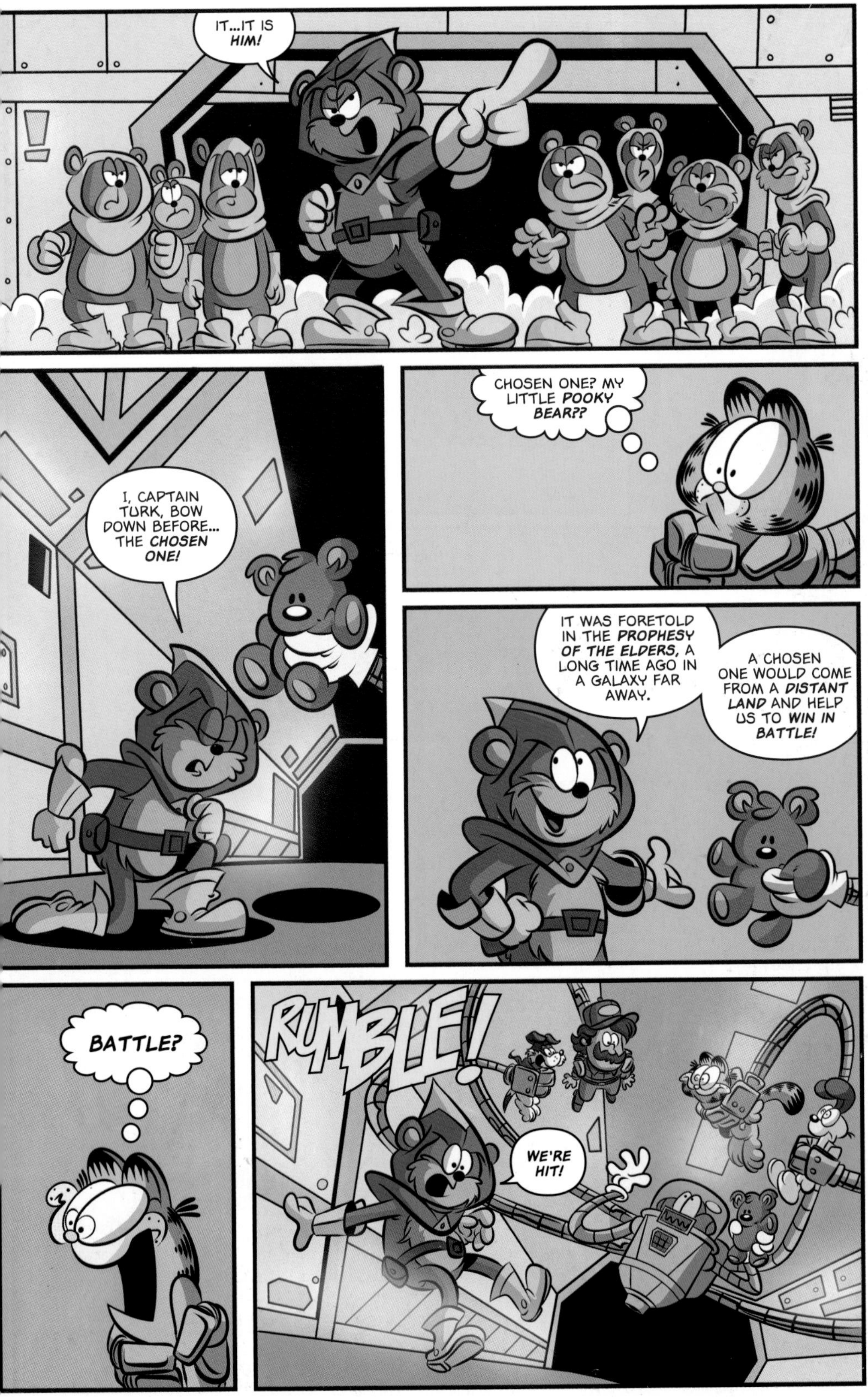
IT...IT IS HIM!
I, CAPTAIN TURK, BOW DOWN BEFORE... THE CHOSEN ONE!
CHOSEN ONE? MY LITTLE POOKY BEAR??
IT WAS FORETOLD IN THE PROPHESY OF THE ELDERS, A LONG TIME AGO IN A GALAXY FAR AWAY.
A CHOSEN ONE WOULD COME FROM A DISTANT LAND AND HELP US TO WIN IN BATTLE!
BATTLE?
RUMBLE!
WE'RE HIT!

WE ARE UNDER ATTACK! REPEAT: WE ARE UNDER ATTACK!

CREW TO BATTLE STATIONS! REPEAT: CREW TO BATTLE STATIONS!

I NEED TO GET *OFF THIS SHIP!* REPEAT: I NEED TO GET OFF THIS SHIP!

WE WILL TAKE THE CHOSEN ONE TO THE BRIDGE. THERE WE WILL PLACE HIM IN THE THRONE OF HONOR.

THESE OTHERS MAY BE TAKEN TO THE INSPECTION LAB FOR... PROBING.

AFFIRMATIVE, CAPTAIN!

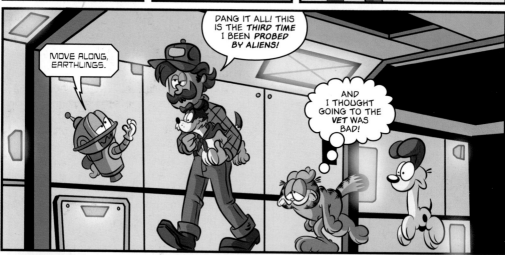

MOVE ALONG, EARTHLINGS.

DANG IT ALL! THIS IS THE *THIRD TIME* I BEEN *PROBED* BY ALIENS!

AND I THOUGHT GOING TO THE *VET* WAS BAD!

CHOOM KABOOM!

CHOOM

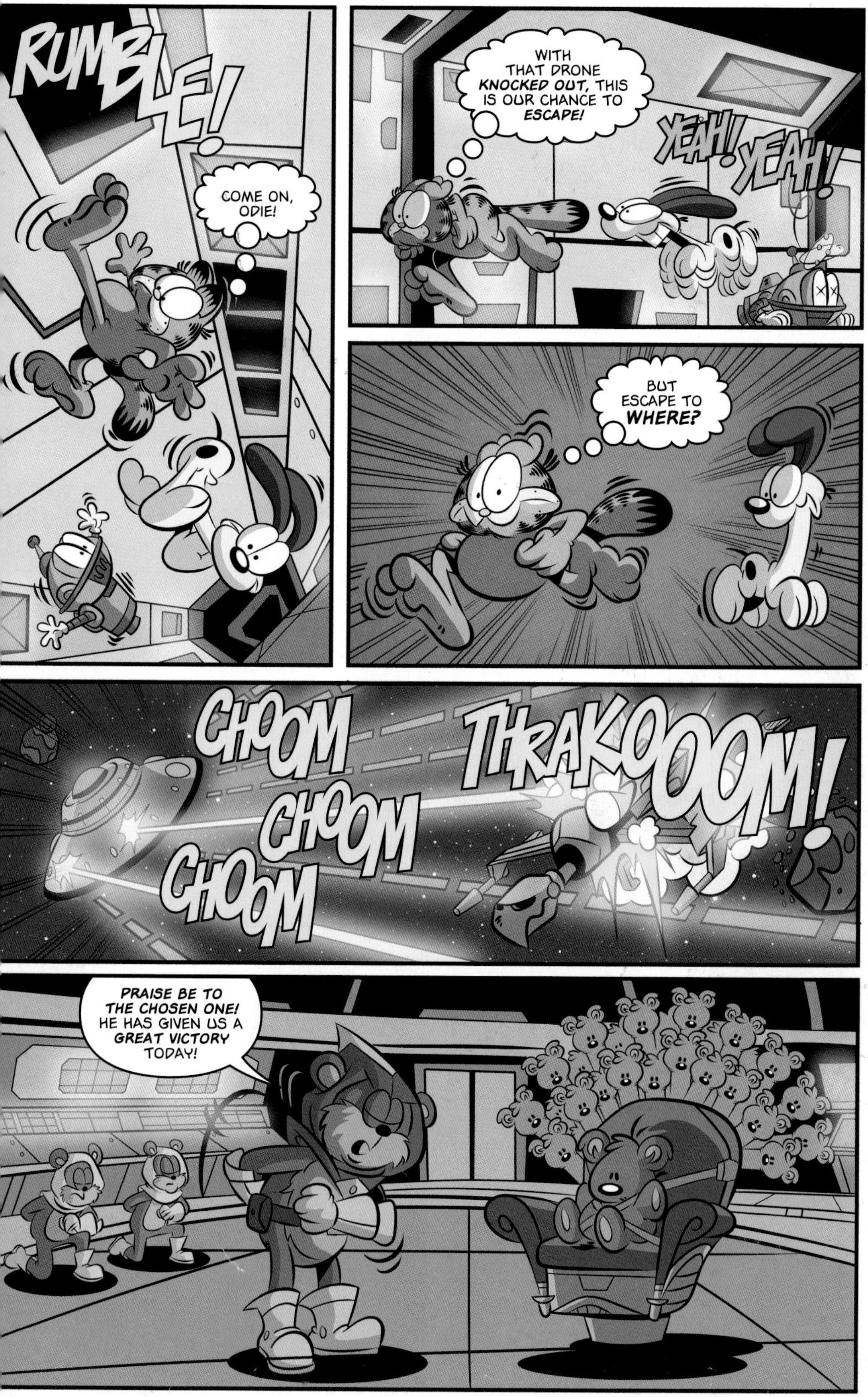
RUMBLE!
COME ON, ODIE!
WITH THAT DRONE KNOCKED OUT, THIS IS OUR CHANCE TO ESCAPE!
YEAH! YEAH!
BUT ESCAPE TO WHERE?
CHOOM
CHOOM
CHOOM
THRAKOOOM!
PRAISE BE TO THE CHOSEN ONE! HE HAS GIVEN US A GREAT VICTORY TODAY!

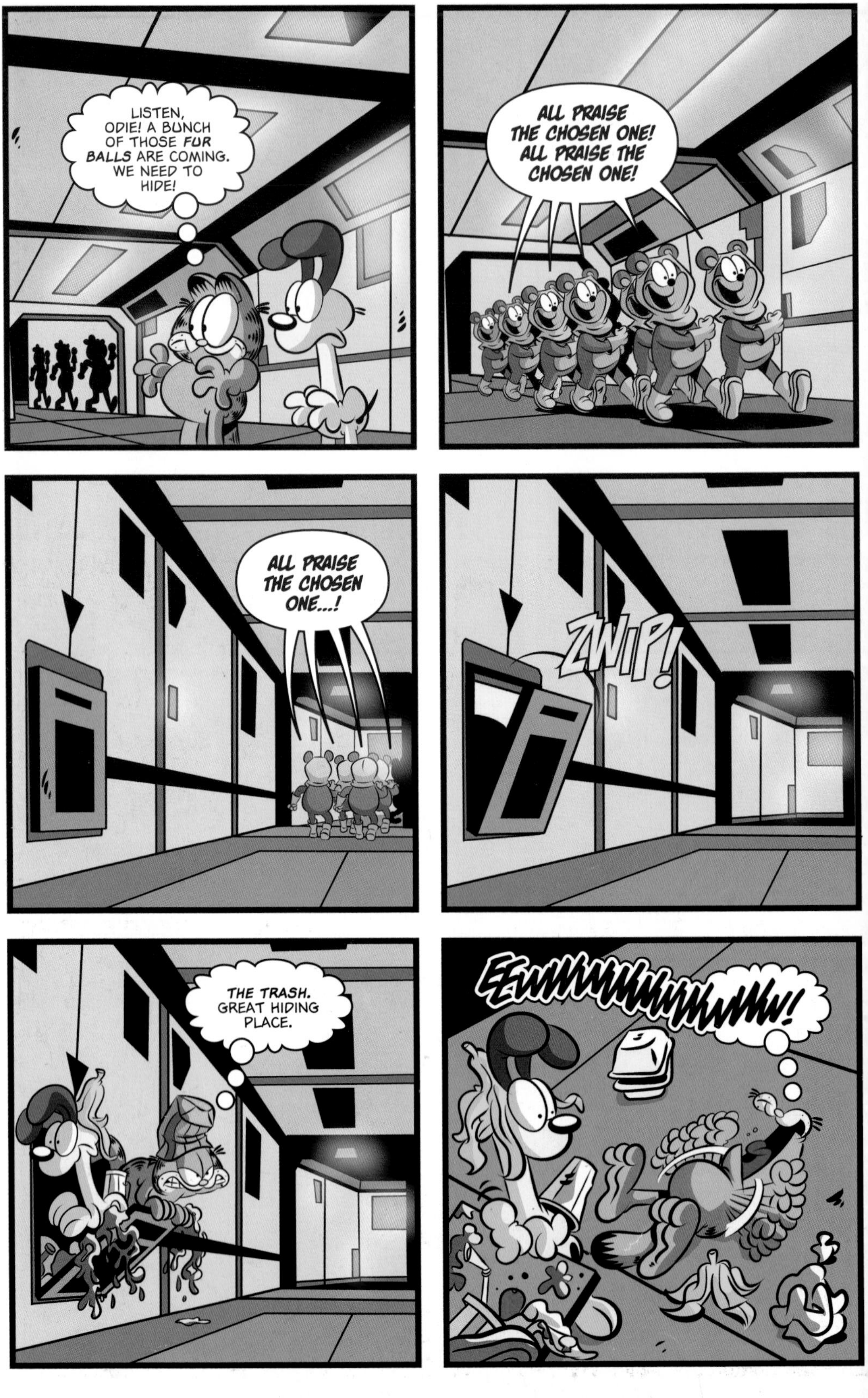
LISTEN, ODIE! A BUNCH OF THOSE FUR BALLS ARE COMING. WE NEED TO HIDE!
ALL PRAISE THE CHOSEN ONE! ALL PRAISE THE CHOSEN ONE!
ALL PRAISE THE CHOSEN ONE...!
ZWIP!
THE TRASH. GREAT HIDING PLACE.
EEWWWWWWWWWWWW!

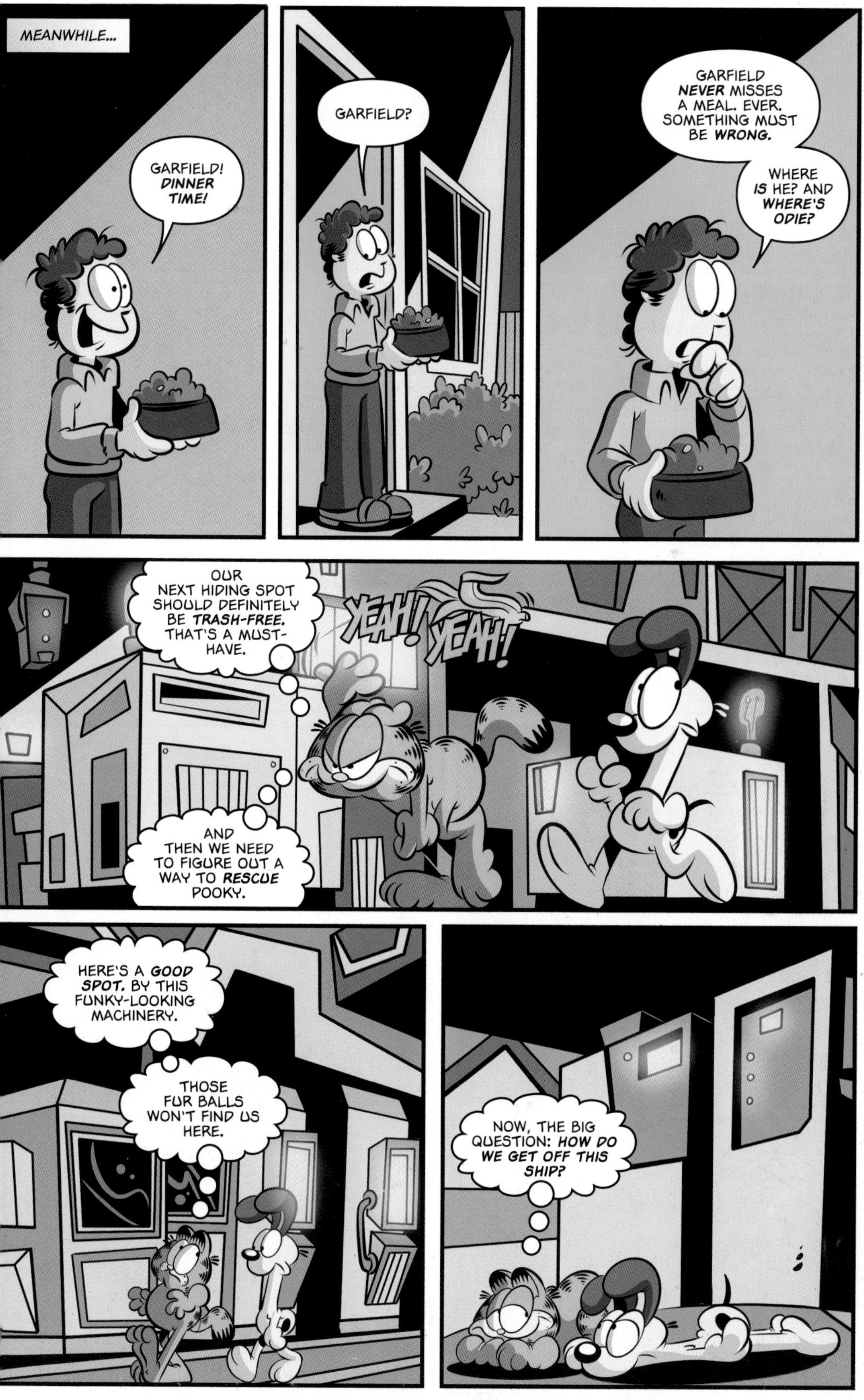
MEANWHILE...
GARFIELD! DINNER TIME!
GARFIELD?
GARFIELD NEVER MISSES A MEAL. EVER. SOMETHING MUST BE WRONG.
WHERE IS HE? AND WHERE'S ODIE?
OUR NEXT HIDING SPOT SHOULD DEFINITELY BE TRASH-FREE. THAT'S A MUST-HAVE.
YEAH! YEAH!
AND THEN WE NEED TO FIGURE OUT A WAY TO RESCUE POOKY.
HERE'S A GOOD SPOT. BY THIS FUNKY-LOOKING MACHINERY.
THOSE FUR BALLS WON'T FIND US HERE.
NOW, THE BIG QUESTION: HOW DO WE GET OFF THIS SHIP?

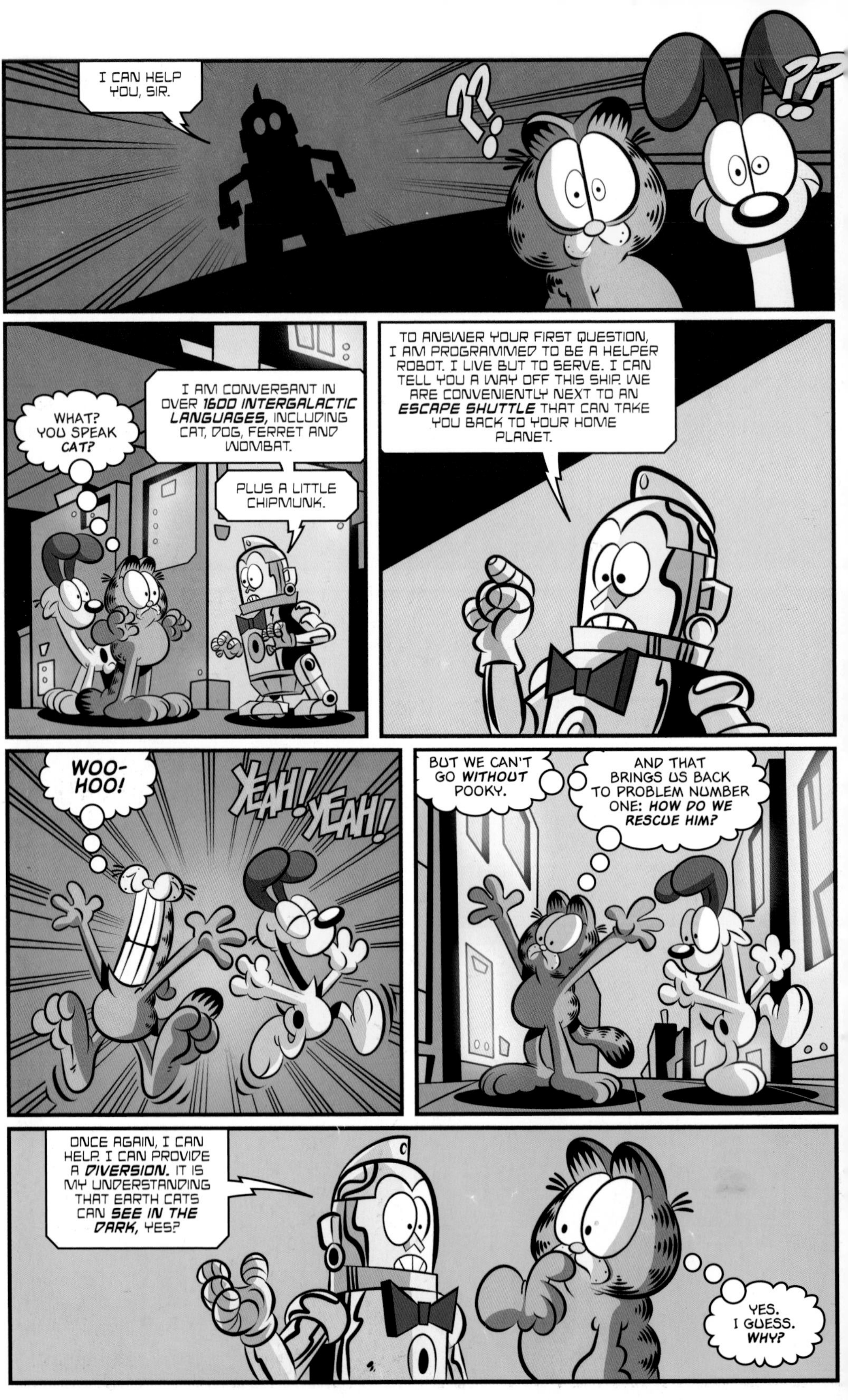

I CAN HELP YOU, SIR.
??
??
WHAT? YOU SPEAK CAT?
I AM CONVERSANT IN OVER 1600 INTERGALACTIC LANGUAGES, INCLUDING CAT, DOG, FERRET AND WOMBAT.
PLUS A LITTLE CHIPMUNK.
TO ANSWER YOUR FIRST QUESTION, I AM PROGRAMMED TO BE A HELPER ROBOT. I LIVE BUT TO SERVE. I CAN TELL YOU A WAY OFF THIS SHIP. WE ARE CONVENIENTLY NEXT TO AN ESCAPE SHUTTLE THAT CAN TAKE YOU BACK TO YOUR HOME PLANET.
WOO-HOO!
YEAH! YEAH!
BUT WE CAN'T GO WITHOUT POOKY.
AND THAT BRINGS US BACK TO PROBLEM NUMBER ONE: HOW DO WE RESCUE HIM?
ONCE AGAIN, I CAN HELP. I CAN PROVIDE A DIVERSION. IT IS MY UNDERSTANDING THAT EARTH CATS CAN SEE IN THE DARK, YES?
YES. I GUESS. WHY?

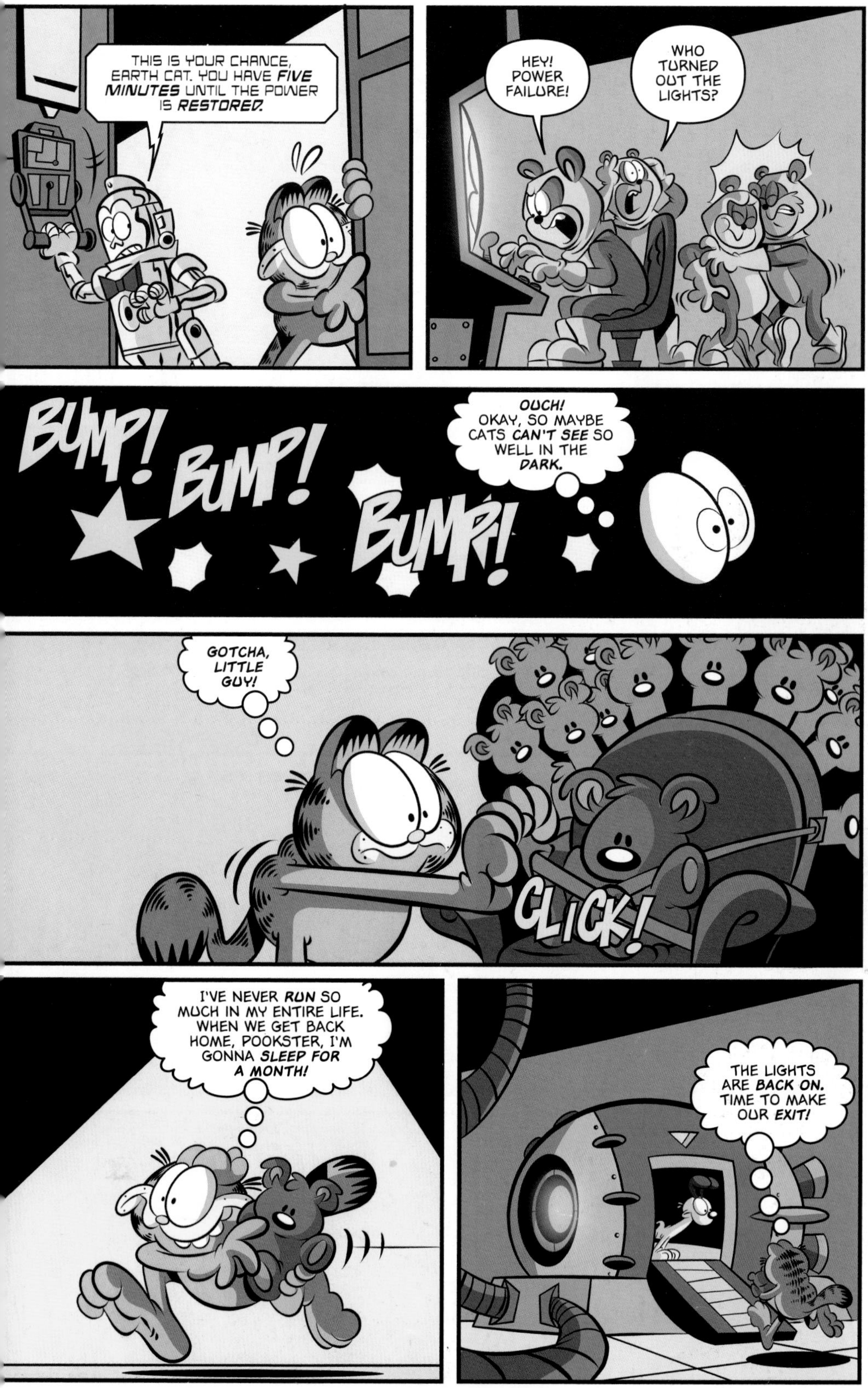

THIS IS YOUR CHANCE, EARTH CAT. YOU HAVE FIVE MINUTES UNTIL THE POWER IS RESTORED.
HEY! POWER FAILURE!
WHO TURNED OUT THE LIGHTS?
BUMP! BUMP!
OUCH! OKAY, SO MAYBE CATS CAN'T SEE SO WELL IN THE DARK.
BUMP!
GOTCHA, LITTLE GUY!
CLICK!
I'VE NEVER RUN SO MUCH IN MY ENTIRE LIFE. WHEN WE GET BACK HOME, POOKSTER, I'M GONNA SLEEP FOR A MONTH!
THE LIGHTS ARE BACK ON. TIME TO MAKE OUR EXIT!

WOW! LOOK AT ALL THESE CONTROLS! IS THERE AN "ON" BUTTON?

DO NOT WORRY, EARTH CAT. I WILL ENGAGE AUTOPILOT. YOUR COORDINATES HAVE BEEN *LOCKED IN.*

PREPARE FOR *LIFT-OFF!*

PHEW! YOU *ARE* A HELPER!

THE EARTHLING IS *ESCAPING.* AND HE HAS THE *CHOSEN ONE!*

STOP HIM!

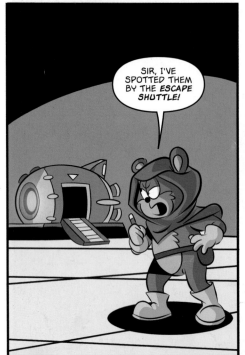

SIR, I'VE SPOTTED THEM BY THE *ESCAPE SHUTTLE!*

PEW

PEW PEW

PEW PEW

KRA-POW

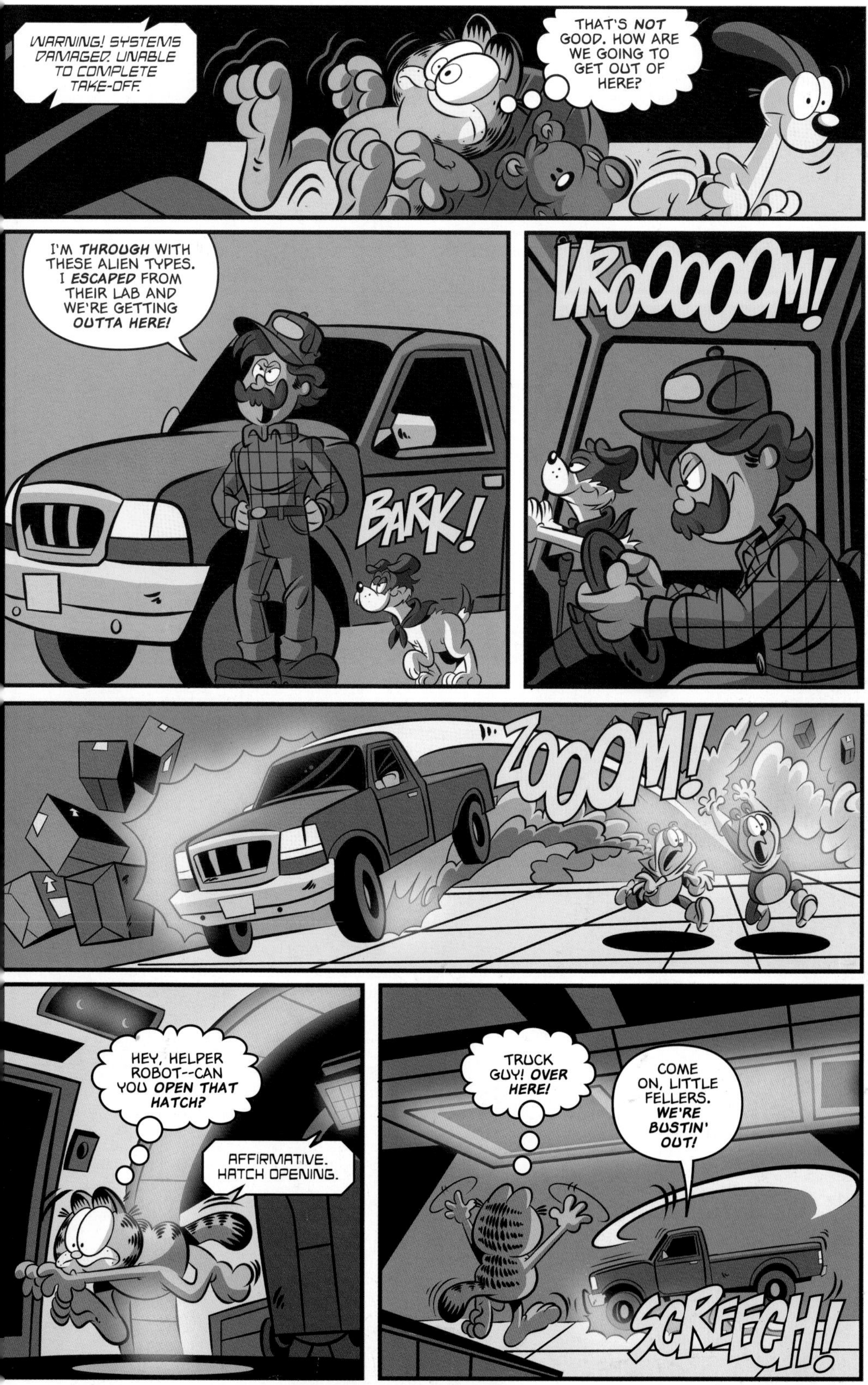
WARNING! SYSTEMS DAMAGED. UNABLE TO COMPLETE TAKE-OFF.
THAT'S NOT GOOD. HOW ARE WE GOING TO GET OUT OF HERE?
I'M THROUGH WITH THESE ALIEN TYPES. I ESCAPED FROM THEIR LAB AND WE'RE GETTING OUTTA HERE!
BARK!
VROOOOOM!
ZOOOM!
HEY, HELPER ROBOT--CAN YOU OPEN THAT HATCH?
AFFIRMATIVE. HATCH OPENING.
TRUCK GUY! OVER HERE!
COME ON, LITTLE FELLERS. WE'RE BUSTIN' OUT!
SCREECH!

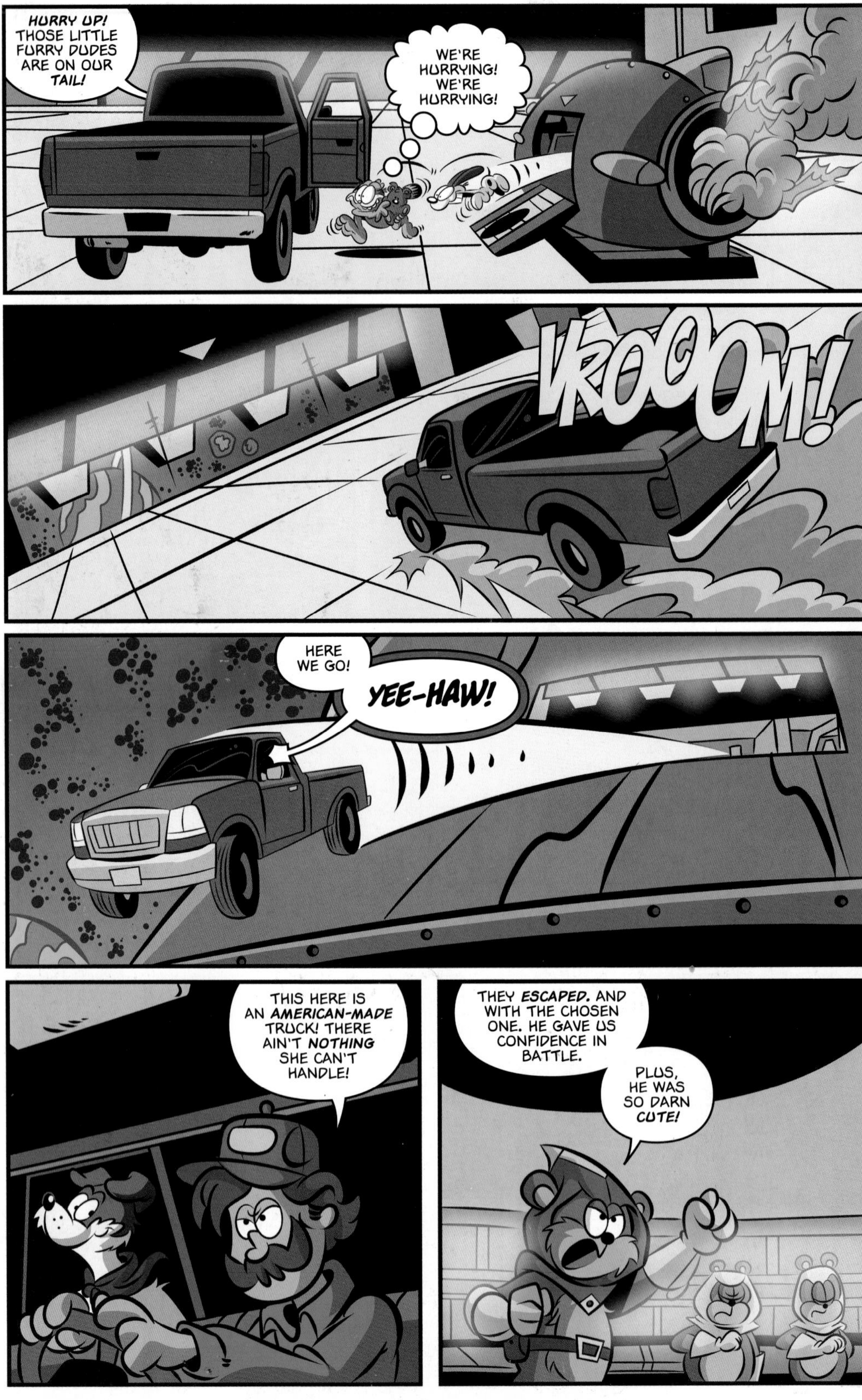
HURRY UP! THOSE LITTLE FURRY DUDES ARE ON OUR TAIL!
WE'RE HURRYING! WE'RE HURRYING!
VROOOOM!!
HERE WE GO!
YEE-HAW!
THIS HERE IS AN AMERICAN-MADE TRUCK! THERE AIN'T NOTHING SHE CAN'T HANDLE!
THEY ESCAPED. AND WITH THE CHOSEN ONE. HE GAVE US CONFIDENCE IN BATTLE.
PLUS, HE WAS SO DARN CUTE!

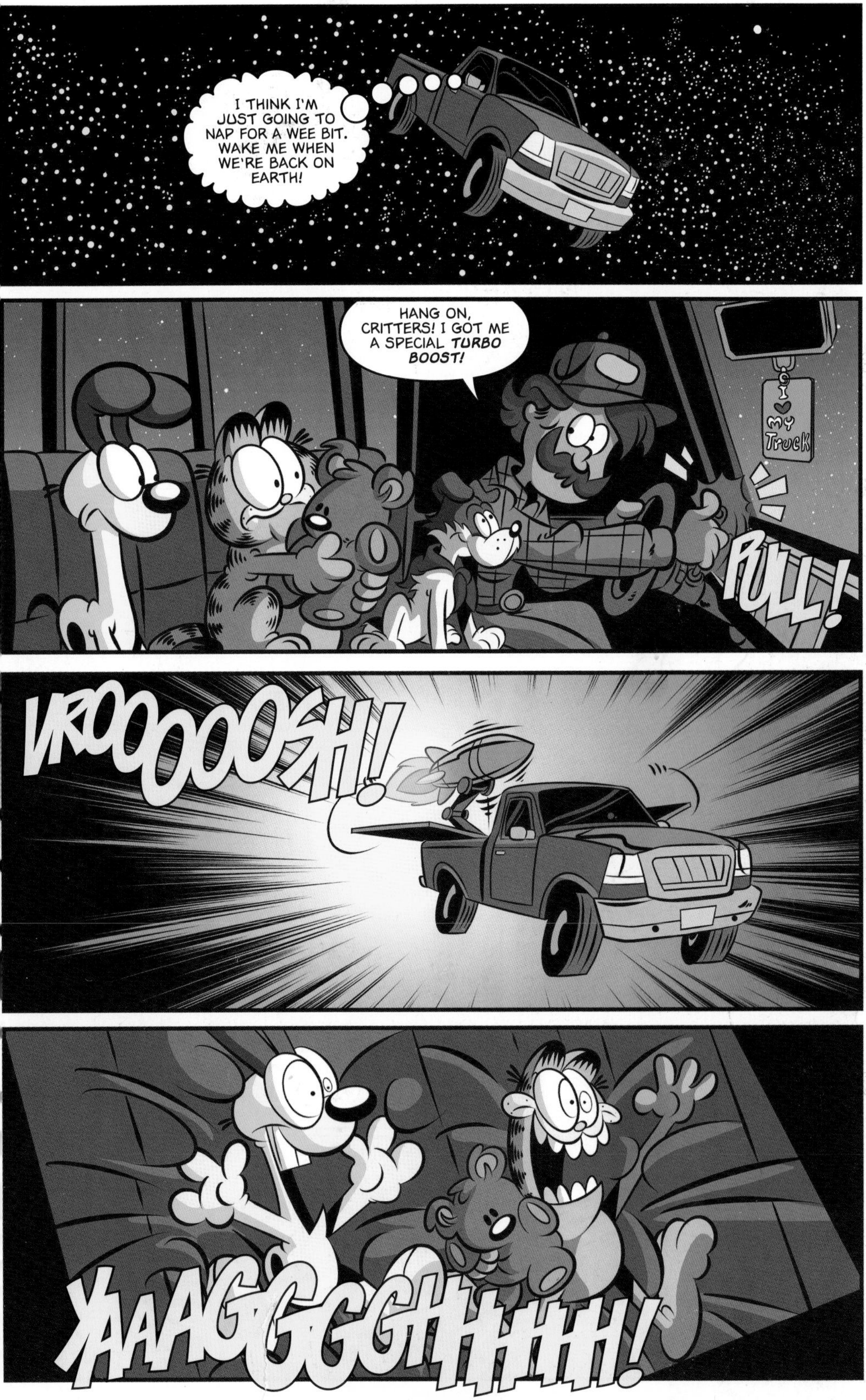
I THINK I'M JUST GOING TO NAP FOR A WEE BIT. WAKE ME WHEN WE'RE BACK ON EARTH!
HANG ON, CRITTERS! I GOT ME A SPECIAL *TURBO BOOST!*
I ♥ my Truck
PULL!
VROOOOOSH!
YAAAGGGGHHHHHH!

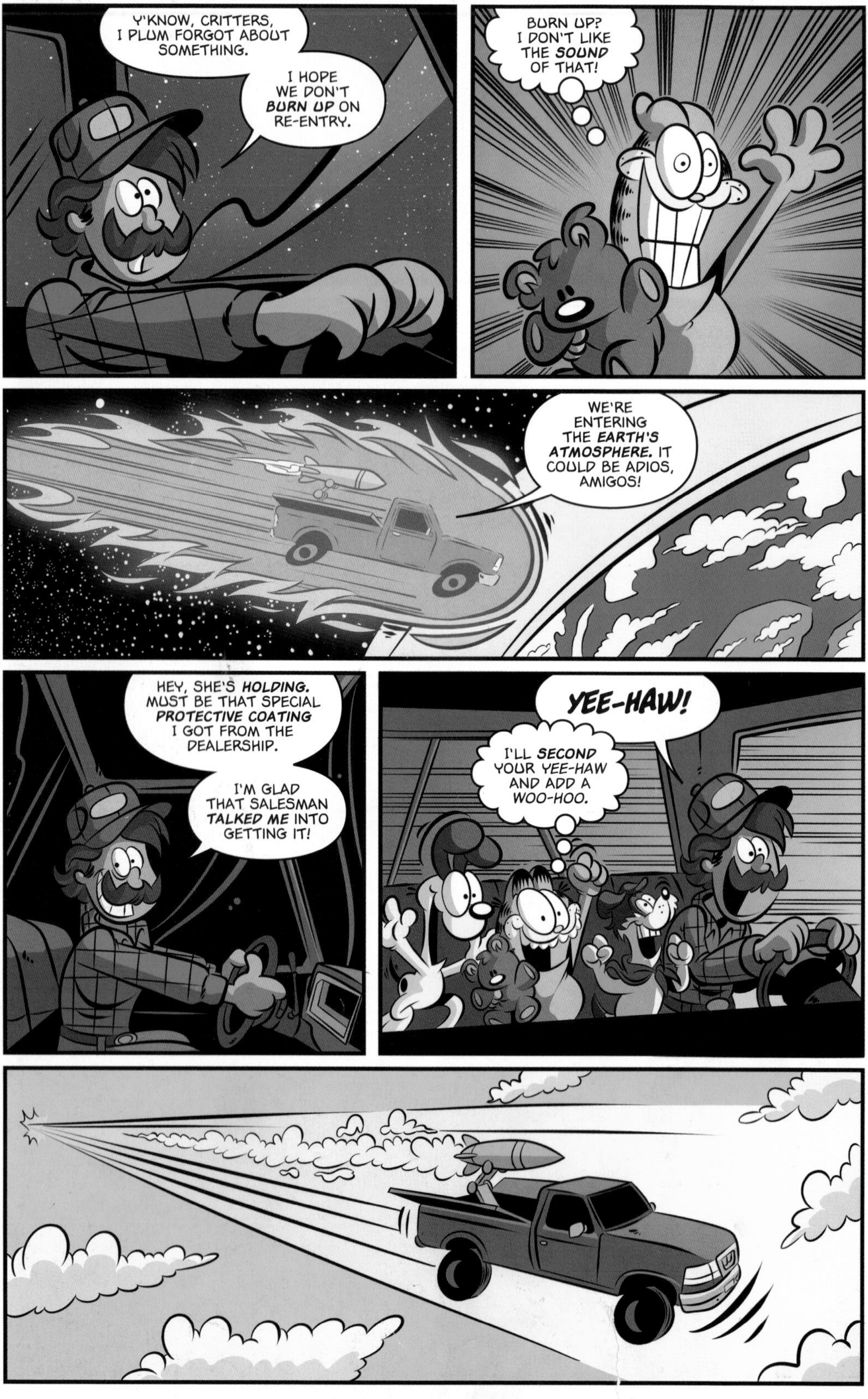
Y'KNOW, CRITTERS, I PLUM FORGOT ABOUT SOMETHING.
I HOPE WE DON'T BURN UP ON RE-ENTRY.
BURN UP? I DON'T LIKE THE SOUND OF THAT!
WE'RE ENTERING THE EARTH'S ATMOSPHERE. IT COULD BE ADIOS, AMIGOS!
HEY, SHE'S HOLDING. MUST BE THAT SPECIAL PROTECTIVE COATING I GOT FROM THE DEALERSHIP.
I'M GLAD THAT SALESMAN TALKED ME INTO GETTING IT!
YEE-HAW!
I'LL SECOND YOUR YEE-HAW AND ADD A WOO-HOO.

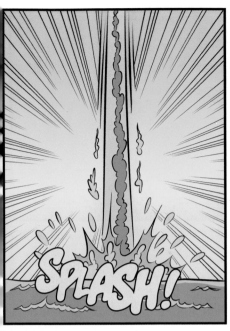

SPLASH!

WE MADE IT!

HEY, EARL. A TRUCK DONE *FELL FROM THE SKY* AND LANDED IN OUR *POND*.

AGAIN.

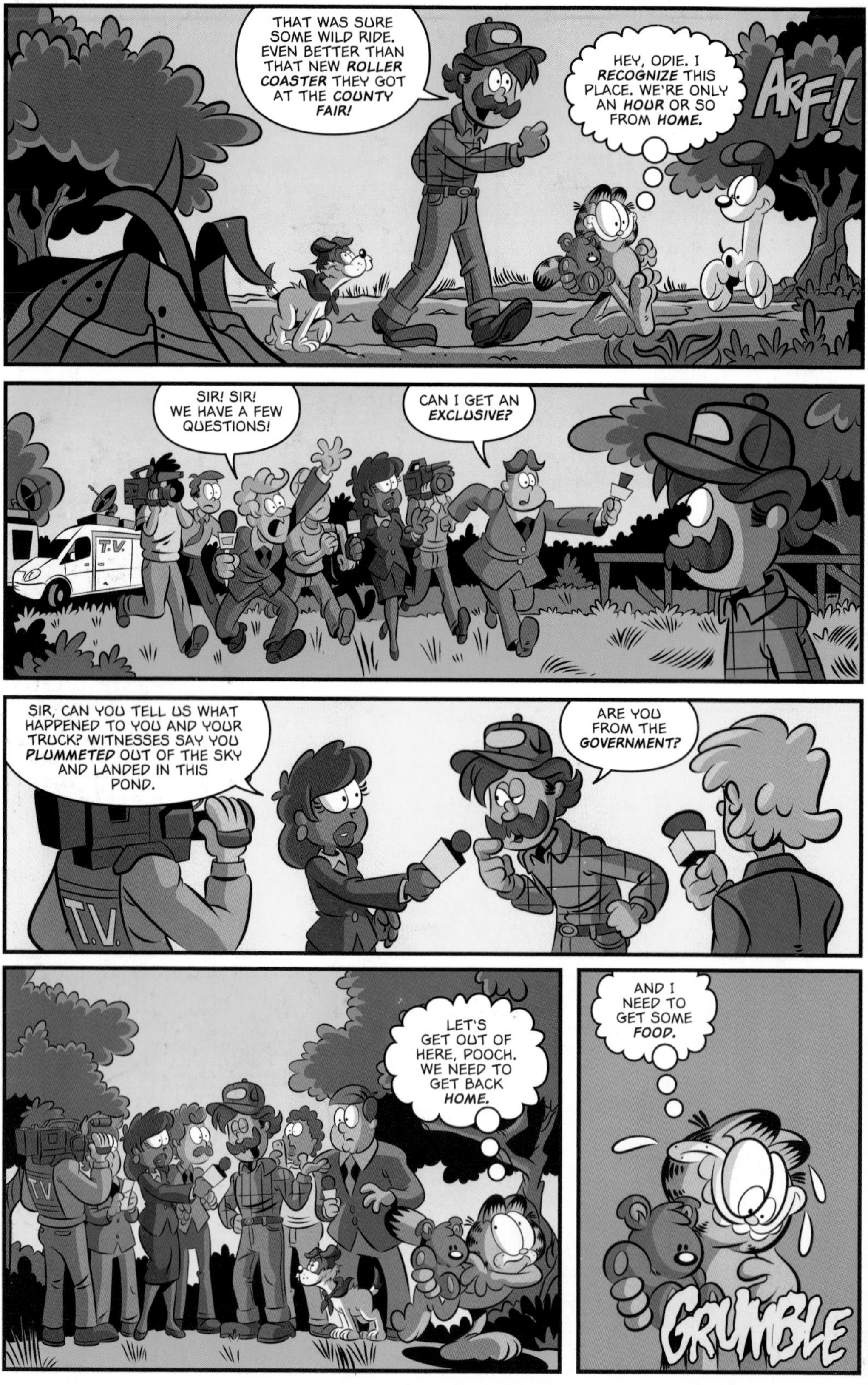
THAT WAS SURE SOME WILD RIDE. EVEN BETTER THAN THAT NEW ROLLER COASTER THEY GOT AT THE COUNTY FAIR!
HEY, ODIE. I RECOGNIZE THIS PLACE. WE'RE ONLY AN HOUR OR SO FROM HOME.
ARF!
SIR! SIR! WE HAVE A FEW QUESTIONS!
CAN I GET AN EXCLUSIVE?
T.V.
SIR, CAN YOU TELL US WHAT HAPPENED TO YOU AND YOUR TRUCK? WITNESSES SAY YOU PLUMMETED OUT OF THE SKY AND LANDED IN THIS POND.
ARE YOU FROM THE GOVERNMENT?
T.V.
LET'S GET OUT OF HERE, POOCH. WE NEED TO GET BACK HOME.
TV
AND I NEED TO GET SOME FOOD.
GRUMBLE

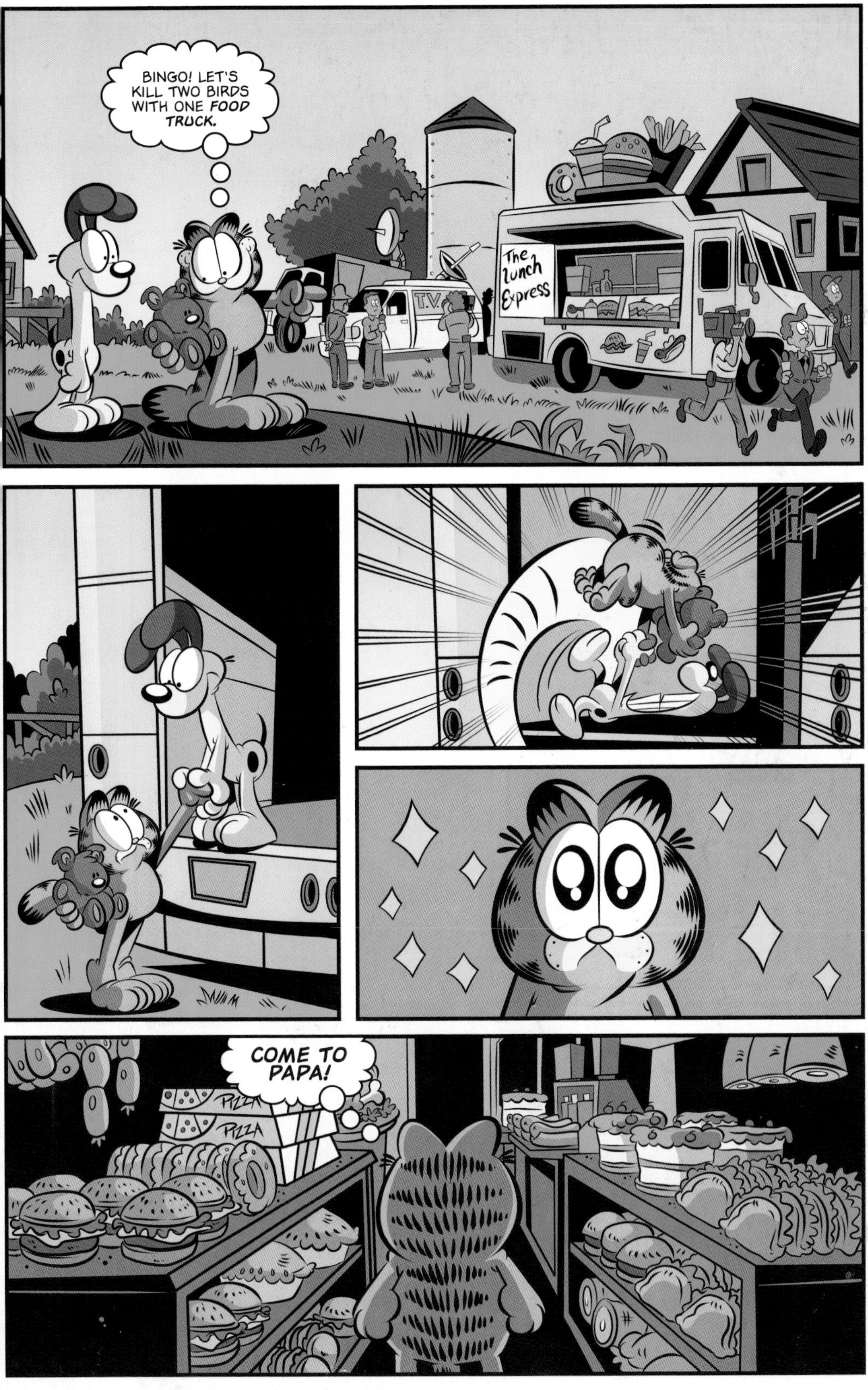
BINGO! LET'S KILL TWO BIRDS WITH ONE FOOD TRUCK.
T.V.
The Lunch Express
COME TO PAPA!
PIZZA
PIZZA

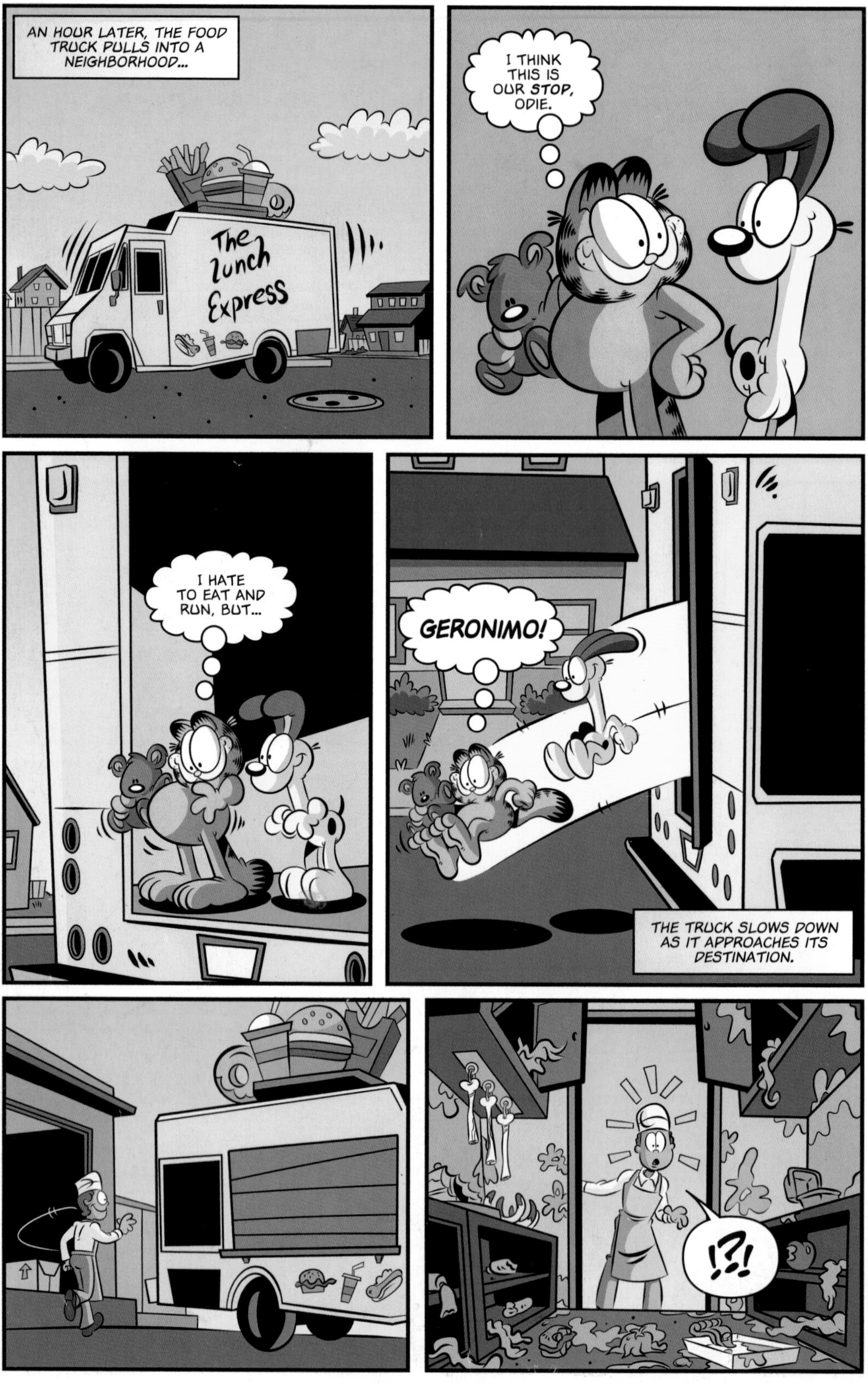
AN HOUR LATER, THE FOOD TRUCK PULLS INTO A NEIGHBORHOOD...
The Lunch Express
I THINK THIS IS OUR STOP, ODIE.
I HATE TO EAT AND RUN, BUT...
GERONIMO!
THE TRUCK SLOWS DOWN AS IT APPROACHES ITS DESTINATION.
!?!

I'M STILL *WORRIED* ABOUT GARFIELD. HE'S BEEN GONE FOR HOURS.

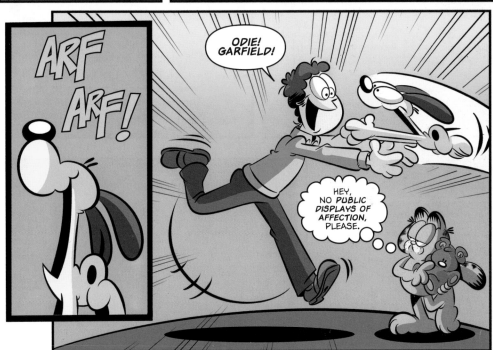

ARF ARF!

ODIE! GARFIELD!

HEY, NO *PUBLIC* DISPLAYS OF AFFECTION, PLEASE.

WHERE *WERE* YOU TWO? I WAS WORRIED.

ARE YOU *HUNGRY?*

I JUST *DEVOURED* THE CONTENTS OF A FOOD TRUCK...

BUT I COULD EAT.

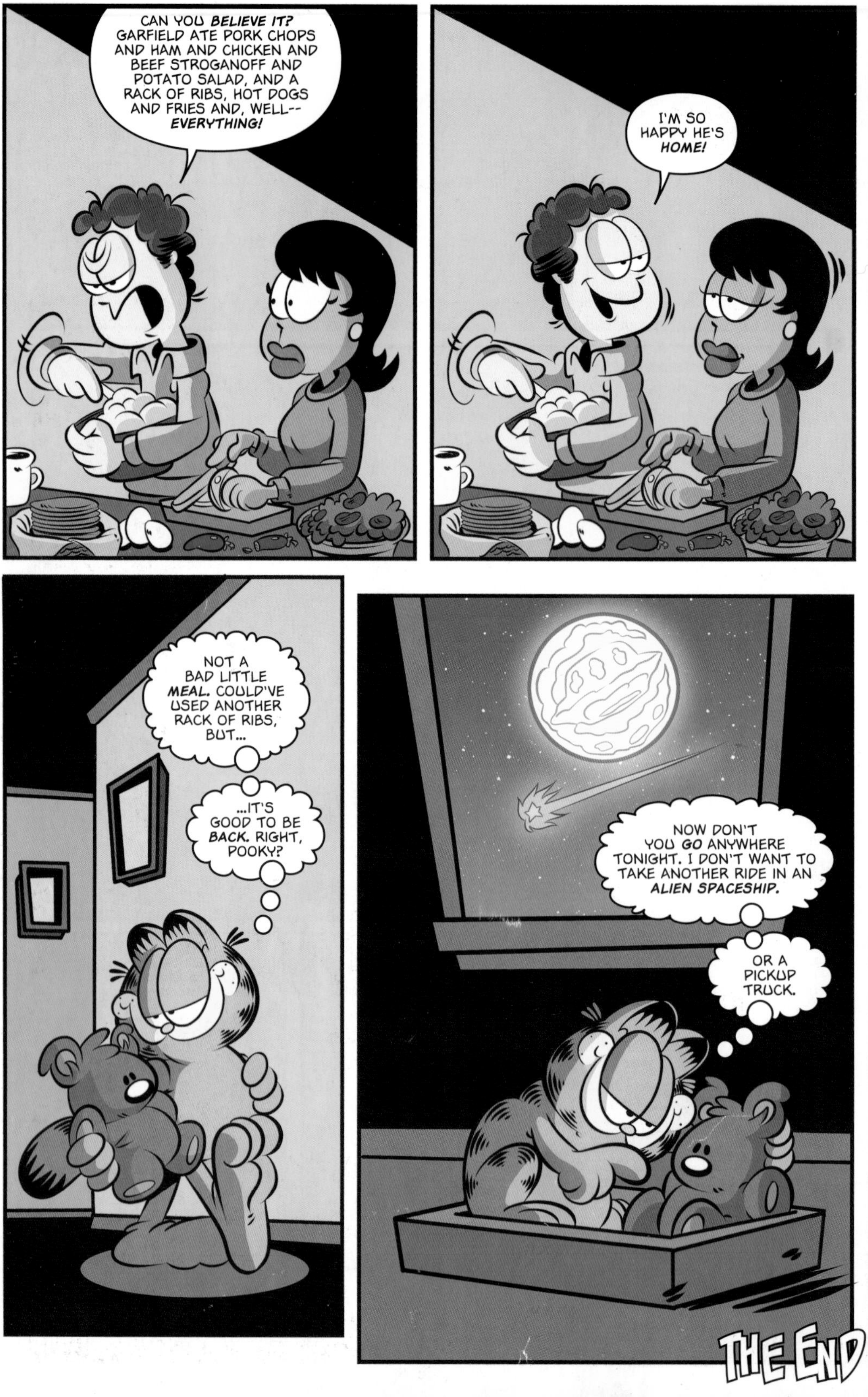
CAN YOU **BELIEVE IT?** GARFIELD ATE PORK CHOPS AND HAM AND CHICKEN AND BEEF STROGANOFF AND POTATO SALAD, AND A RACK OF RIBS, HOT DOGS AND FRIES AND, WELL-- **EVERYTHING!**
I'M SO HAPPY HE'S **HOME!**
NOT A BAD LITTLE **MEAL.** COULD'VE USED ANOTHER RACK OF RIBS, BUT...
...IT'S GOOD TO BE **BACK.** RIGHT, POOKY?
NOW DON'T YOU **GO** ANYWHERE TONIGHT. I DON'T WANT TO TAKE ANOTHER RIDE IN AN **ALIEN SPACESHIP.**
OR A PICKUP TRUCK.
THE END

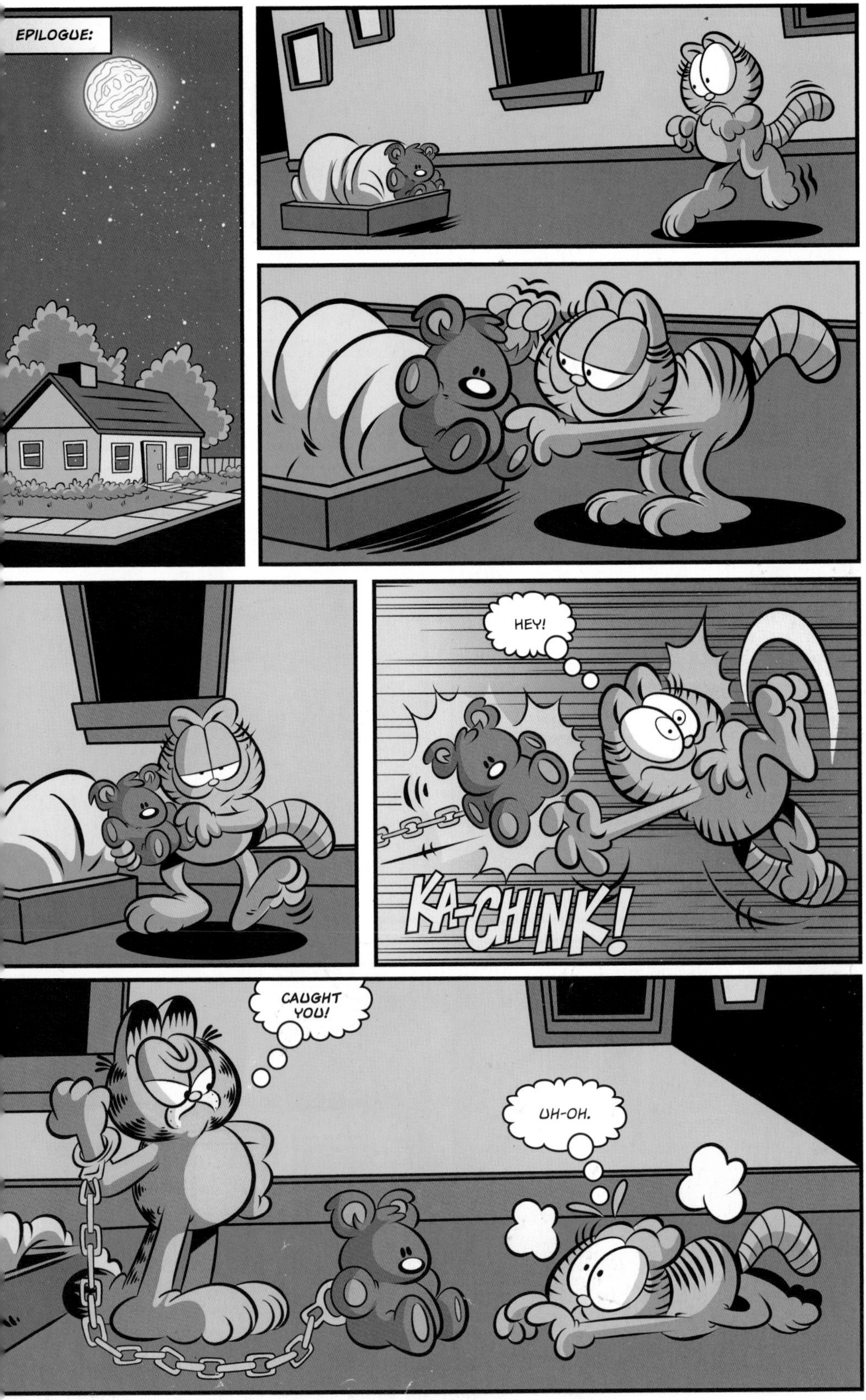
EPILOGUE:
HEY!
KA-CHINK!
CAUGHT YOU!
UH-OH.

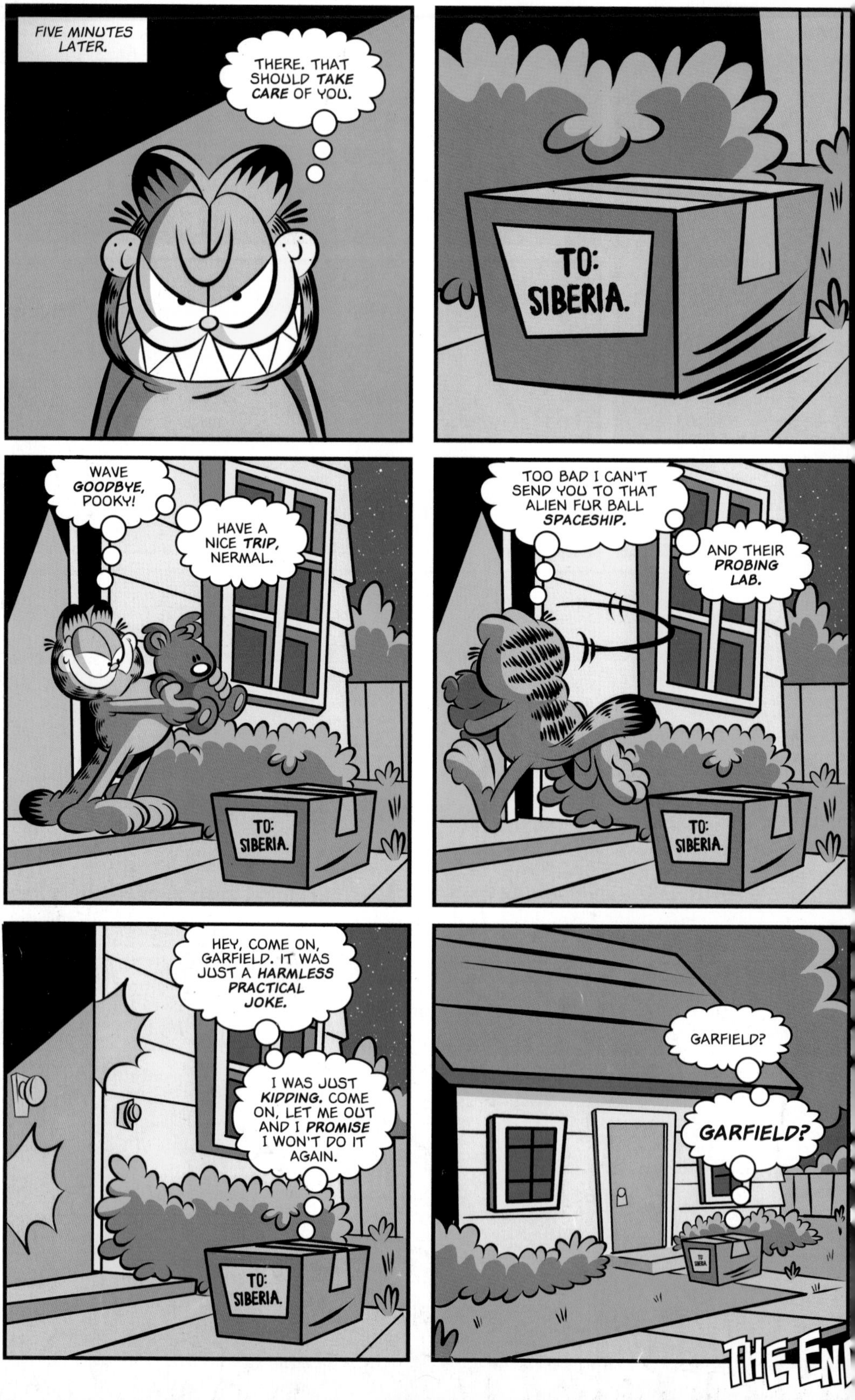
FIVE MINUTES LATER.
THERE. THAT SHOULD TAKE CARE OF YOU.
TO: SIBERIA.
WAVE GOODBYE, POOKY!
HAVE A NICE TRIP, NERMAL.
TO: SIBERIA.
TOO BAD I CAN'T SEND YOU TO THAT ALIEN FUR BALL SPACESHIP.
AND THEIR PROBING LAB.
TO: SIBERIA.
HEY, COME ON, GARFIELD. IT WAS JUST A HARMLESS PRACTICAL JOKE.
I WAS JUST KIDDING. COME ON, LET ME OUT AND I PROMISE I WON'T DO IT AGAIN.
TO: SIBERIA.
GARFIELD?
GARFIELD?
THE END

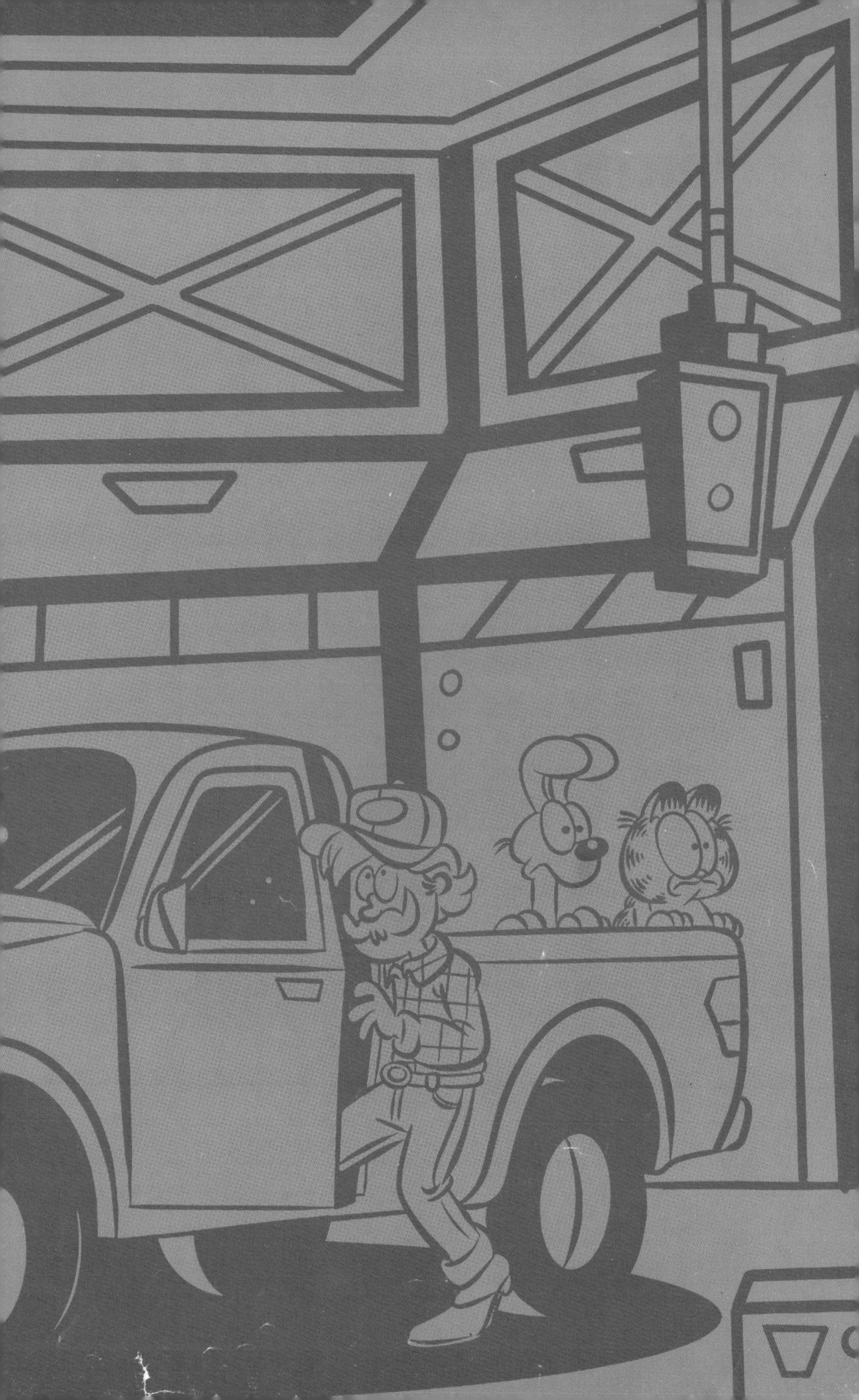

"PRINCESS PRISCILLA"

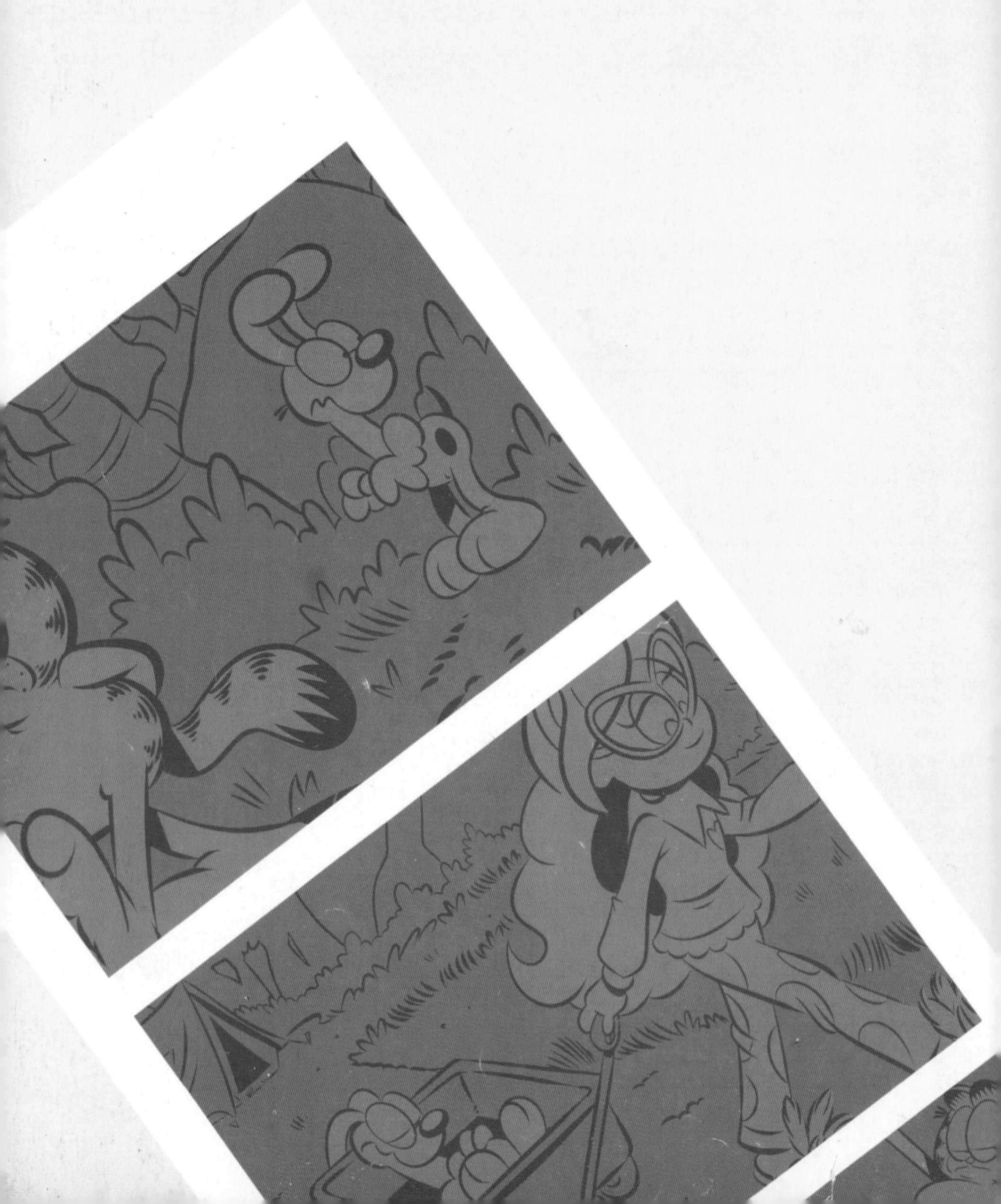

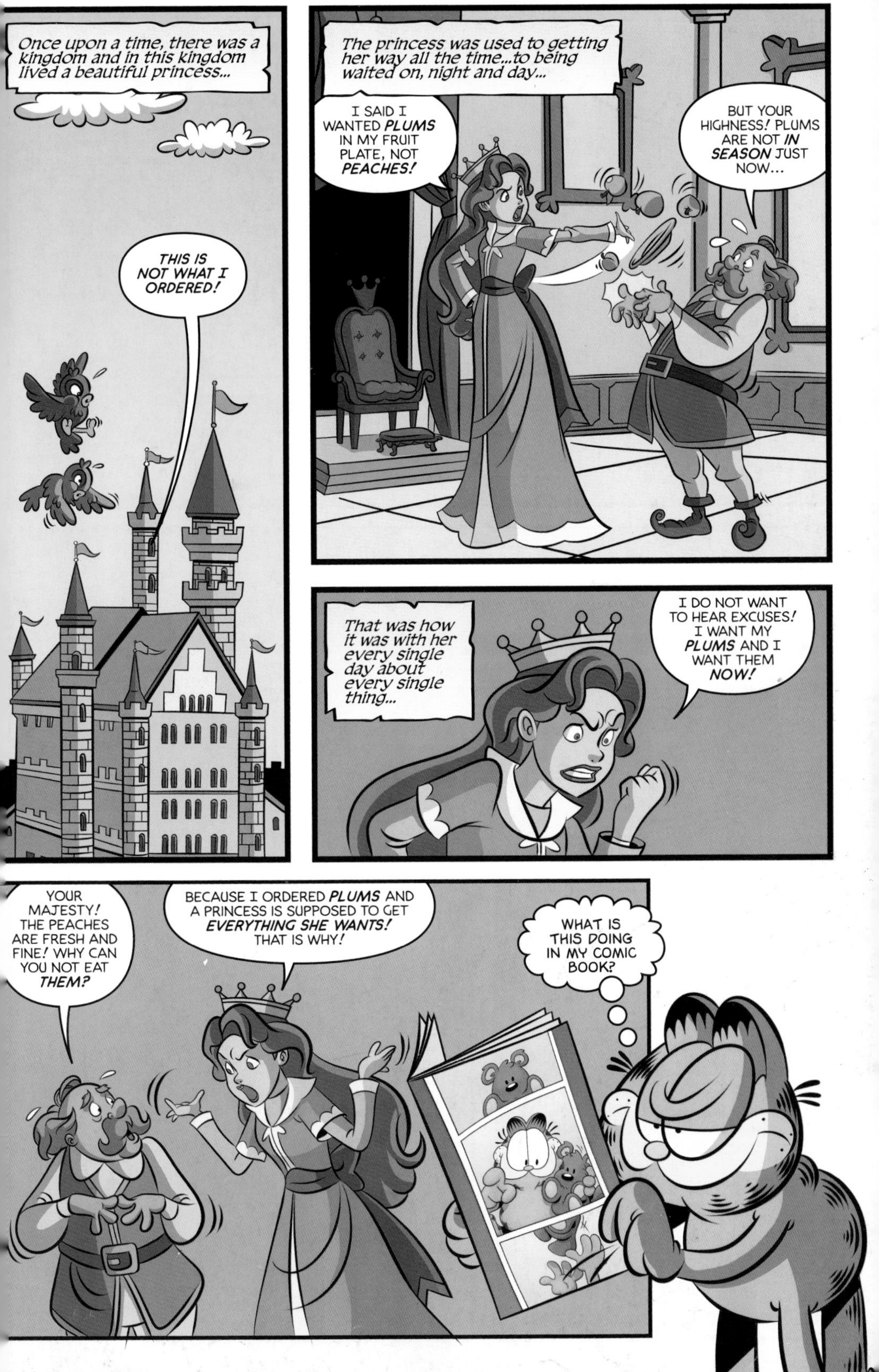
Once upon a time, there was a kingdom and in this kingdom lived a beautiful princess...
THIS IS NOT WHAT I ORDERED!
The princess was used to getting her way all the time...to being waited on, night and day...
I SAID I WANTED PLUMS IN MY FRUIT PLATE, NOT PEACHES!
BUT YOUR HIGHNESS! PLUMS ARE NOT IN SEASON JUST NOW...
That was how it was with her every single day about every single thing...
I DO NOT WANT TO HEAR EXCUSES! I WANT MY PLUMS AND I WANT THEM NOW!
YOUR MAJESTY! THE PEACHES ARE FRESH AND FINE! WHY CAN YOU NOT EAT THEM?
BECAUSE I ORDERED PLUMS AND A PRINCESS IS SUPPOSED TO GET EVERYTHING SHE WANTS! THAT IS WHY!
WHAT IS THIS DOING IN MY COMIC BOOK?

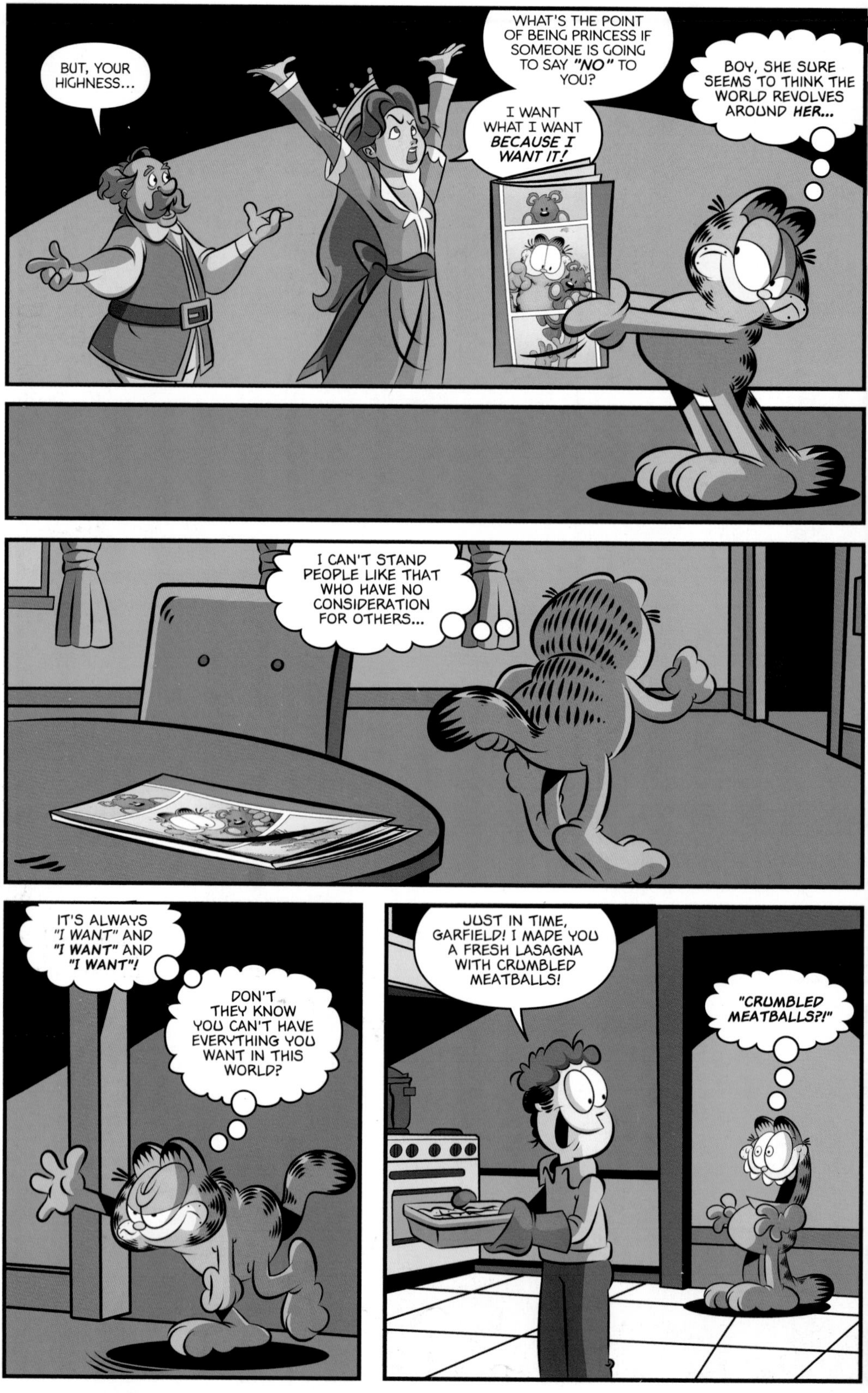
BUT, YOUR HIGHNESS...
WHAT'S THE POINT OF BEING PRINCESS IF SOMEONE IS GOING TO SAY "NO" TO YOU?
I WANT WHAT I WANT BECAUSE I WANT IT!
BOY, SHE SURE SEEMS TO THINK THE WORLD REVOLVES AROUND HER...
I CAN'T STAND PEOPLE LIKE THAT WHO HAVE NO CONSIDERATION FOR OTHERS...
IT'S ALWAYS "I WANT" AND "I WANT" AND "I WANT"!
DON'T THEY KNOW YOU CAN'T HAVE EVERYTHING YOU WANT IN THIS WORLD?
JUST IN TIME, GARFIELD! I MADE YOU A FRESH LASAGNA WITH CRUMBLED MEATBALLS!
"CRUMBLED MEATBALLS?!"

I DON'T WANT LASAGNA WITH CRUMBLED MEATBALLS!
I WOULD NEVER IN A MILLION YEARS EAT LASAGNA WITH CRUMBLED MEATBALLS!
WRONG, WRONG, WRONG!
OH, THAT'S RIGHT! YOU WANTED LASAGNA WITH SAUSAGE!
I'M ALL OUT OF SAUSAGE, GARFIELD! I'LL RUN TO THE STORE AND GET SOME!
BACK IN A JIF!
WHAT ARE YOU LOOKING AT, PUP?
ARF ARF! ARF ARF ARF ARF!
ARF ARF ARF!
YOU'RE SAYING I REMIND YOU OF SOMEONE?
WHO DO I REMIND YOU OF?
OKAY, I'LL FOLLOW YOU.
BUT TELL ME: WHO DO I REMIND YOU OF?

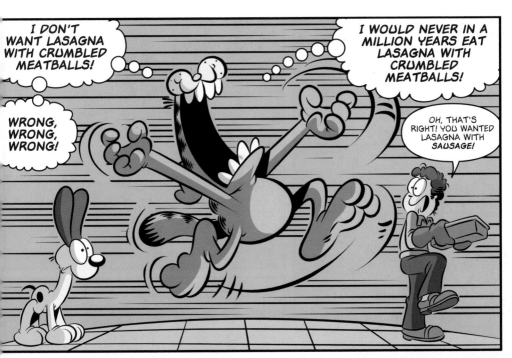

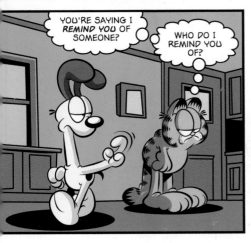

OH.

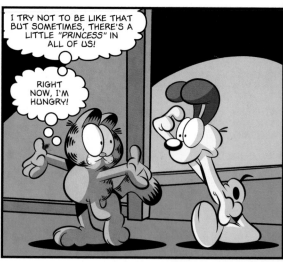

I TRY NOT TO BE LIKE THAT BUT SOMETIMES, THERE'S A LITTLE "PRINCESS" IN ALL OF US!

RIGHT NOW, I'M HUNGRY!

IT'LL TAKE JON TWENTY MINUTES TO GET BACK FROM THE MARKET...TWO MORE HOURS TO BAKE A NEW LASAGNA WITH SAUSAGE...

YEAH, I KNOW ⇒GULP!⇐ I SAID I'D NEVER EAT LASAGNA WITH CRUMBLED MEATBALLS BUT ⇒GULP!⇐ I FORGOT...

THE WRONG LASAGNA IS STILL ⇒SLOBBER!⇐ BETTER THAN ⇒GULP!⇐ NO LASAGNA!

HUH?

YUM!

CHEW!

SLURP!

GULP!

The next day, Jon decided to take his pets camping...

...Which calls to mind another story, one that also begins with "Once Upon a Time"...

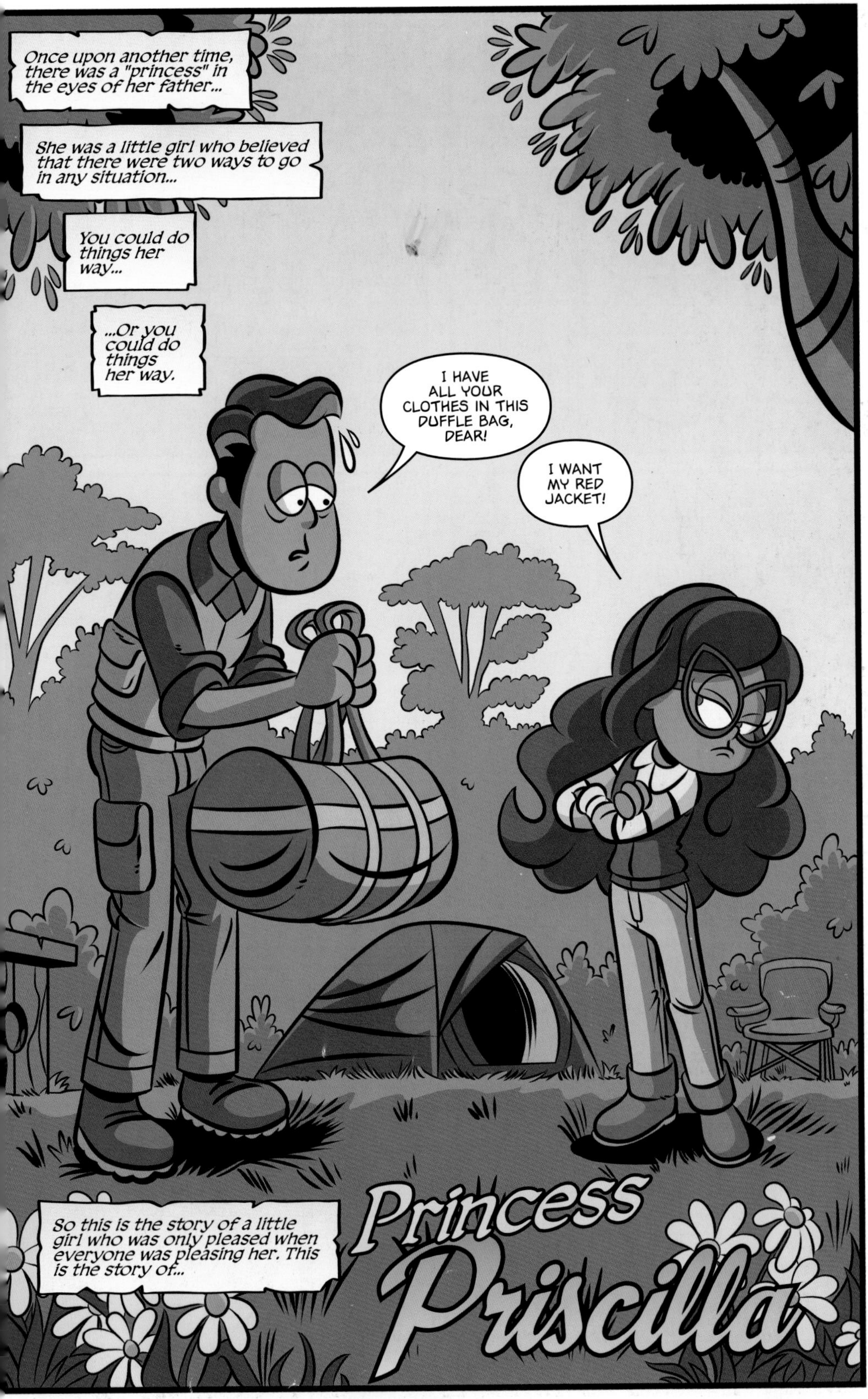
Once upon another time, there was a "princess" in the eyes of her father...
She was a little girl who believed that there were two ways to go in any situation...
You could do things her way...
...Or you could do things her way.
I HAVE ALL YOUR CLOTHES IN THIS DUFFLE BAG, DEAR!
I WANT MY RED JACKET!
So this is the story of a little girl who was only pleased when everyone was pleasing her. This is the story of...
Princess Priscilla

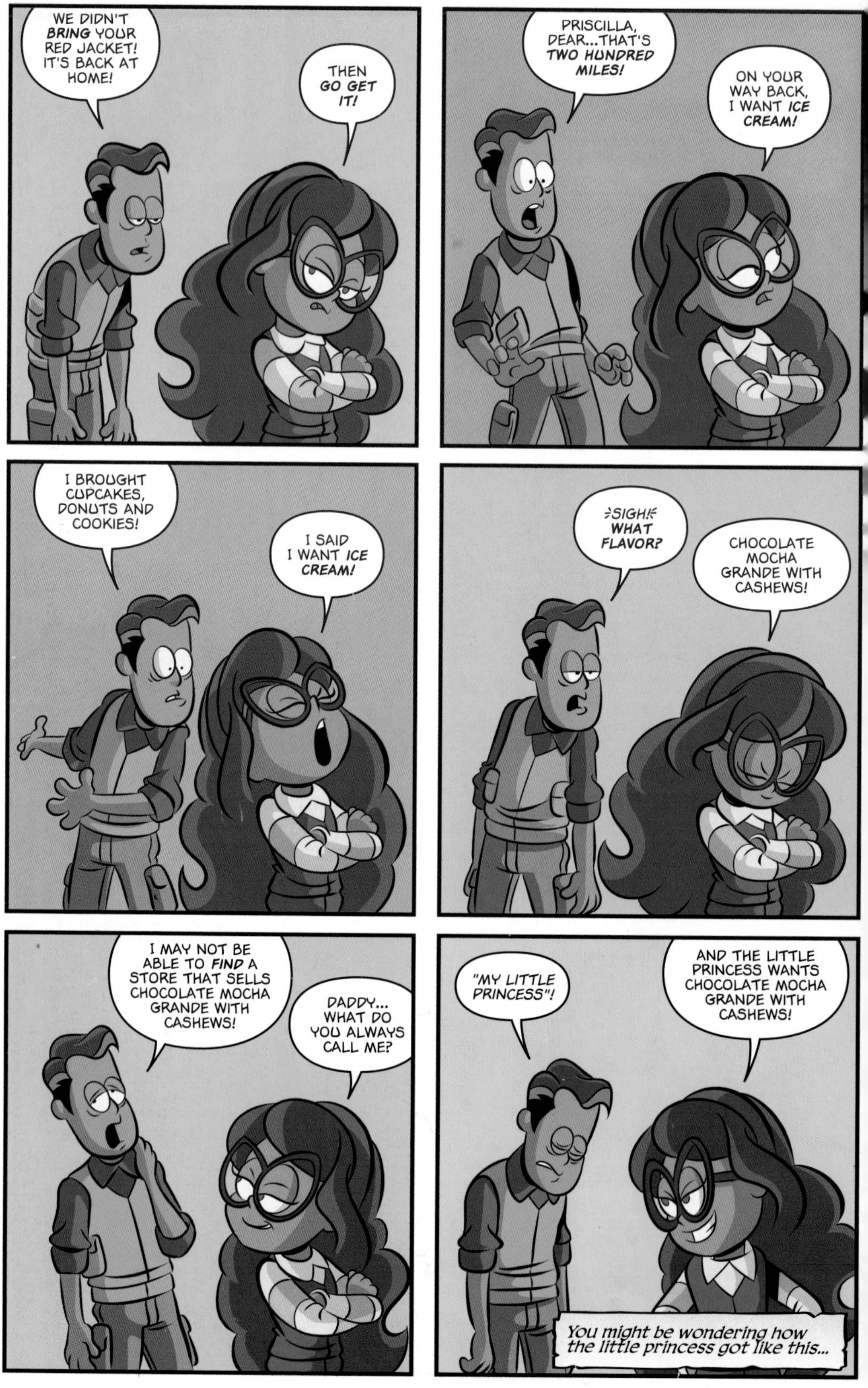
WE DIDN'T BRING YOUR RED JACKET! IT'S BACK AT HOME!
THEN GO GET IT!
PRISCILLA, DEAR...THAT'S TWO HUNDRED MILES!
ON YOUR WAY BACK, I WANT ICE CREAM!
I BROUGHT CUPCAKES, DONUTS AND COOKIES!
I SAID I WANT ICE CREAM!
SIGH! WHAT FLAVOR?
CHOCOLATE MOCHA GRANDE WITH CASHEWS!
I MAY NOT BE ABLE TO FIND A STORE THAT SELLS CHOCOLATE MOCHA GRANDE WITH CASHEWS!
DADDY... WHAT DO YOU ALWAYS CALL ME?
"MY LITTLE PRINCESS"!
AND THE LITTLE PRINCESS WANTS CHOCOLATE MOCHA GRANDE WITH CASHEWS!
You might be wondering how the little princess got like this...

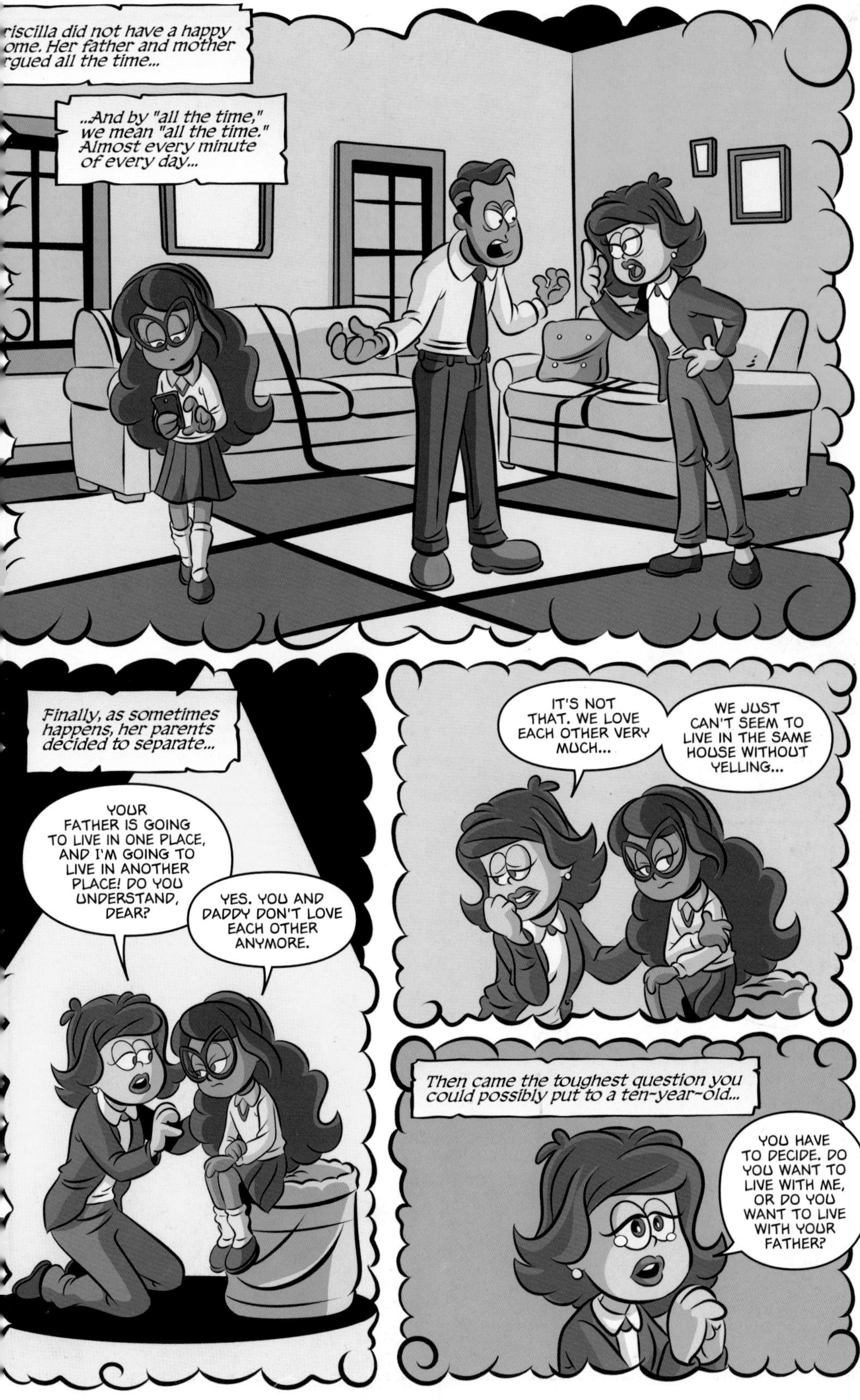
riscilla did not have a happy ome. Her father and mother rgued all the time...
...And by "all the time," we mean "all the time." Almost every minute of every day...
Finally, as sometimes happens, her parents decided to separate...
YOUR FATHER IS GOING TO LIVE IN ONE PLACE, AND I'M GOING TO LIVE IN ANOTHER PLACE! DO YOU UNDERSTAND, DEAR?
YES. YOU AND DADDY DON'T LOVE EACH OTHER ANYMORE.
IT'S NOT THAT. WE LOVE EACH OTHER VERY MUCH...
WE JUST CAN'T SEEM TO LIVE IN THE SAME HOUSE WITHOUT YELLING...
Then came the toughest question you could possibly put to a ten-year-old...
YOU HAVE TO DECIDE. DO YOU WANT TO LIVE WITH ME, OR DO YOU WANT TO LIVE WITH YOUR FATHER?

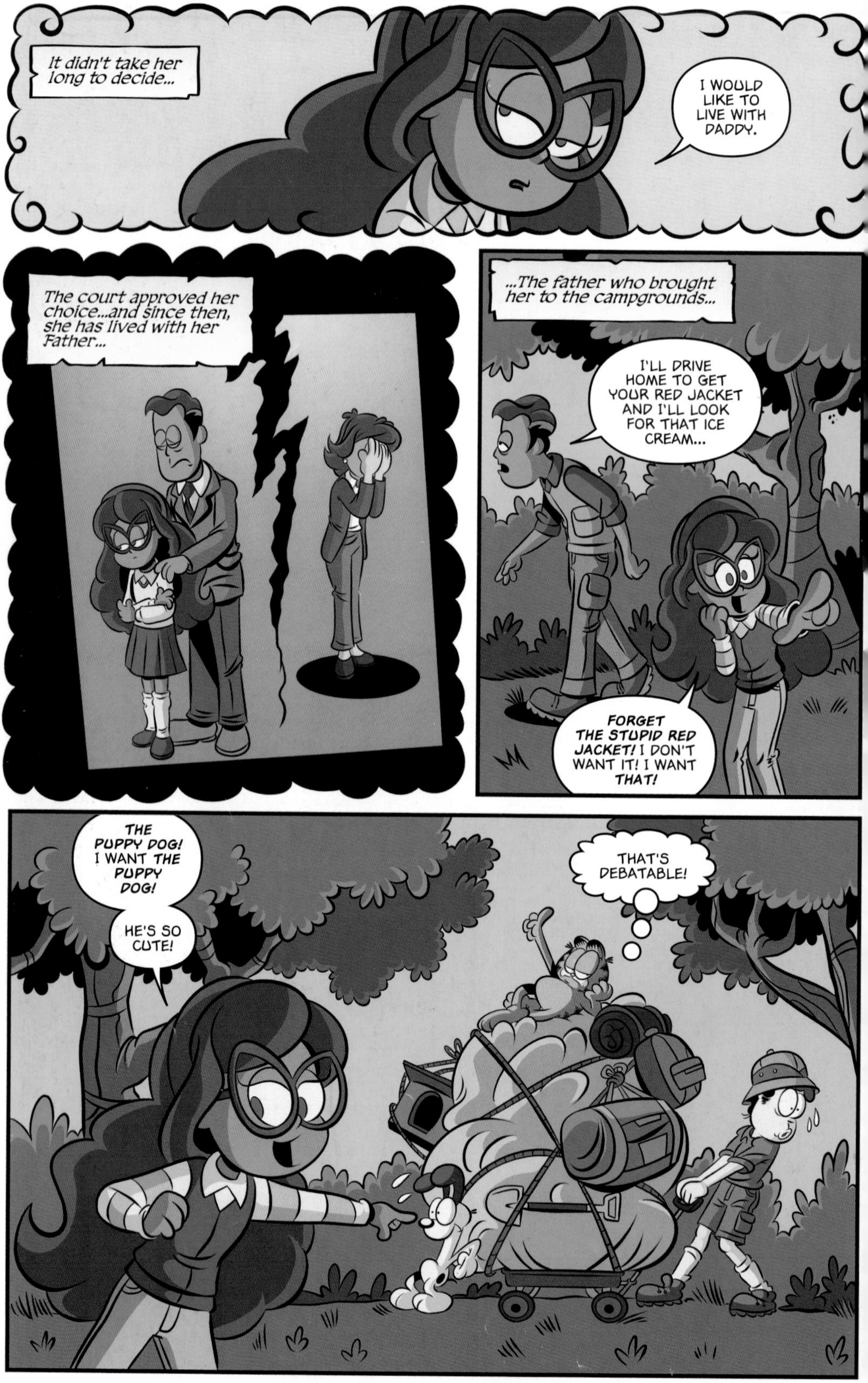
It didn't take her long to decide...
I WOULD LIKE TO LIVE WITH DADDY.
The court approved her choice...and since then, she has lived with her Father...
...The father who brought her to the campgrounds...
I'LL DRIVE HOME TO GET YOUR RED JACKET AND I'LL LOOK FOR THAT ICE CREAM...
FORGET THE STUPID RED JACKET! I DON'T WANT IT! I WANT THAT!
THE PUPPY DOG! I WANT THE PUPPY DOG!
HE'S SO CUTE!
THAT'S DEBATABLE!

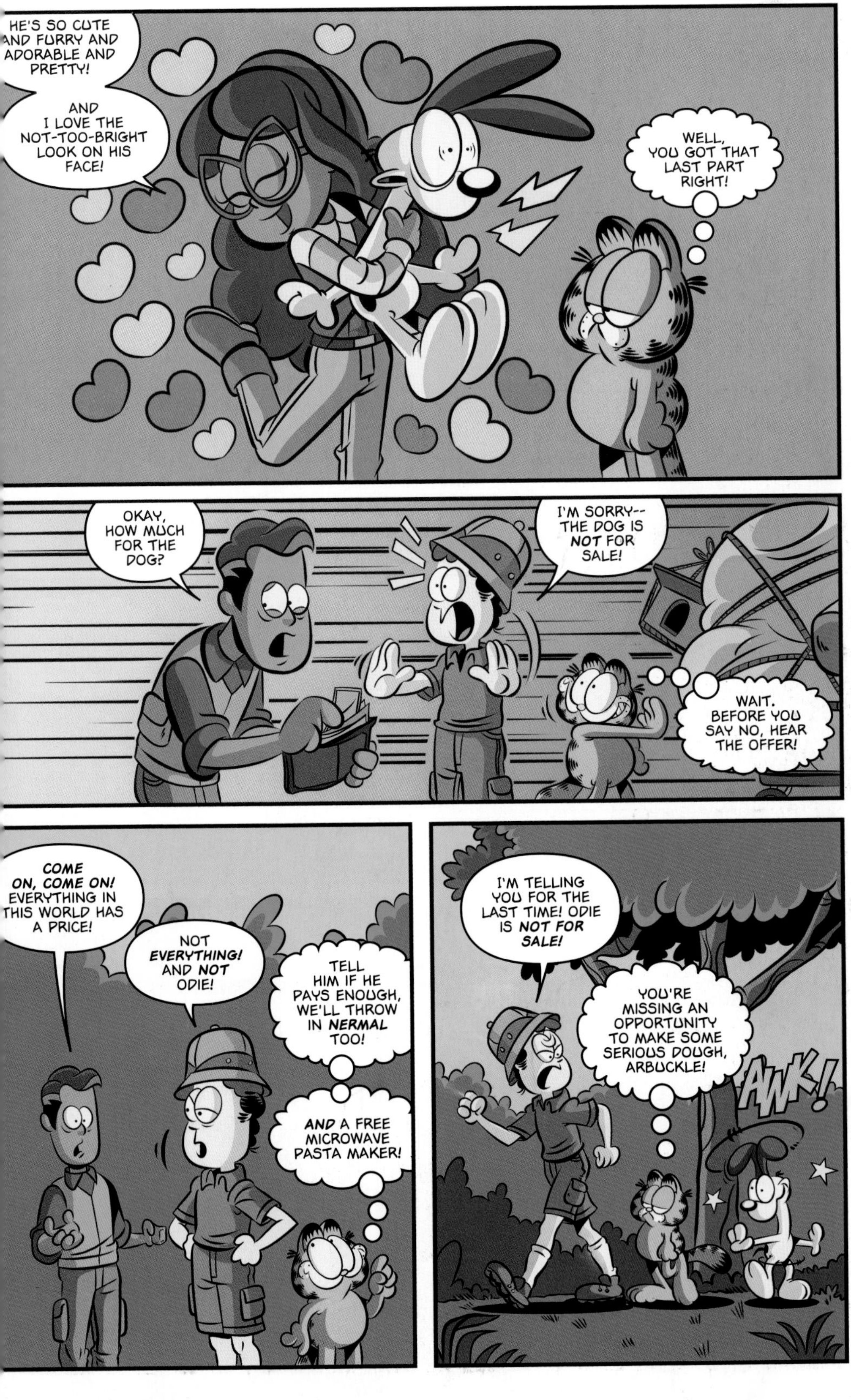
HE'S SO CUTE AND FURRY AND ADORABLE AND PRETTY!
AND I LOVE THE NOT-TOO-BRIGHT LOOK ON HIS FACE!
WELL, YOU GOT THAT LAST PART RIGHT!
OKAY, HOW MUCH FOR THE DOG?
I'M SORRY-- THE DOG IS NOT FOR SALE!
WAIT. BEFORE YOU SAY NO, HEAR THE OFFER!
COME ON, COME ON! EVERYTHING IN THIS WORLD HAS A PRICE!
NOT EVERYTHING! AND NOT ODIE!
TELL HIM IF HE PAYS ENOUGH, WE'LL THROW IN NERMAL TOO!
AND A FREE MICROWAVE PASTA MAKER!
I'M TELLING YOU FOR THE LAST TIME! ODIE IS NOT FOR SALE!
YOU'RE MISSING AN OPPORTUNITY TO MAKE SOME SERIOUS DOUGH, ARBUCKLE!
AWK!

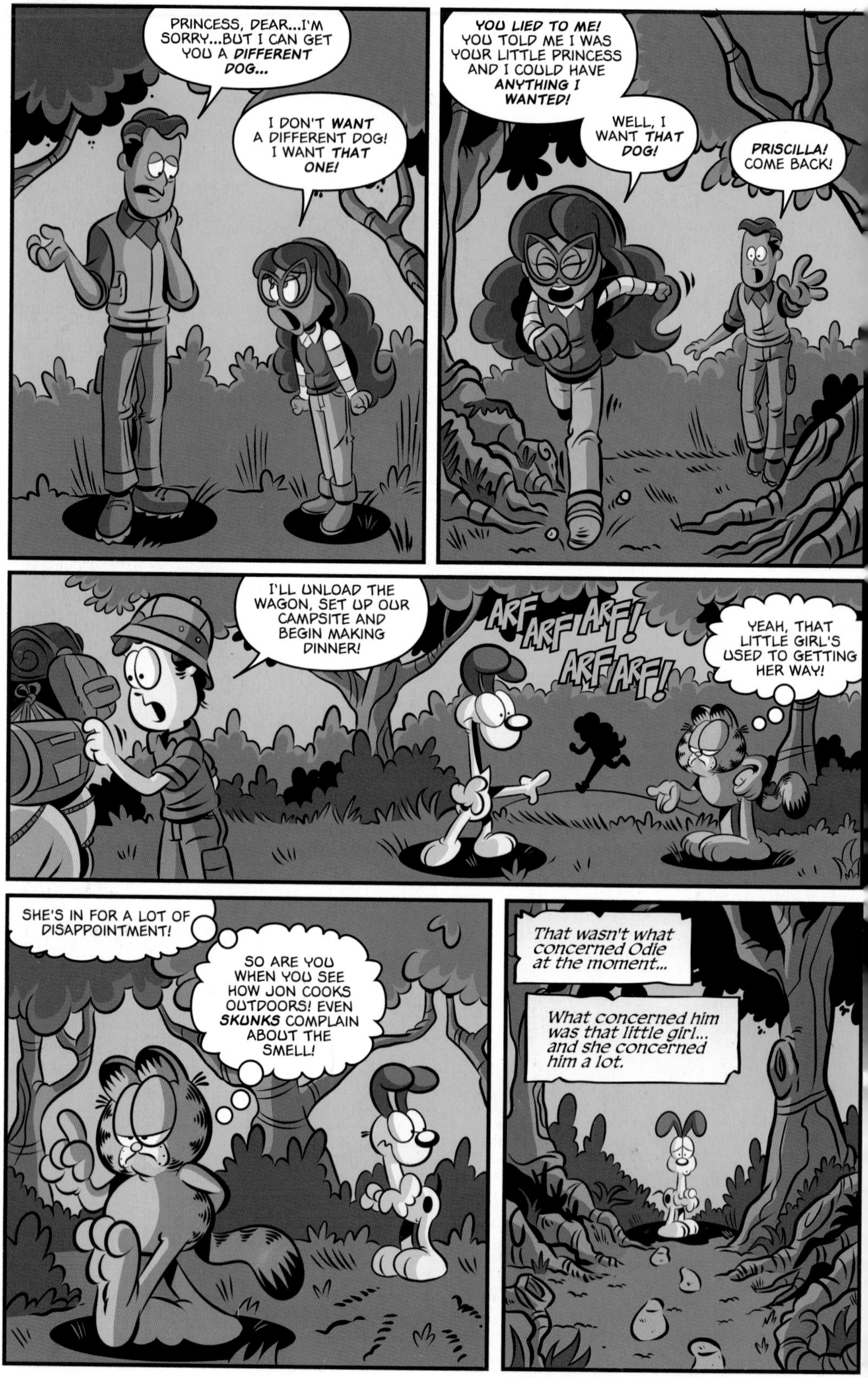
PRINCESS, DEAR...I'M SORRY...BUT I CAN GET YOU A DIFFERENT DOG...
I DON'T WANT A DIFFERENT DOG! I WANT THAT ONE!
YOU LIED TO ME! YOU TOLD ME I WAS YOUR LITTLE PRINCESS AND I COULD HAVE ANYTHING I WANTED!
WELL, I WANT THAT DOG!
PRISCILLA! COME BACK!
I'LL UNLOAD THE WAGON, SET UP OUR CAMPSITE AND BEGIN MAKING DINNER!
ARF ARF ARF!
ARF ARF!
YEAH, THAT LITTLE GIRL'S USED TO GETTING HER WAY!
SHE'S IN FOR A LOT OF DISAPPOINTMENT!
SO ARE YOU WHEN YOU SEE HOW JON COOKS OUTDOORS! EVEN SKUNKS COMPLAIN ABOUT THE SMELL!
That wasn't what concerned Odie at the moment...
What concerned him was that little girl... and she concerned him a lot.

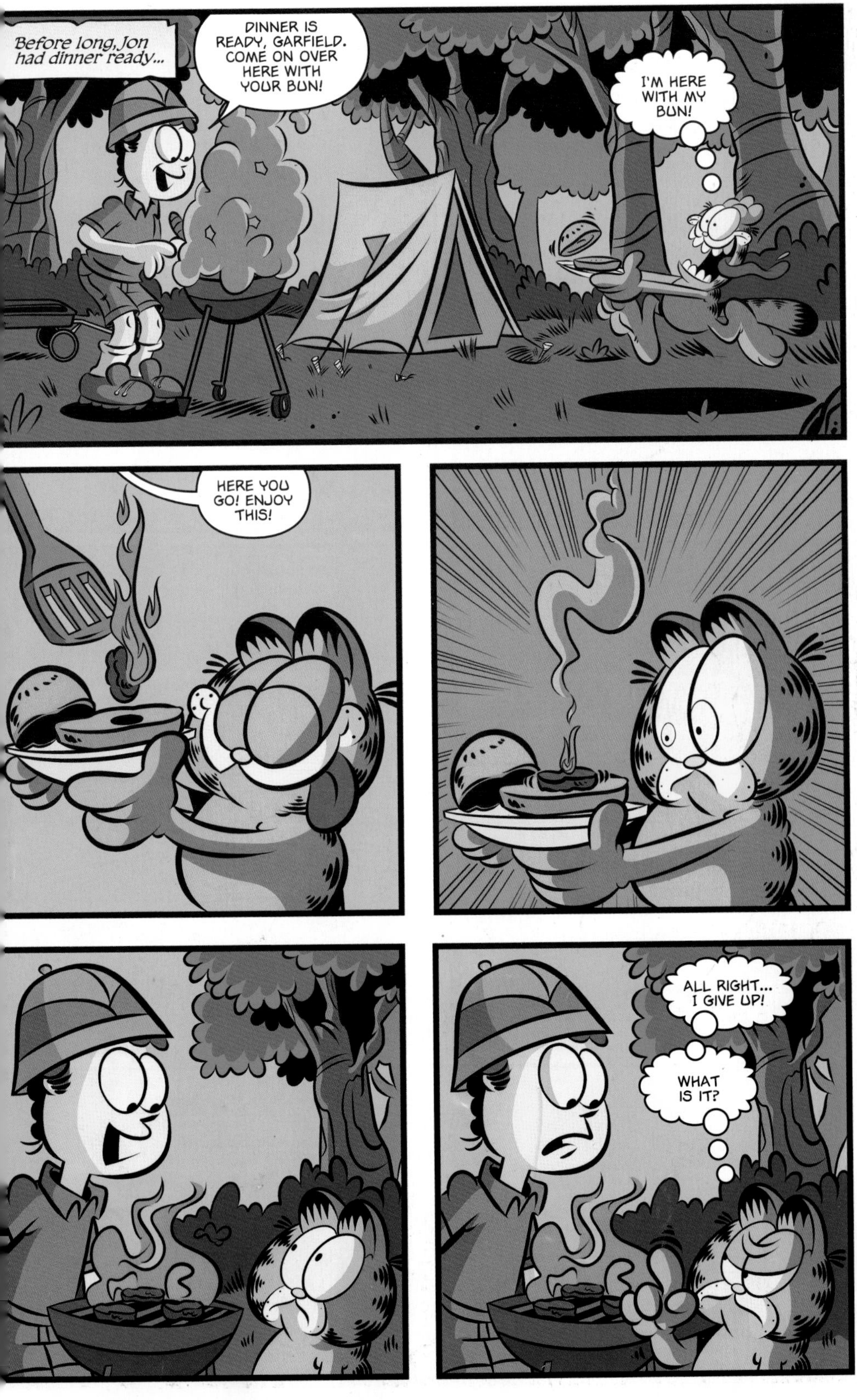
Before long, Jon had dinner ready...
DINNER IS READY, GARFIELD. COME ON OVER HERE WITH YOUR BUN!
I'M HERE WITH MY BUN!
HERE YOU GO! ENJOY THIS!
ALL RIGHT... I GIVE UP!
WHAT IS IT?

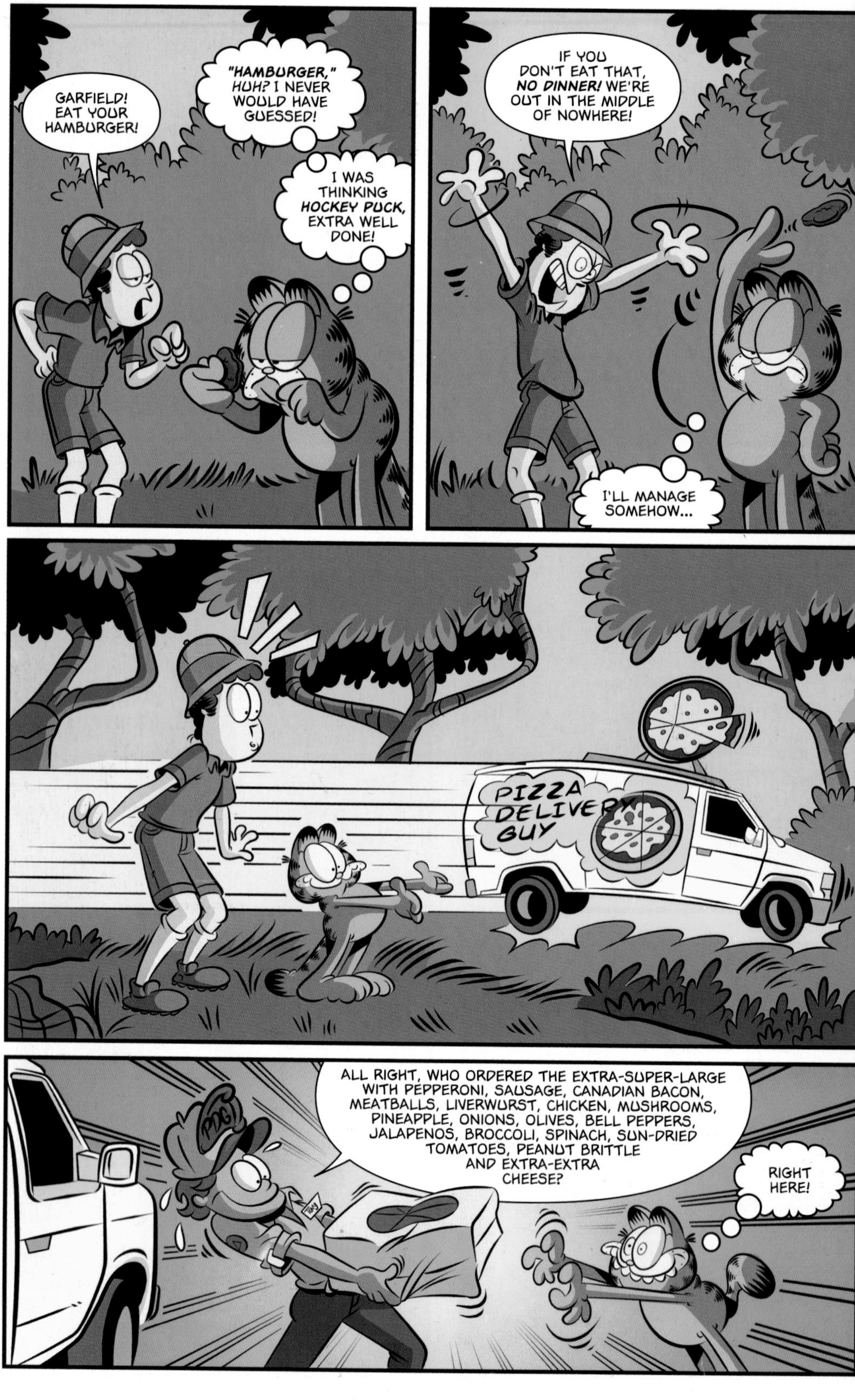
GARFIELD! EAT YOUR HAMBURGER!
"HAMBURGER," HUH? I NEVER WOULD HAVE GUESSED!
I WAS THINKING HOCKEY PUCK, EXTRA WELL DONE!
IF YOU DON'T EAT THAT, NO DINNER! WE'RE OUT IN THE MIDDLE OF NOWHERE!
I'LL MANAGE SOMEHOW...
PIZZA DELIVERY GUY
PDG
ALL RIGHT, WHO ORDERED THE EXTRA-SUPER-LARGE WITH PEPPERONI, SAUSAGE, CANADIAN BACON, MEATBALLS, LIVERWURST, CHICKEN, MUSHROOMS, PINEAPPLE, ONIONS, OLIVES, BELL PEPPERS, JALAPENOS, BROCCOLI, SPINACH, SUN-DRIED TOMATOES, PEANUT BRITTLE AND EXTRA-EXTRA CHEESE?
RIGHT HERE!

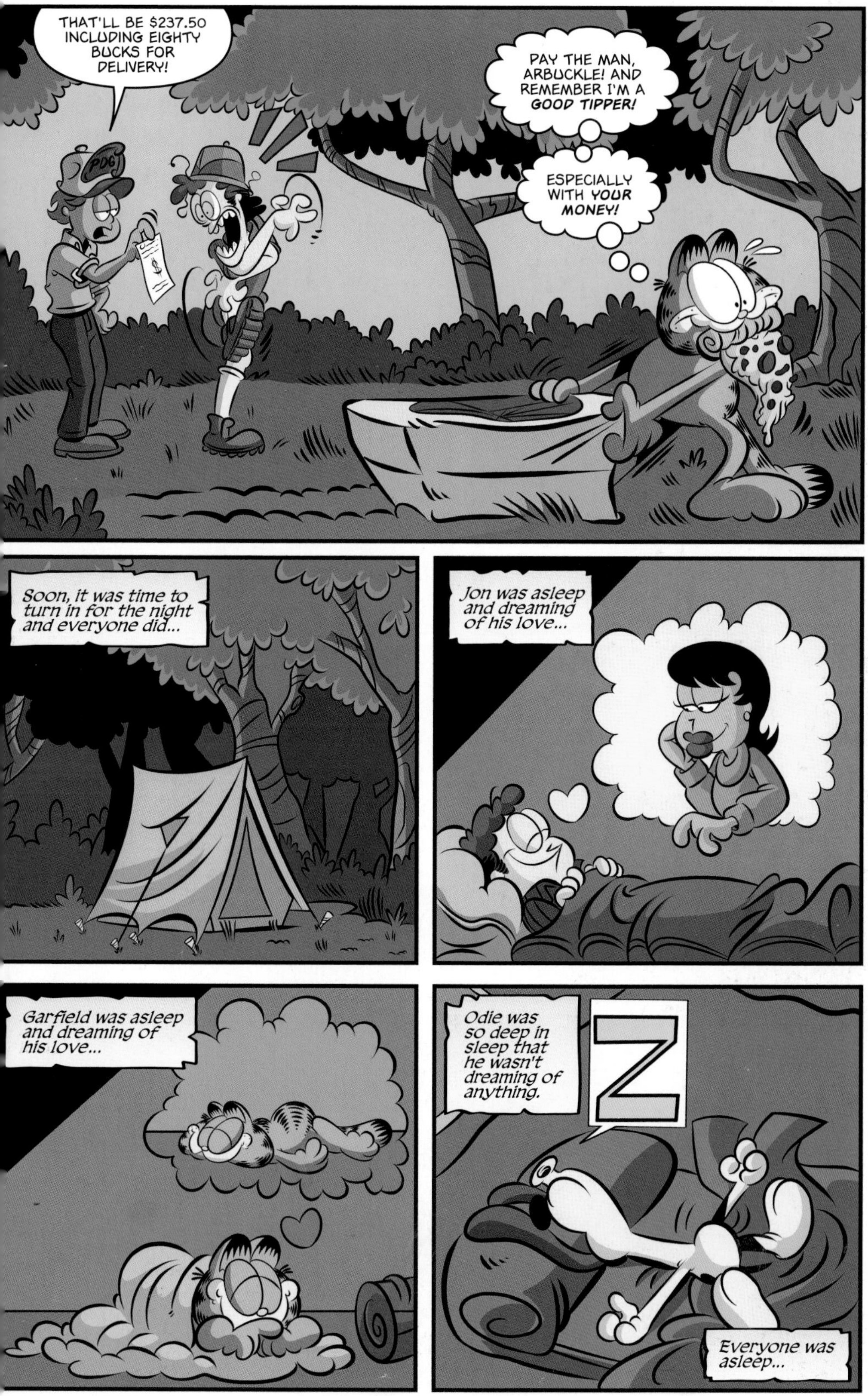
THAT'LL BE $237.50 INCLUDING EIGHTY BUCKS FOR DELIVERY!
PAY THE MAN, ARBUCKLE! AND REMEMBER I'M A GOOD TIPPER!
ESPECIALLY WITH YOUR MONEY!
Soon, it was time to turn in for the night and everyone did...
Jon was asleep and dreaming of his love...
Garfield was asleep and dreaming of his love...
Odie was so deep in sleep that he wasn't dreaming of anything.
Z
Everyone was asleep...

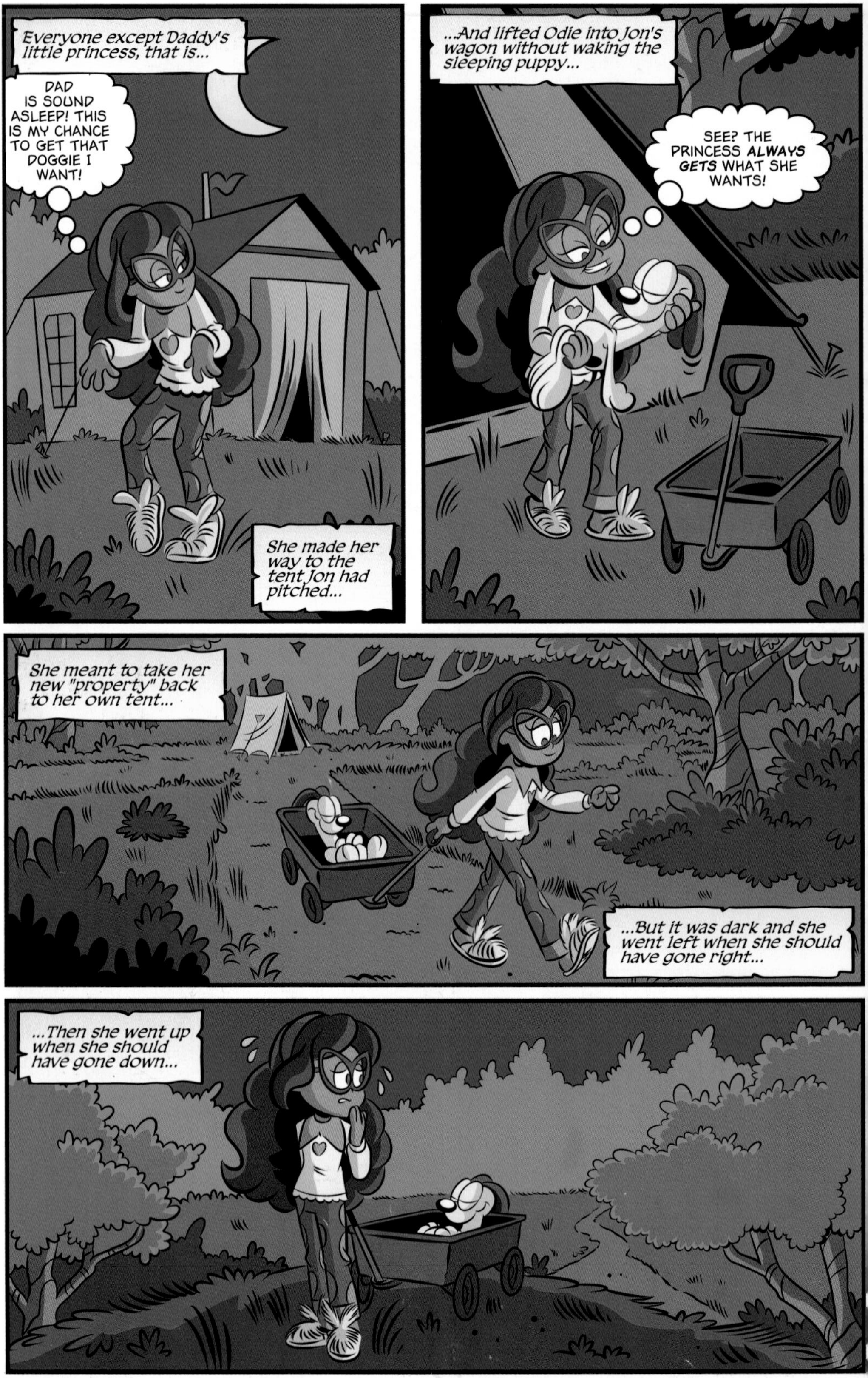
Everyone except Daddy's little princess, that is...
DAD IS SOUND ASLEEP! THIS IS MY CHANCE TO GET THAT DOGGIE I WANT!
She made her way to the tent Jon had pitched...
...And lifted Odie into Jon's wagon without waking the sleeping puppy...
SEE? THE PRINCESS ALWAYS GETS WHAT SHE WANTS!
She meant to take her new "property" back to her own tent...
...But it was dark and she went left when she should have gone right...
...Then she went up when she should have gone down...

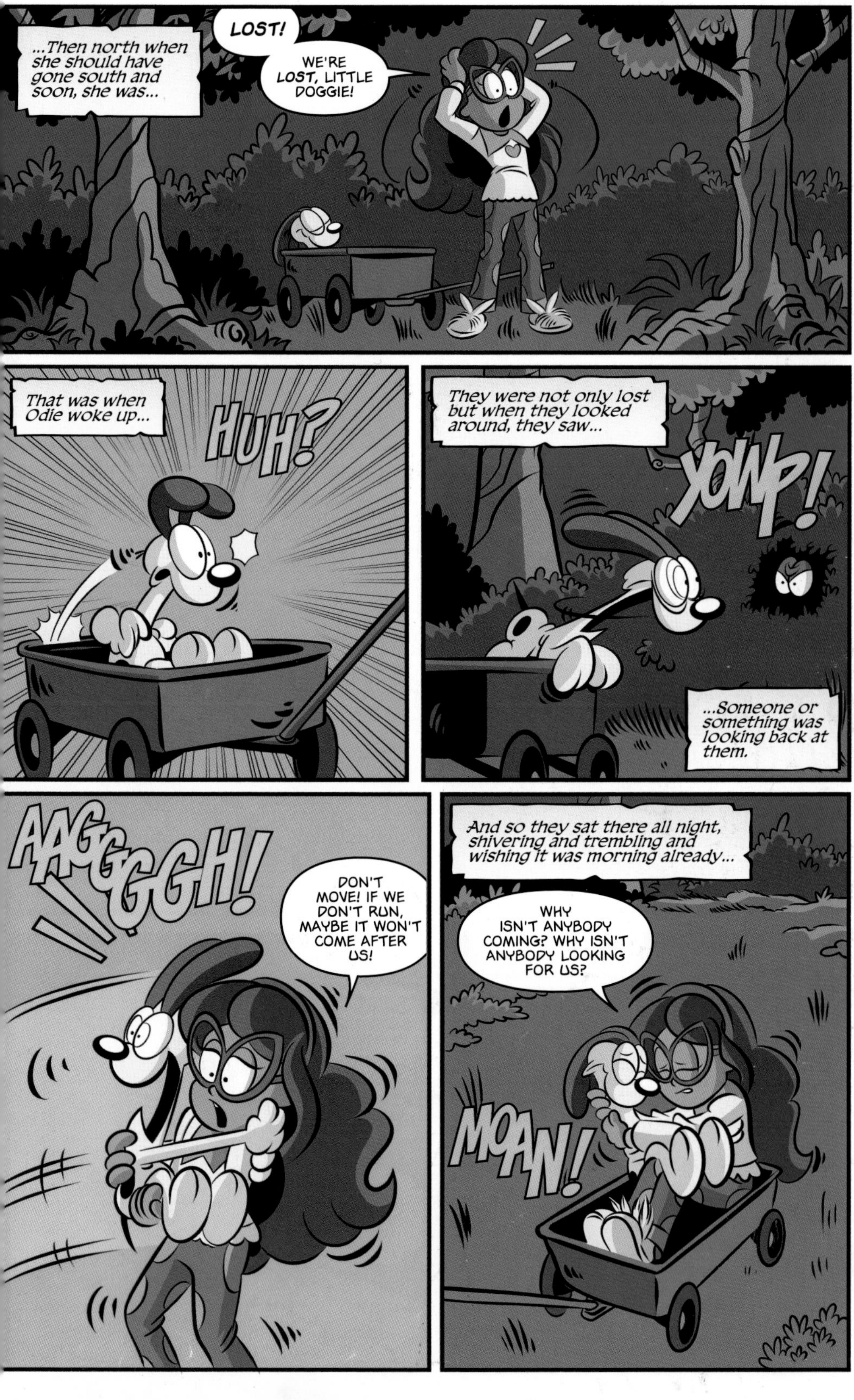
...Then north when she should have gone south and soon, she was...
LOST!
WE'RE LOST, LITTLE DOGGIE!
That was when Odie woke up...
HUH?
They were not only lost but when they looked around, they saw...
YOWP!
...Someone or something was looking back at them.
AAGGGGH!
DON'T MOVE! IF WE DON'T RUN, MAYBE IT WON'T COME AFTER US!
And so they sat there all night, shivering and trembling and wishing it was morning already...
WHY ISN'T ANYBODY COMING? WHY ISN'T ANYBODY LOOKING FOR US?
MOAN!

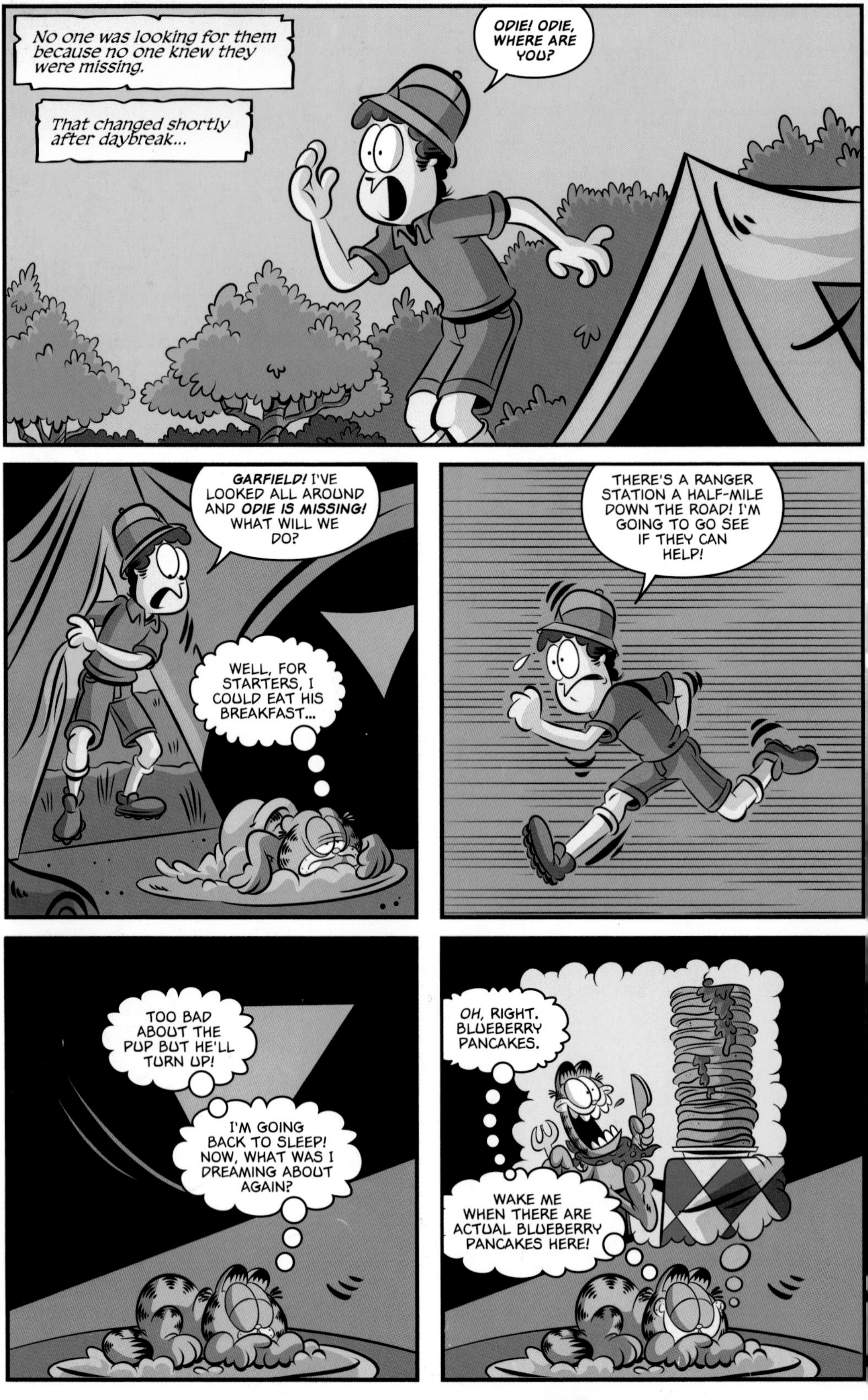
No one was looking for them because no one knew they were missing.
That changed shortly after daybreak...
ODIE! ODIE, WHERE ARE YOU?
GARFIELD! I'VE LOOKED ALL AROUND AND ODIE IS MISSING! WHAT WILL WE DO?
WELL, FOR STARTERS, I COULD EAT HIS BREAKFAST...
THERE'S A RANGER STATION A HALF-MILE DOWN THE ROAD! I'M GOING TO GO SEE IF THEY CAN HELP!
TOO BAD ABOUT THE PUP BUT HE'LL TURN UP!
I'M GOING BACK TO SLEEP! NOW, WHAT WAS I DREAMING ABOUT AGAIN?
OH, RIGHT. BLUEBERRY PANCAKES.
WAKE ME WHEN THERE ARE ACTUAL BLUEBERRY PANCAKES HERE!

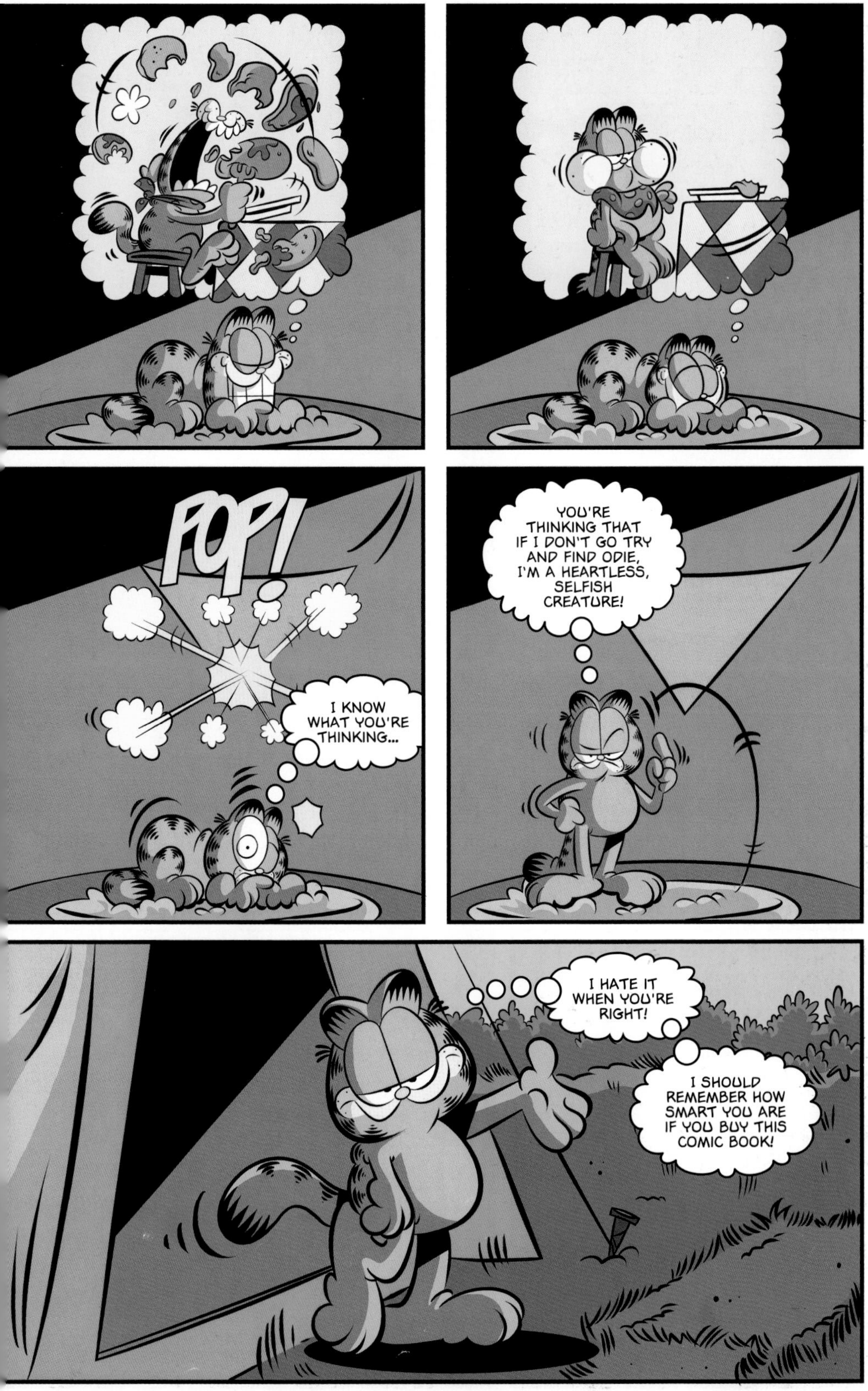
POP!
I KNOW WHAT YOU'RE THINKING...
YOU'RE THINKING THAT IF I DON'T GO TRY AND FIND ODIE, I'M A HEARTLESS, SELFISH CREATURE!
I HATE IT WHEN YOU'RE RIGHT!
I SHOULD REMEMBER HOW SMART YOU ARE IF YOU BUY THIS COMIC BOOK!

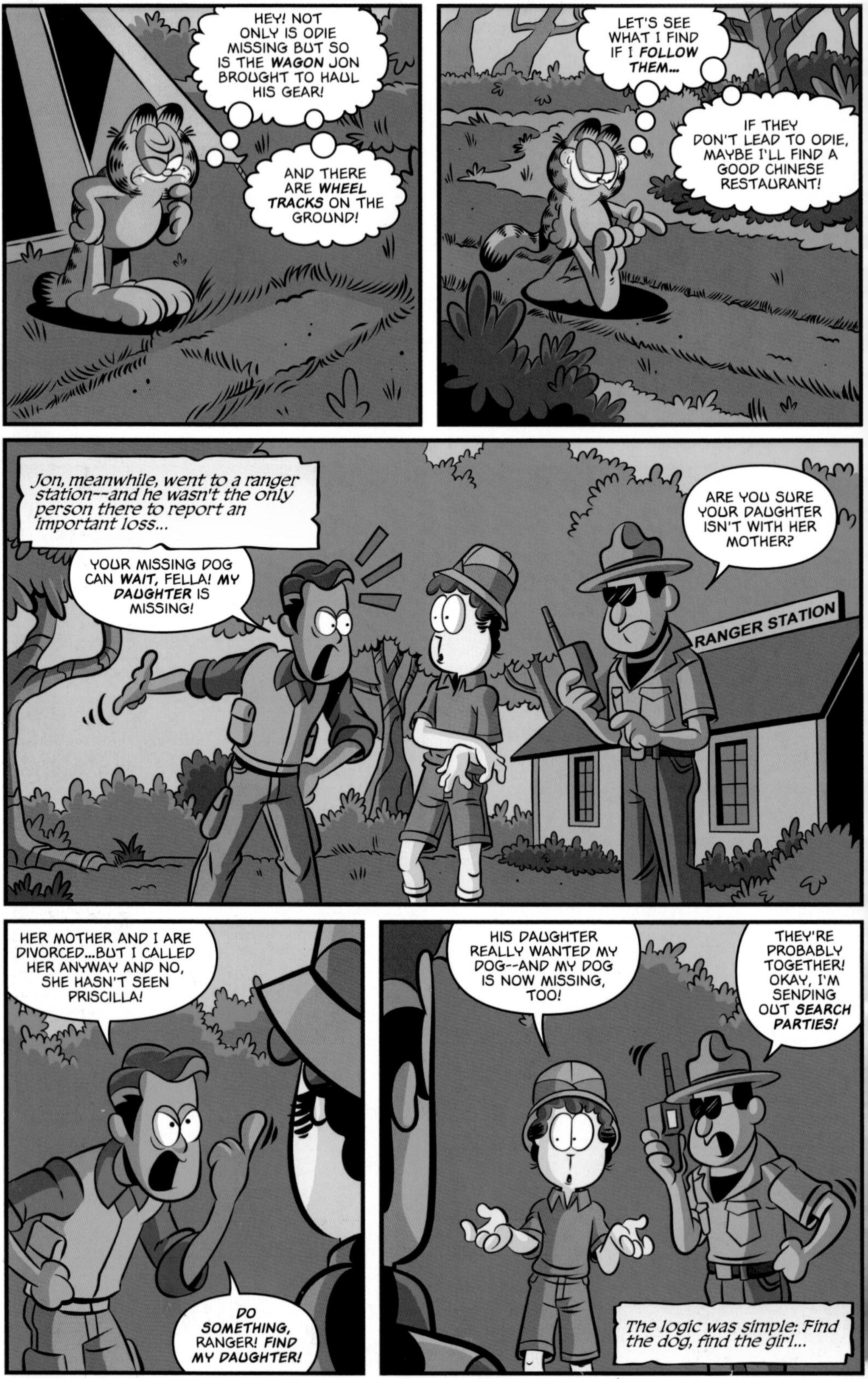
HEY! NOT ONLY IS ODIE MISSING BUT SO IS THE WAGON JON BROUGHT TO HAUL HIS GEAR!
AND THERE ARE WHEEL TRACKS ON THE GROUND!
LET'S SEE WHAT I FIND IF I FOLLOW THEM...
IF THEY DON'T LEAD TO ODIE, MAYBE I'LL FIND A GOOD CHINESE RESTAURANT!
Jon, meanwhile, went to a ranger station--and he wasn't the only person there to report an important loss...
YOUR MISSING DOG CAN WAIT, FELLA! MY DAUGHTER IS MISSING!
ARE YOU SURE YOUR DAUGHTER ISN'T WITH HER MOTHER?
RANGER STATION
HER MOTHER AND I ARE DIVORCED...BUT I CALLED HER ANYWAY AND NO, SHE HASN'T SEEN PRISCILLA!
DO SOMETHING, RANGER! FIND MY DAUGHTER!
HIS DAUGHTER REALLY WANTED MY DOG--AND MY DOG IS NOW MISSING, TOO!
THEY'RE PROBABLY TOGETHER! OKAY, I'M SENDING OUT SEARCH PARTIES!
The logic was simple: Find the dog, find the girl...

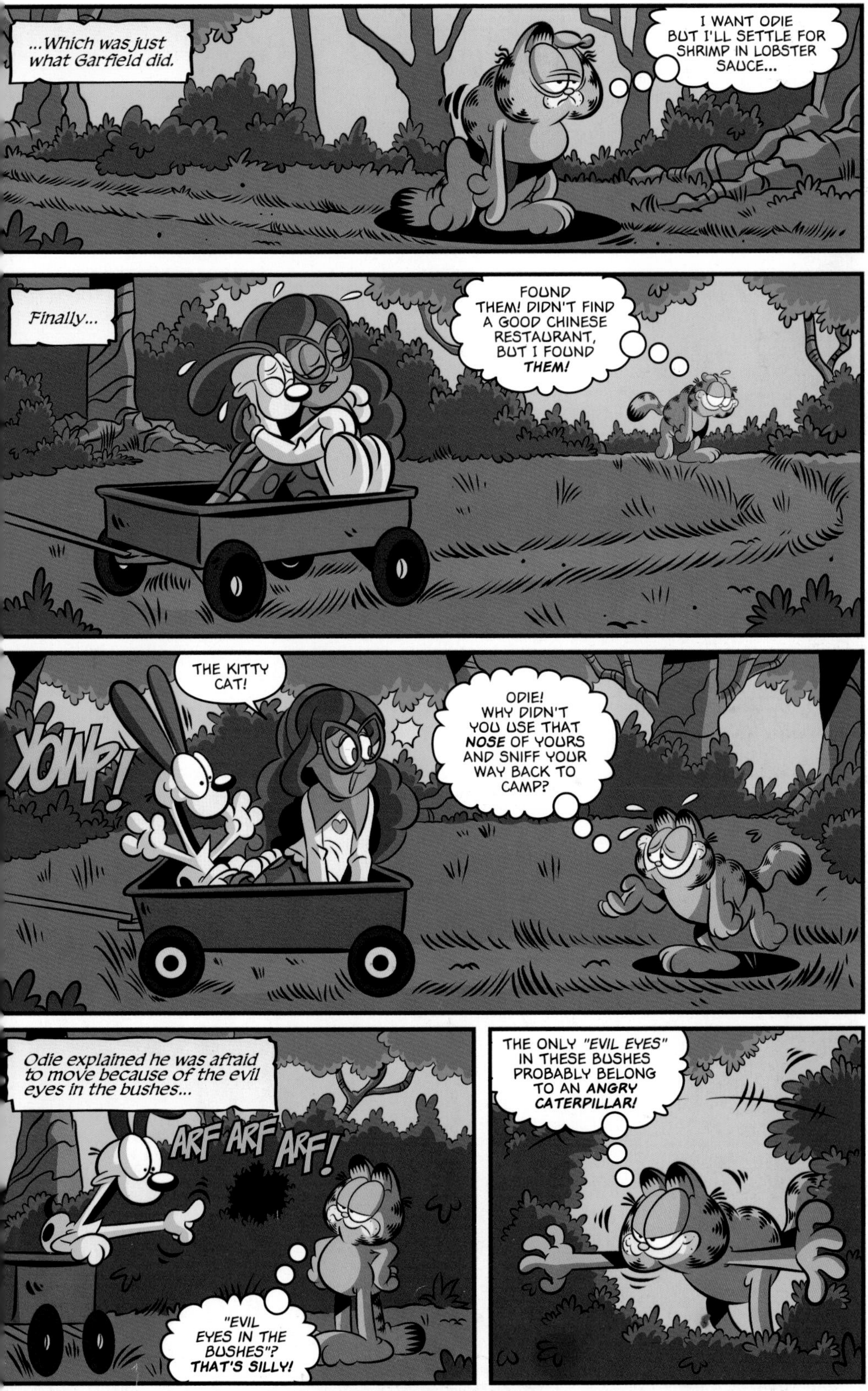
...Which was just what Garfield did.
I WANT ODIE BUT I'LL SETTLE FOR SHRIMP IN LOBSTER SAUCE...
Finally...
FOUND THEM! DIDN'T FIND A GOOD CHINESE RESTAURANT, BUT I FOUND THEM!
YOWP!
THE KITTY CAT!
ODIE! WHY DIDN'T YOU USE THAT NOSE OF YOURS AND SNIFF YOUR WAY BACK TO CAMP?
Odie explained he was afraid to move because of the evil eyes in the bushes...
ARF ARF ARF!
"EVIL EYES IN THE BUSHES"? THAT'S SILLY!
THE ONLY "EVIL EYES" IN THESE BUSHES PROBABLY BELONG TO AN ANGRY CATERPILLAR!

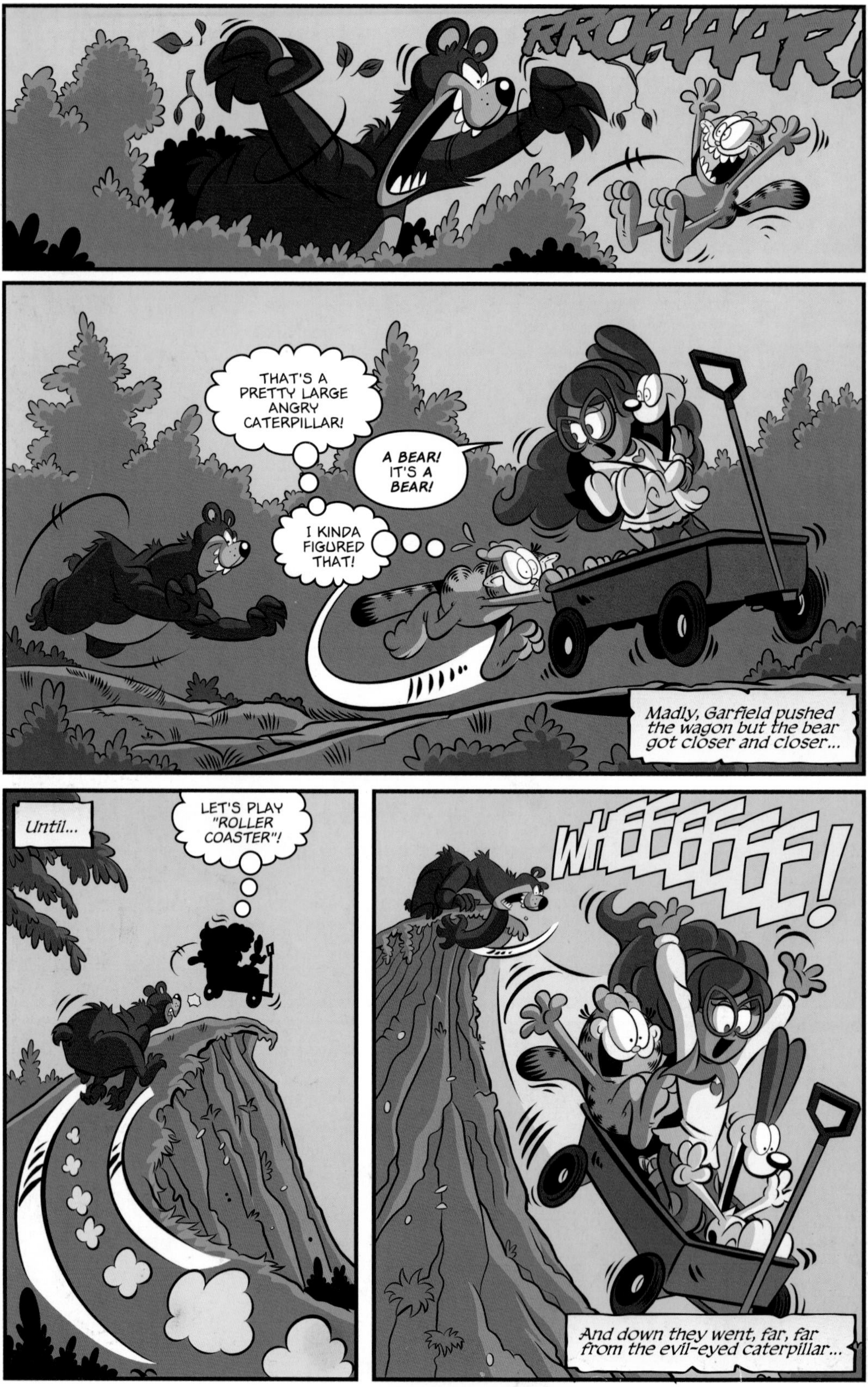
RROAAAR!
THAT'S A PRETTY LARGE ANGRY CATERPILLAR!
A BEAR! IT'S A BEAR!
I KINDA FIGURED THAT!
Madly, Garfield pushed the wagon but the bear got closer and closer...
Until...
LET'S PLAY "ROLLER COASTER"!
WHEEEEEEE!
And down they went, far, far from the evil-eyed caterpillar...

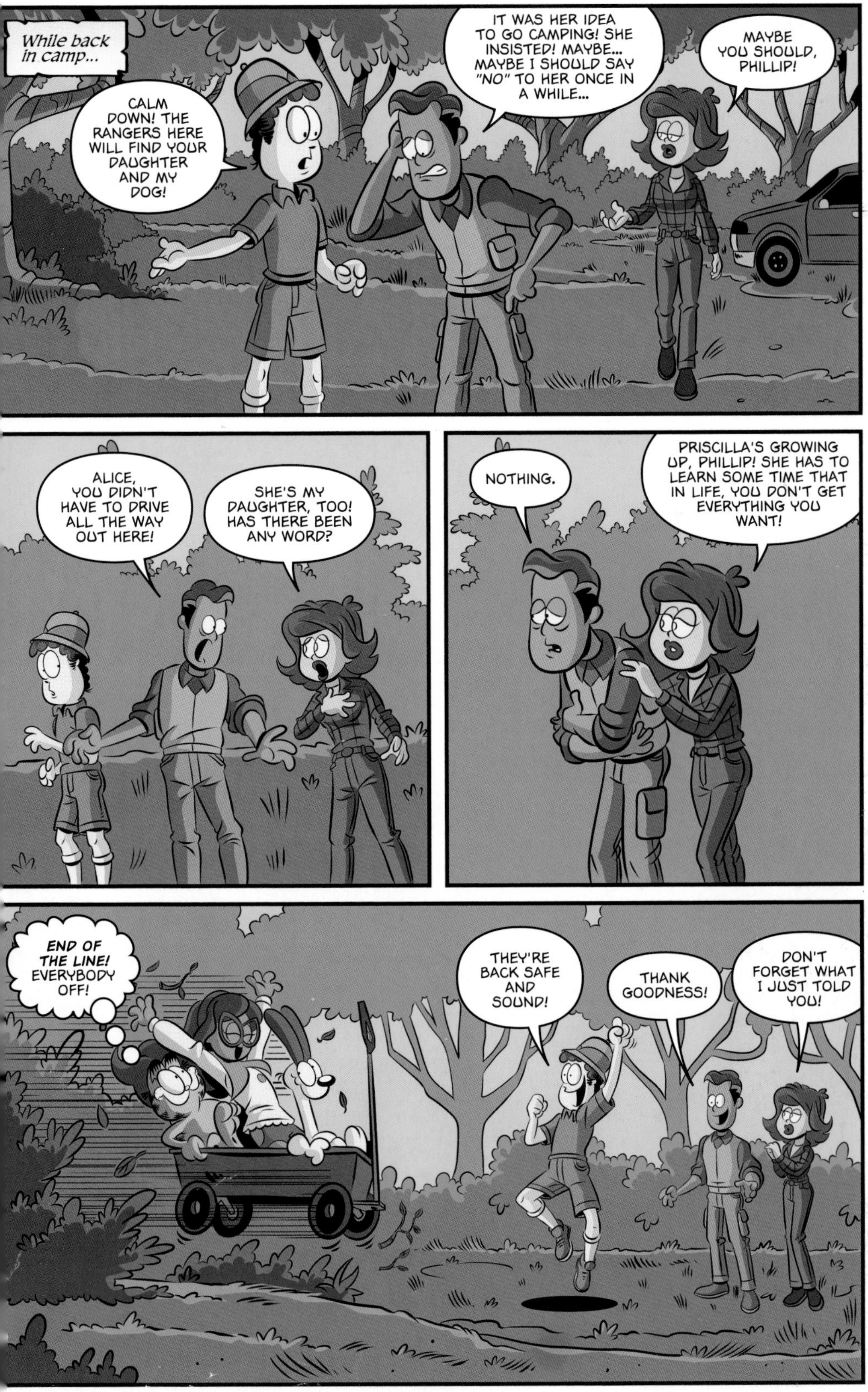
While back in camp...
CALM DOWN! THE RANGERS HERE WILL FIND YOUR DAUGHTER AND MY DOG!
IT WAS HER IDEA TO GO CAMPING! SHE INSISTED! MAYBE... MAYBE I SHOULD SAY "NO" TO HER ONCE IN A WHILE...
MAYBE YOU SHOULD, PHILLIP!
ALICE, YOU DIDN'T HAVE TO DRIVE ALL THE WAY OUT HERE!
SHE'S MY DAUGHTER, TOO! HAS THERE BEEN ANY WORD?
NOTHING.
PRISCILLA'S GROWING UP, PHILLIP! SHE HAS TO LEARN SOME TIME THAT IN LIFE, YOU DON'T GET EVERYTHING YOU WANT!
END OF THE LINE! EVERYBODY OFF!
THEY'RE BACK SAFE AND SOUND!
THANK GOODNESS!
DON'T FORGET WHAT I JUST TOLD YOU!

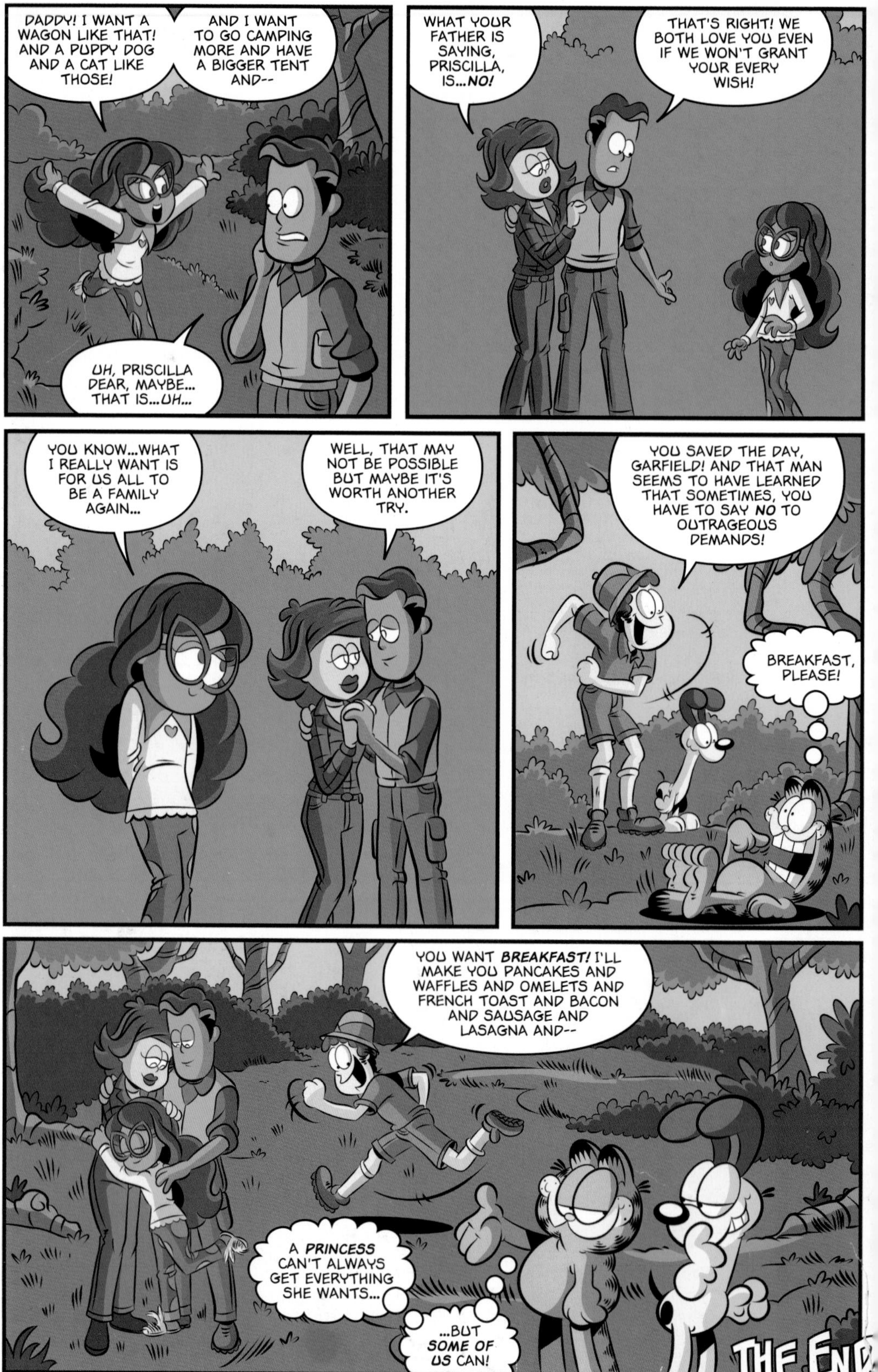
DADDY! I WANT A WAGON LIKE THAT! AND A PUPPY DOG AND A CAT LIKE THOSE!
AND I WANT TO GO CAMPING MORE AND HAVE A BIGGER TENT AND--
UH, PRISCILLA DEAR, MAYBE... THAT IS...UH...
WHAT YOUR FATHER IS SAYING, PRISCILLA, IS...NO!
THAT'S RIGHT! WE BOTH LOVE YOU EVEN IF WE WON'T GRANT YOUR EVERY WISH!
YOU KNOW...WHAT I REALLY WANT IS FOR US ALL TO BE A FAMILY AGAIN...
WELL, THAT MAY NOT BE POSSIBLE BUT MAYBE IT'S WORTH ANOTHER TRY.
YOU SAVED THE DAY, GARFIELD! AND THAT MAN SEEMS TO HAVE LEARNED THAT SOMETIMES, YOU HAVE TO SAY NO TO OUTRAGEOUS DEMANDS!
BREAKFAST, PLEASE!
YOU WANT BREAKFAST! I'LL MAKE YOU PANCAKES AND WAFFLES AND OMELETS AND FRENCH TOAST AND BACON AND SAUSAGE AND LASAGNA AND--
A PRINCESS CAN'T ALWAYS GET EVERYTHING SHE WANTS...
...BUT SOME OF US CAN!
THE END

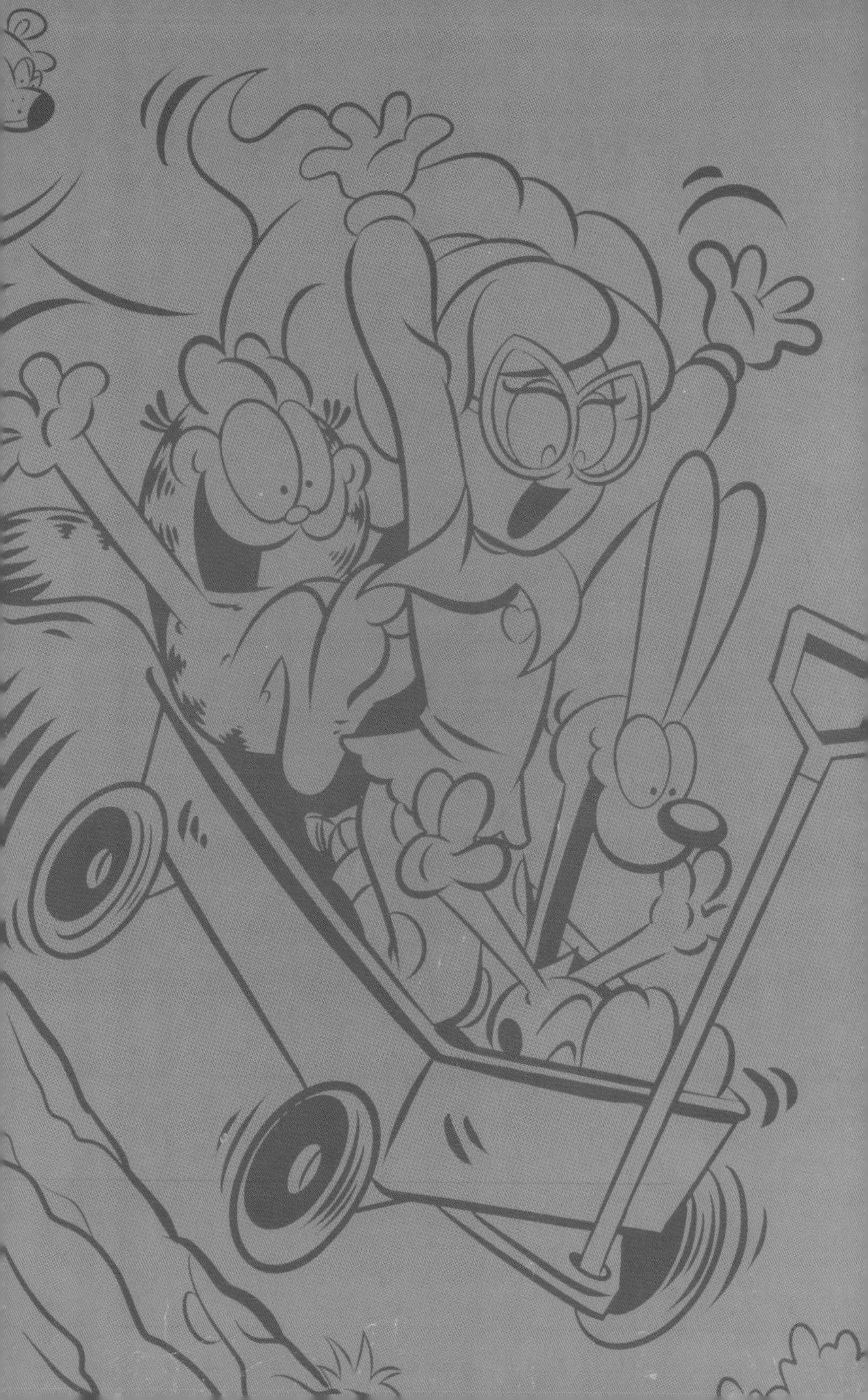

"FRIENDLY FOE"

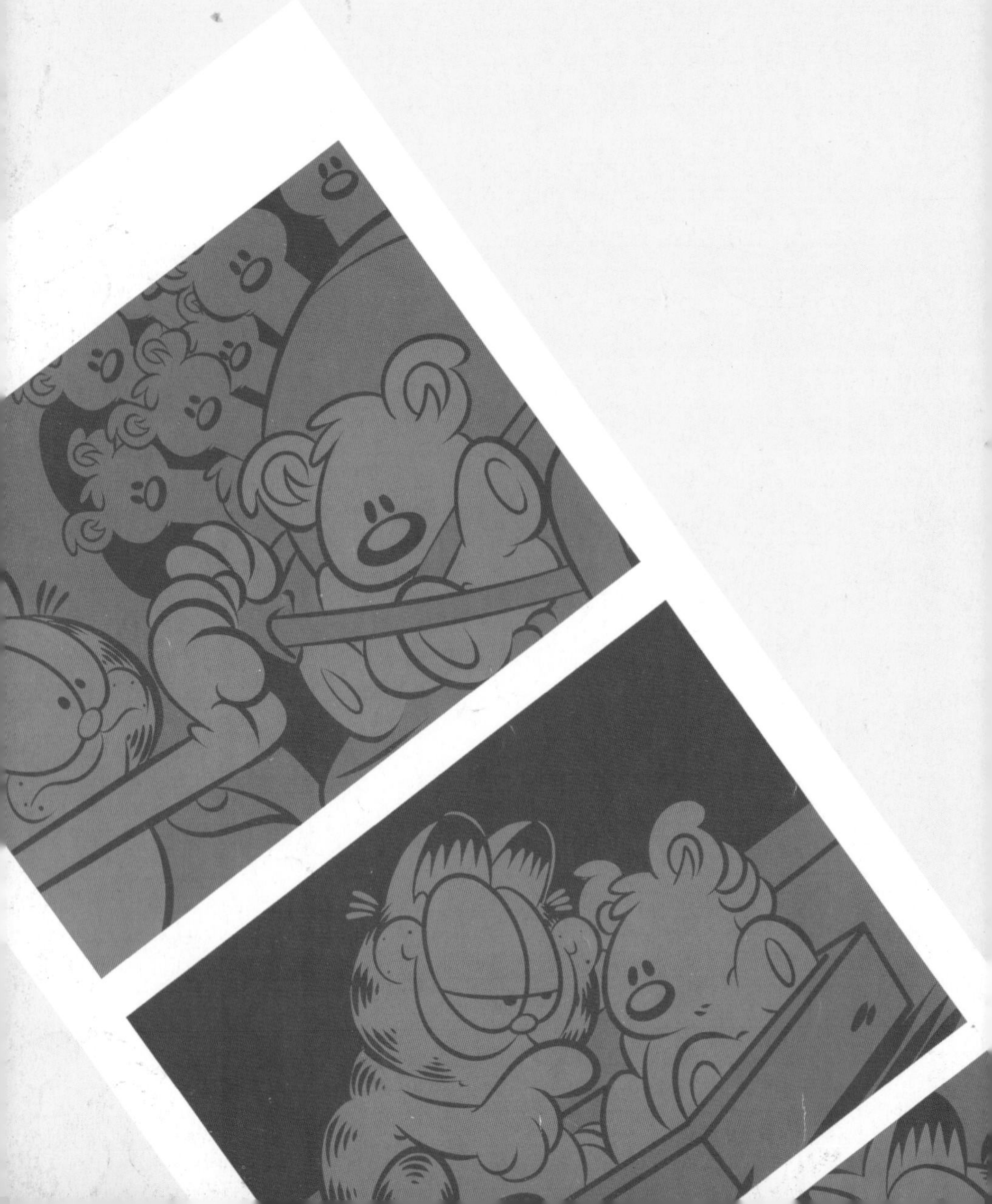

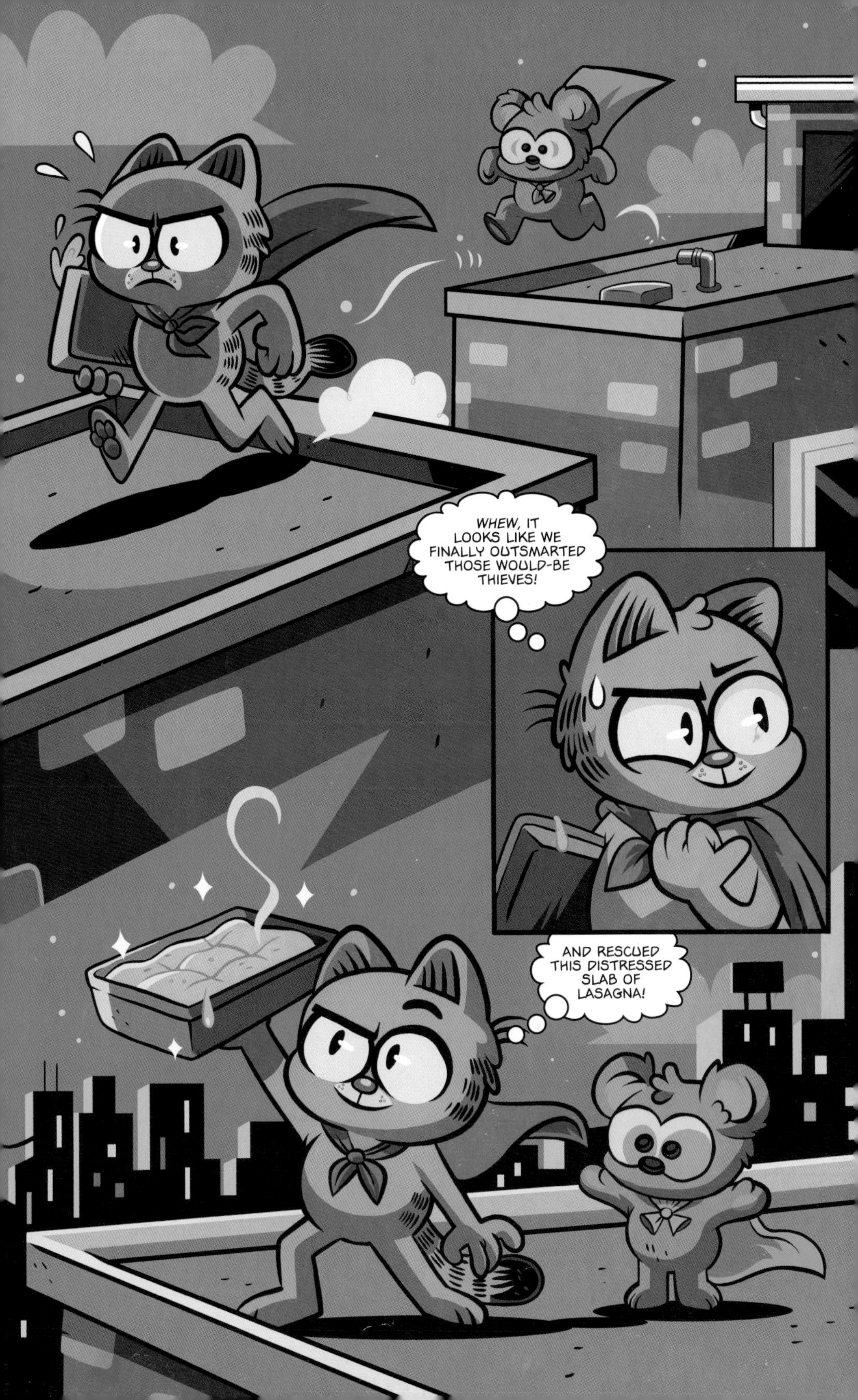
WHEW, IT LOOKS LIKE WE FINALLY OUTSMARTED THOSE WOULD-BE THIEVES!
AND RESCUED THIS DISTRESSED SLAB OF LASAGNA!

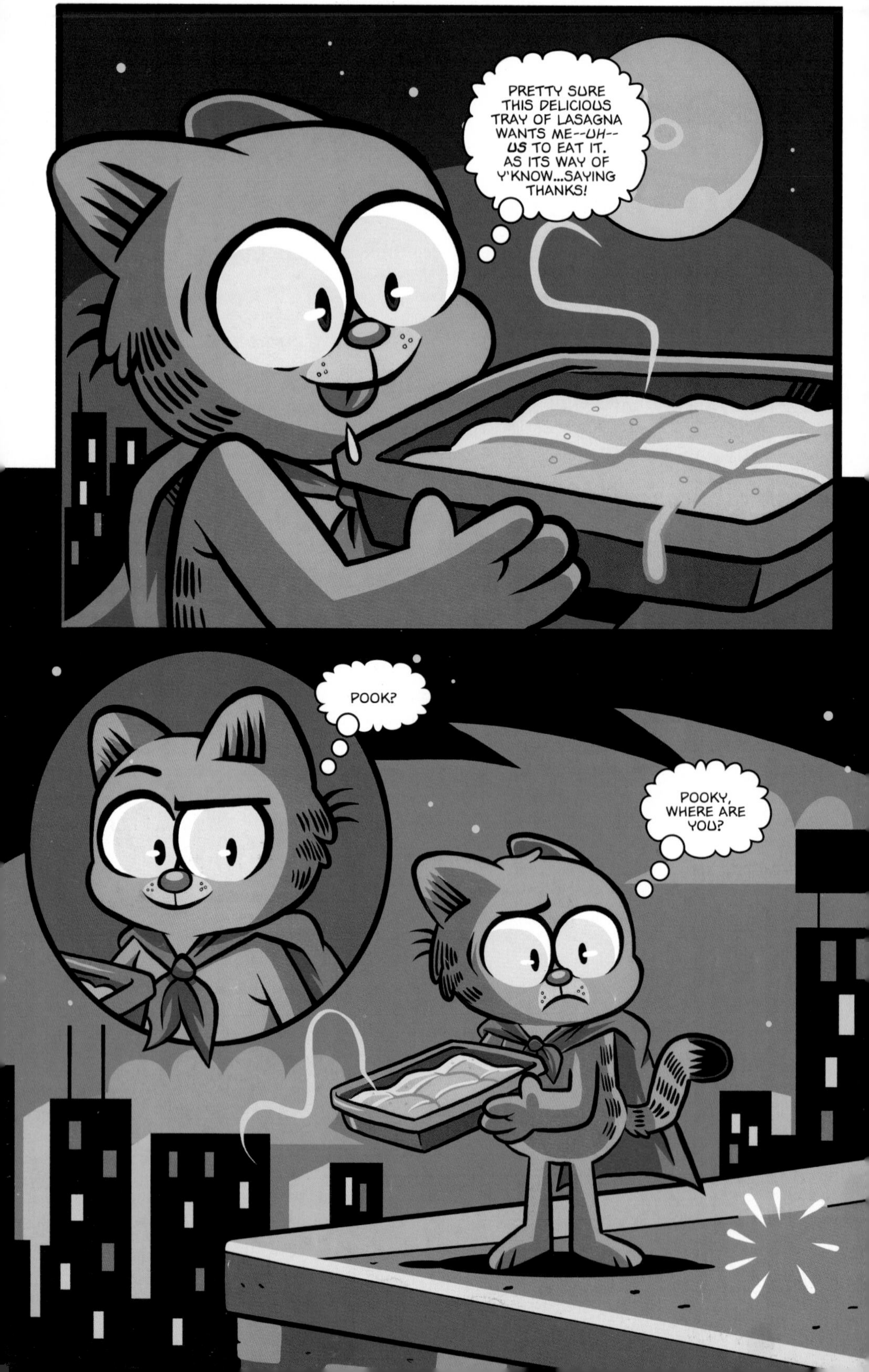
PRETTY SURE THIS DELICIOUS TRAY OF LASAGNA WANTS ME--UH--US TO EAT IT. AS ITS WAY OF Y'KNOW...SAYING THANKS!
POOK?
POOKY, WHERE ARE YOU?

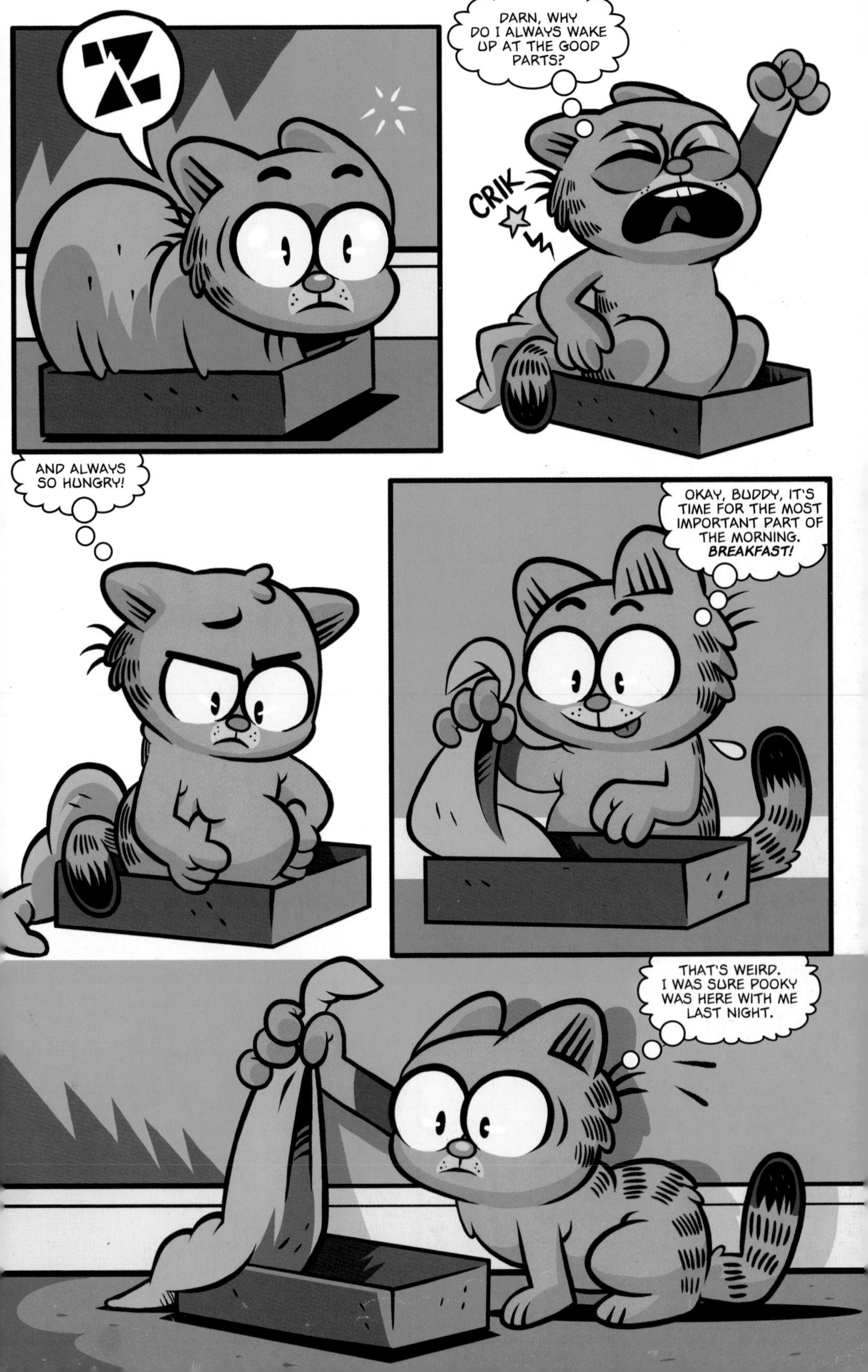
Z
DARN, WHY DO I ALWAYS WAKE UP AT THE GOOD PARTS?
CRIK
AND ALWAYS SO HUNGRY!
OKAY, BUDDY, IT'S TIME FOR THE MOST IMPORTANT PART OF THE MORNING. *BREAKFAST!*
THAT'S WEIRD. I WAS SURE POOKY WAS HERE WITH ME LAST NIGHT.

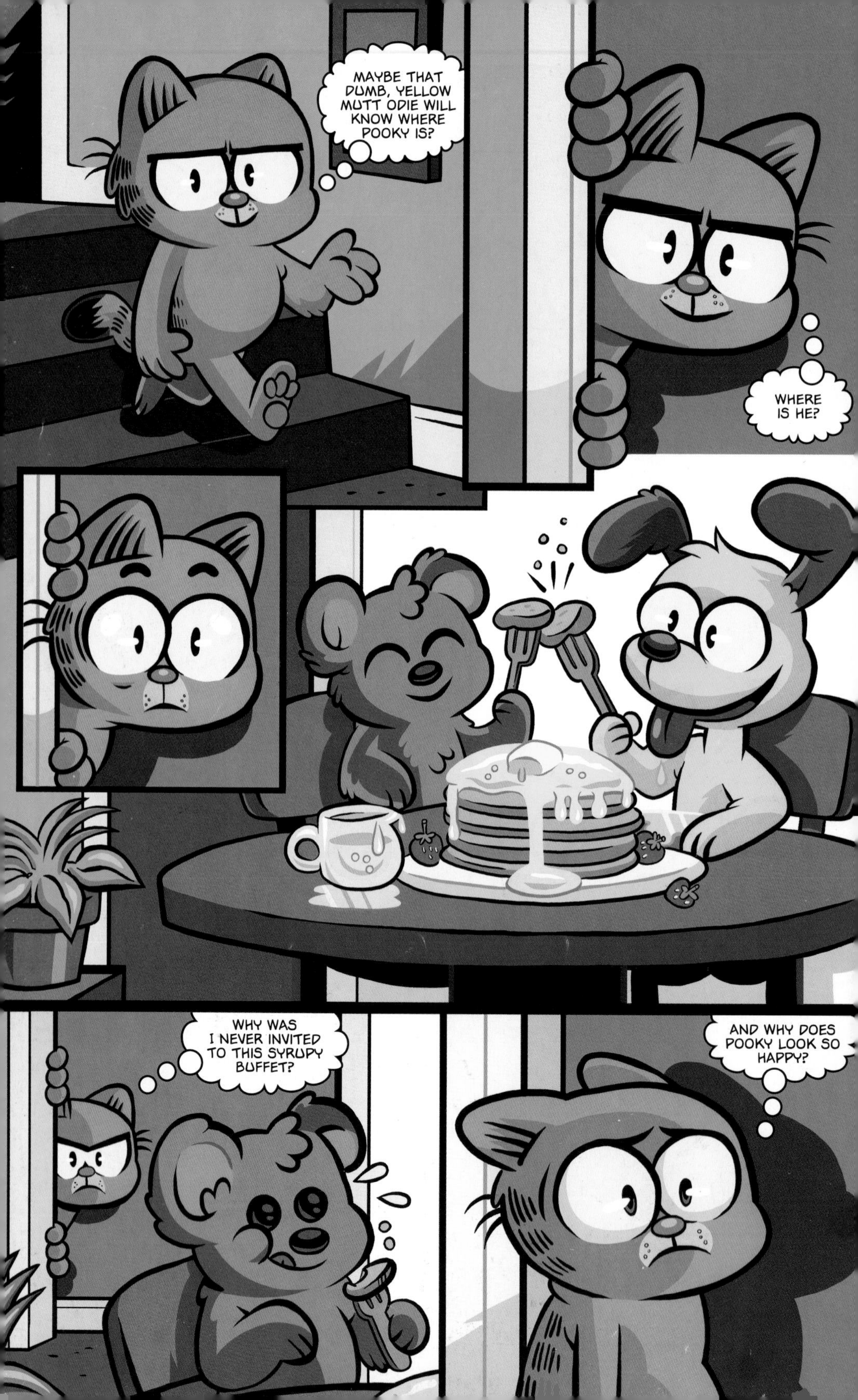
MAYBE THAT DUMB, YELLOW MUTT ODIE WILL KNOW WHERE POOKY IS?
WHERE IS HE?
WHY WAS I NEVER INVITED TO THIS SYRUPY BUFFET?
AND WHY DOES POOKY LOOK SO HAPPY?

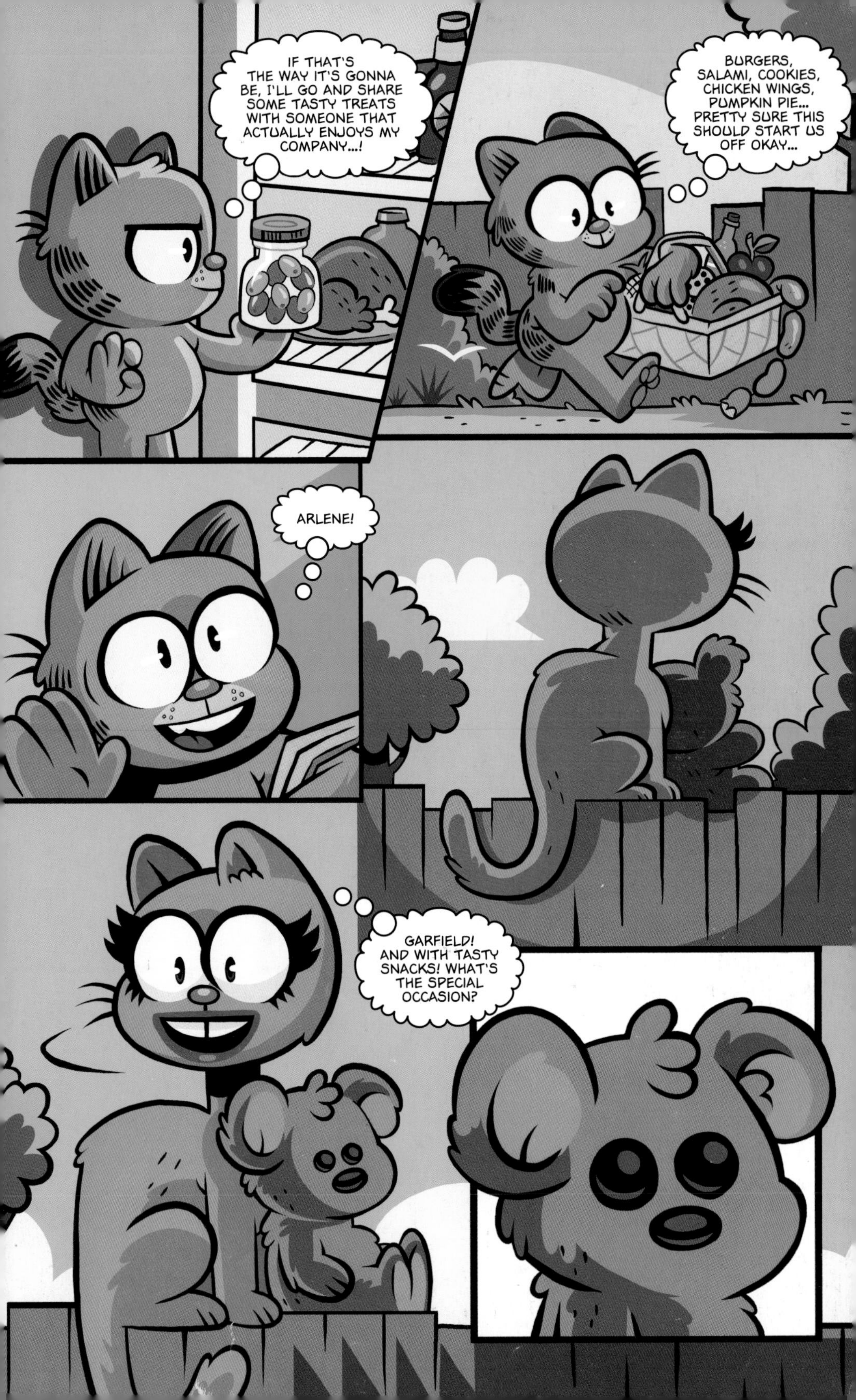
IF THAT'S THE WAY IT'S GONNA BE, I'LL GO AND SHARE SOME TASTY TREATS WITH SOMEONE THAT ACTUALLY ENJOYS MY COMPANY...!
BURGERS, SALAMI, COOKIES, CHICKEN WINGS, PUMPKIN PIE... PRETTY SURE THIS SHOULD START US OFF OKAY...
ARLENE!
GARFIELD! AND WITH TASTY SNACKS! WHAT'S THE SPECIAL OCCASION?

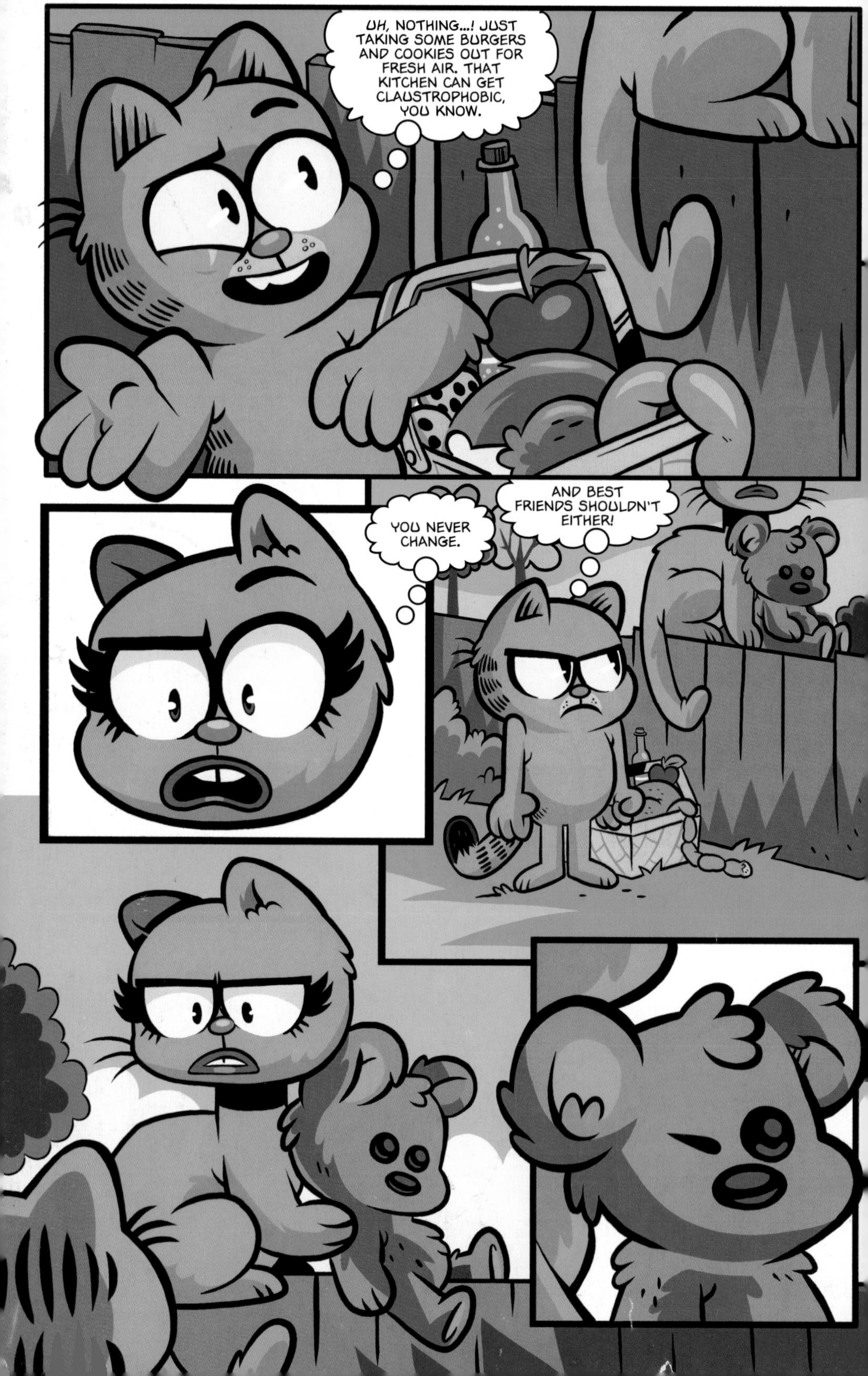
UH, NOTHING...! JUST TAKING SOME BURGERS AND COOKIES OUT FOR FRESH AIR. THAT KITCHEN CAN GET CLAUSTROPHOBIC, YOU KNOW.
YOU NEVER CHANGE.
AND BEST FRIENDS SHOULDN'T EITHER!

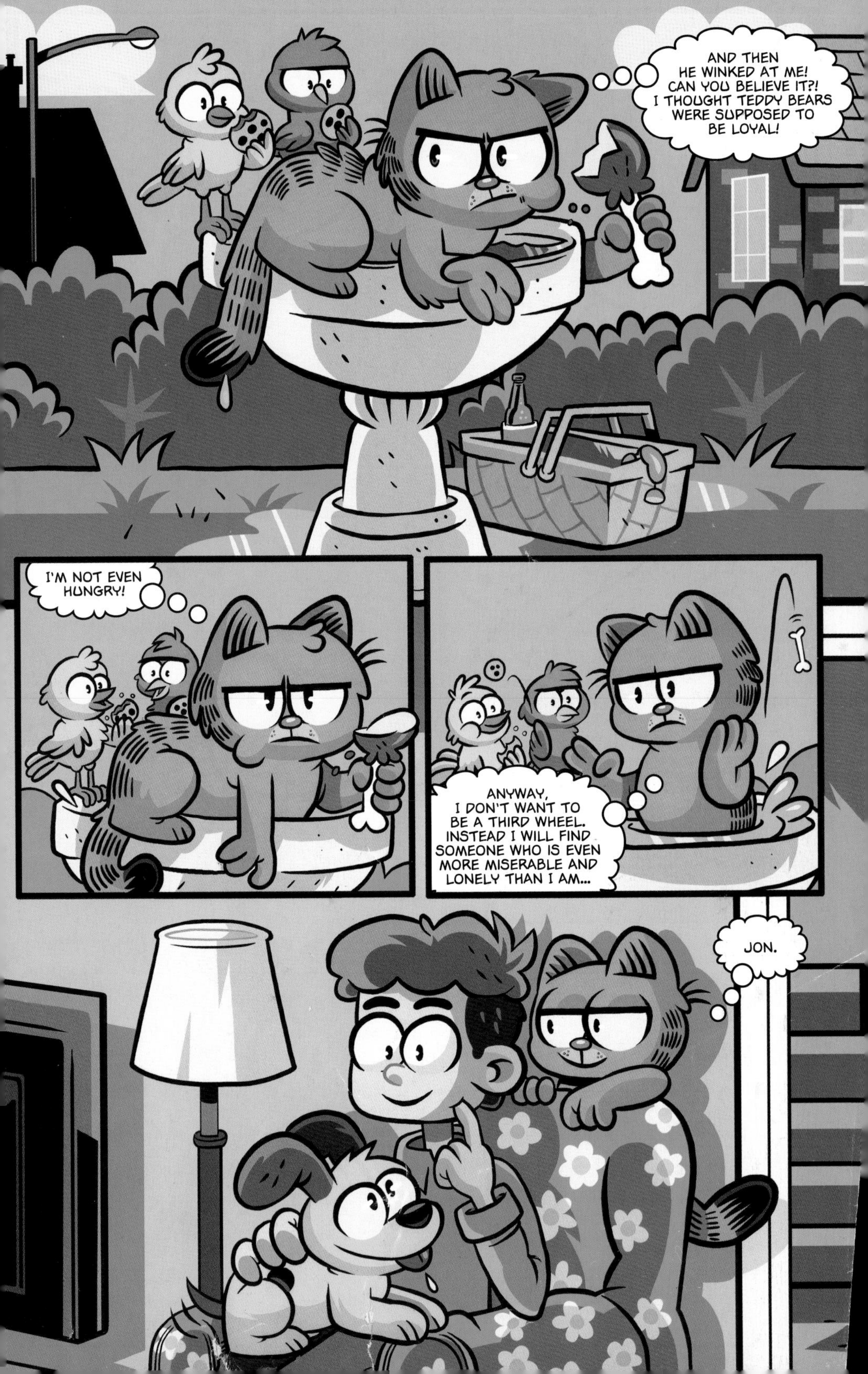
AND THEN HE WINKED AT ME! CAN YOU BELIEVE IT?! I THOUGHT TEDDY BEARS WERE SUPPOSED TO BE LOYAL!
I'M NOT EVEN HUNGRY!
ANYWAY, I DON'T WANT TO BE A THIRD WHEEL. INSTEAD I WILL FIND SOMEONE WHO IS EVEN MORE MISERABLE AND LONELY THAN I AM...
JON.

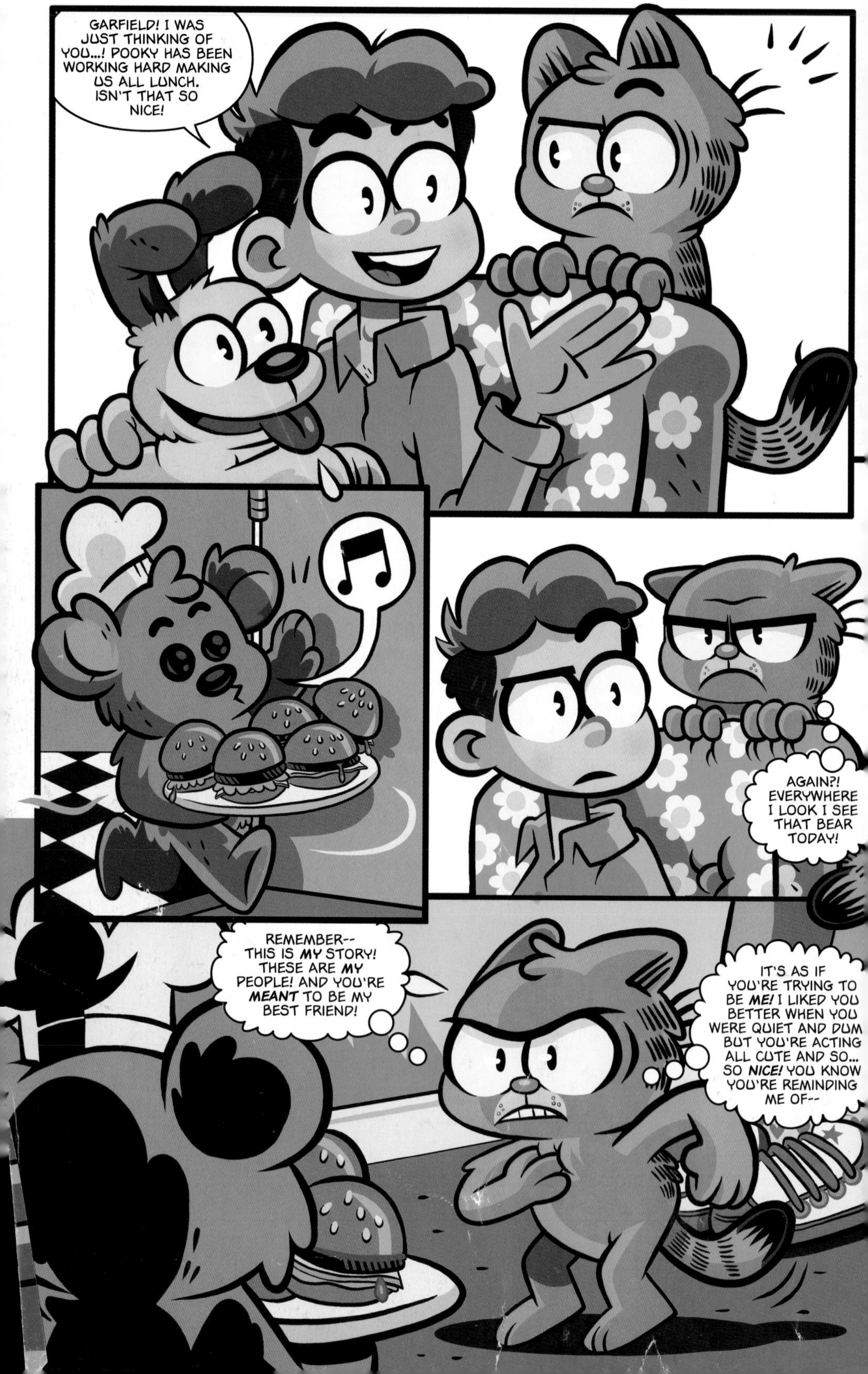
GARFIELD! I WAS JUST THINKING OF YOU...! POOKY HAS BEEN WORKING HARD MAKING US ALL LUNCH. ISN'T THAT SO NICE!
AGAIN?! EVERYWHERE I LOOK I SEE THAT BEAR TODAY!
REMEMBER-- THIS IS MY STORY! THESE ARE MY PEOPLE! AND YOU'RE MEANT TO BE MY BEST FRIEND!
IT'S AS IF YOU'RE TRYING TO BE ME! I LIKED YOU BETTER WHEN YOU WERE QUIET AND DUM BUT YOU'RE ACTING ALL CUTE AND SO... SO NICE! YOU KNOW YOU'RE REMINDING ME OF--

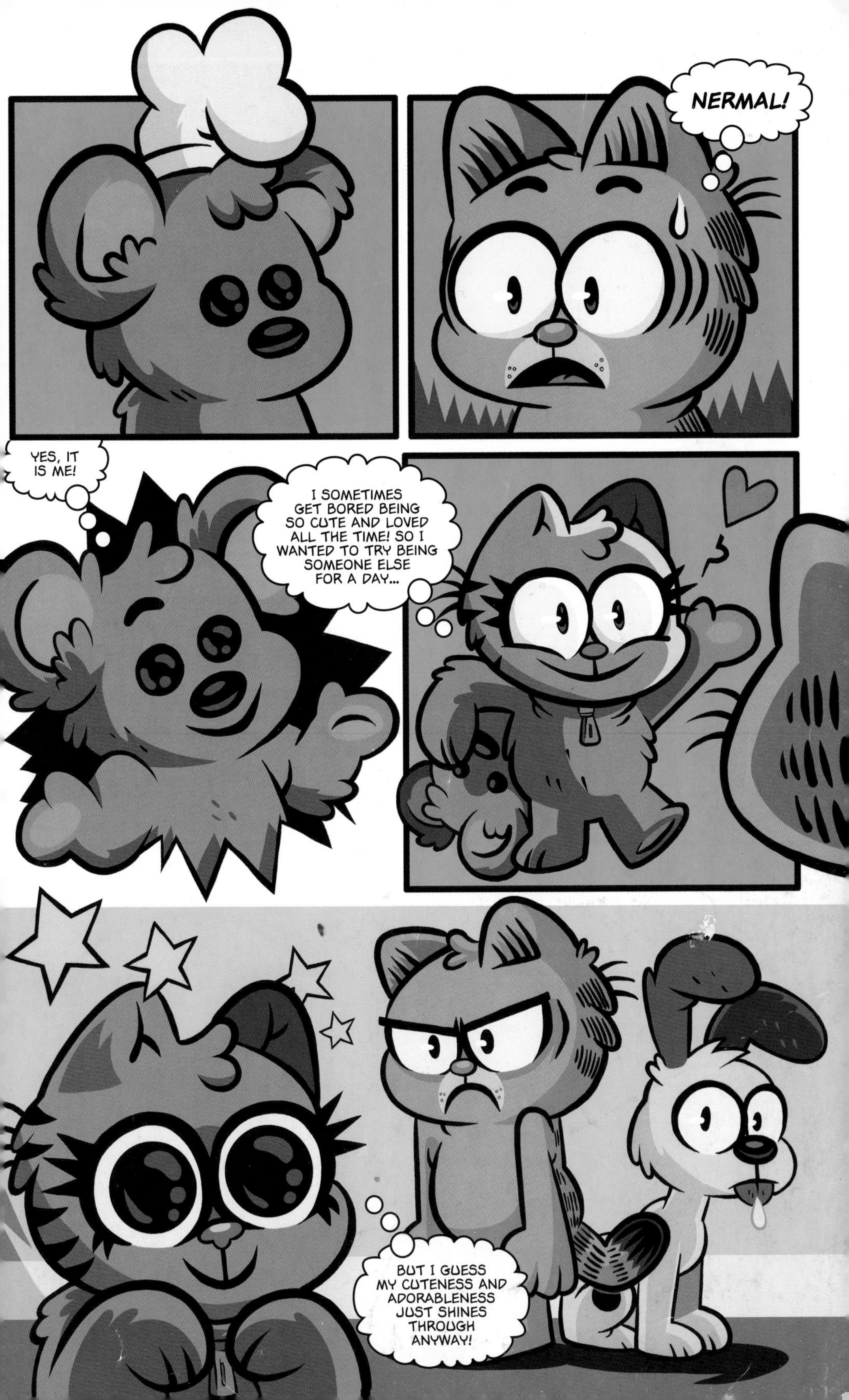
NERMAL!
YES, IT IS ME!
I SOMETIMES GET BORED BEING SO CUTE AND LOVED ALL THE TIME! SO I WANTED TO TRY BEING SOMEONE ELSE FOR A DAY...
BUT I GUESS MY CUTENESS AND ADORABLENESS JUST SHINES THROUGH ANYWAY!

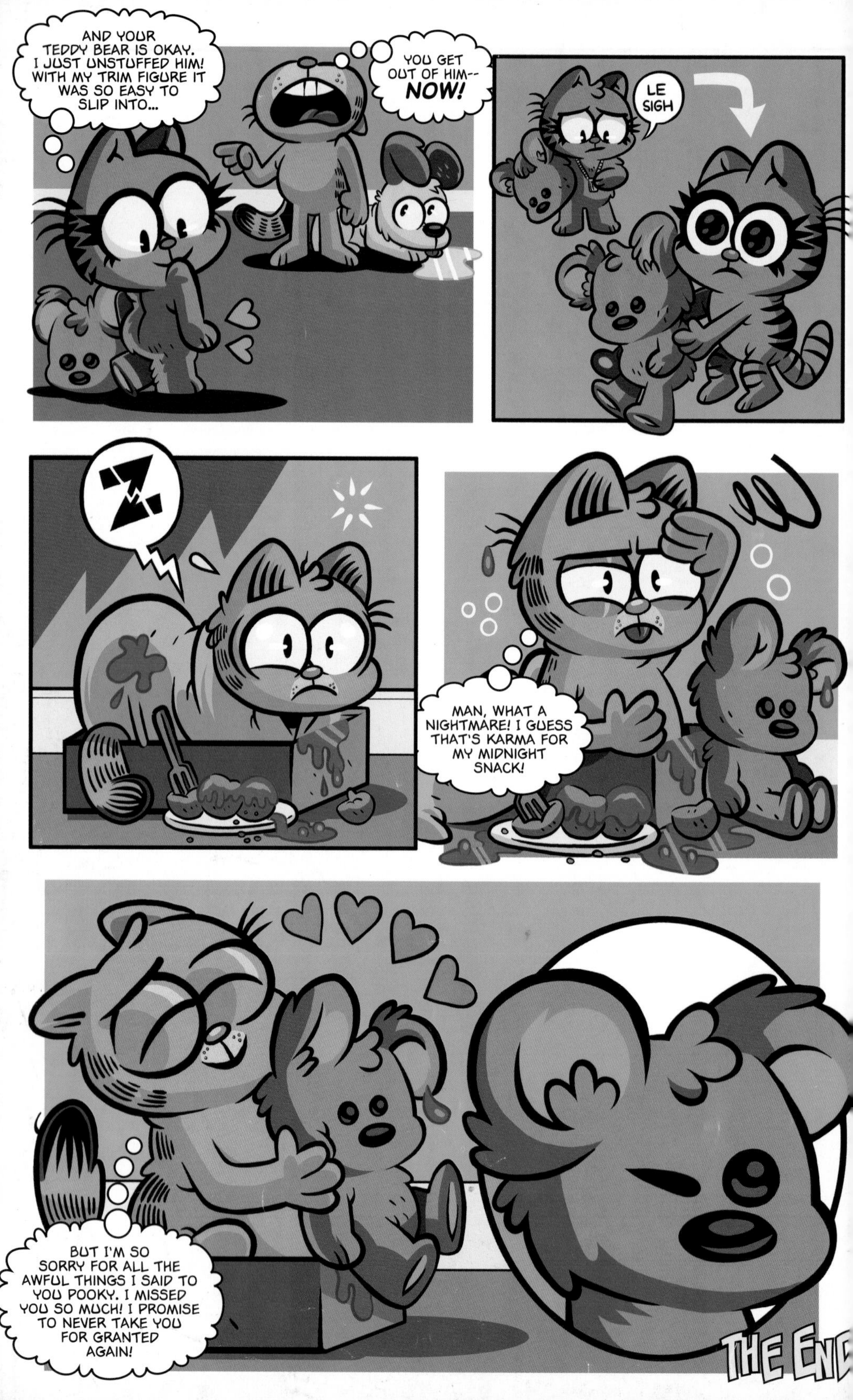
AND YOUR TEDDY BEAR IS OKAY. I JUST UNSTUFFED HIM! WITH MY TRIM FIGURE IT WAS SO EASY TO SLIP INTO...
YOU GET OUT OF HIM-- NOW!
LE SIGH
Z
MAN, WHAT A NIGHTMARE! I GUESS THAT'S KARMA FOR MY MIDNIGHT SNACK!
BUT I'M SO SORRY FOR ALL THE AWFUL THINGS I SAID TO YOU POOKY. I MISSED YOU SO MUCH! I PROMISE TO NEVER TAKE YOU FOR GRANTED AGAIN!
THE END

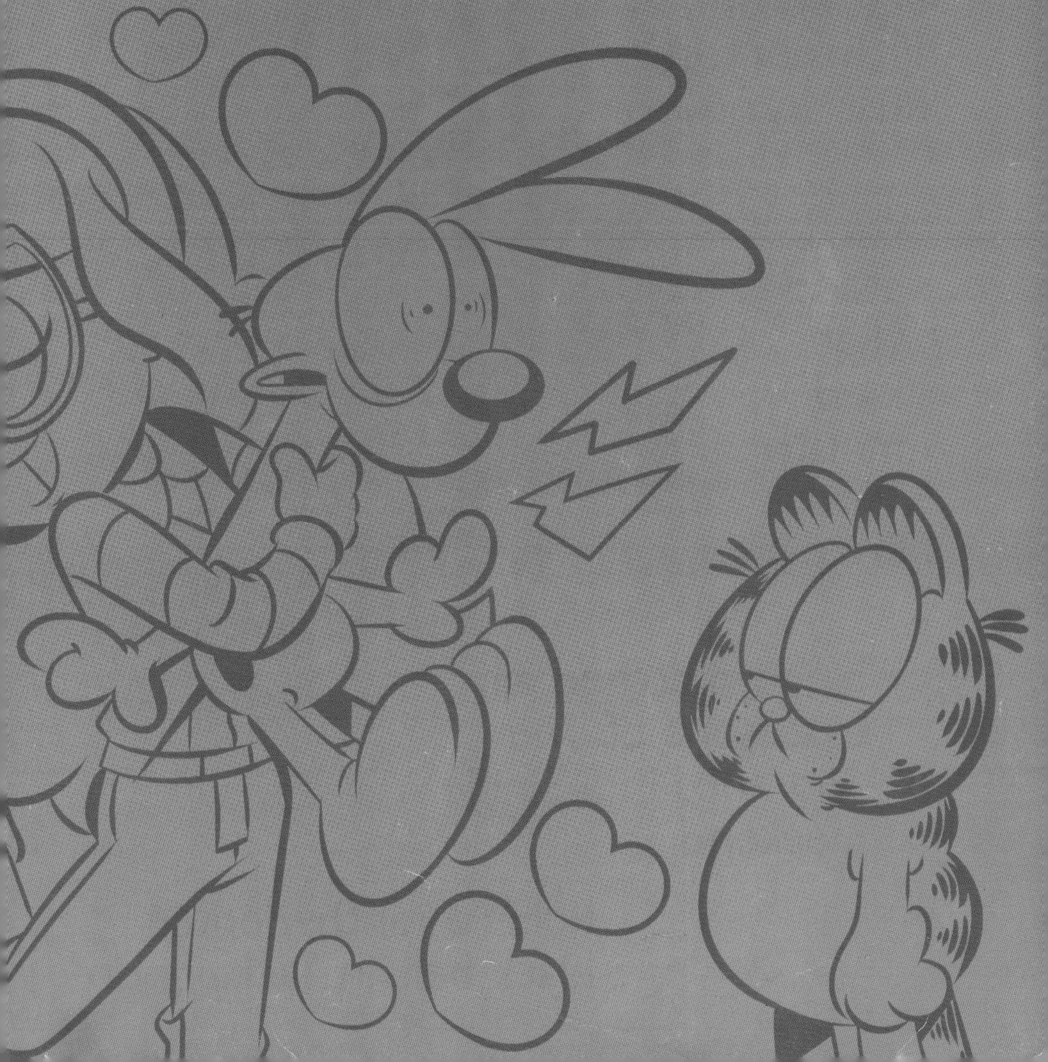

5 THINGS YOU DON'T KNOW ABOUT POOKY

Big fan of 19th-Century Russian novels

Can't stand that loud-mouth Teddy Ruxpin

Briefly toured with WHAM! in the 80s

Binge-watched all 6 seasons of *The Sopranos* in a single weekend

Holds a ninth-degree black belt in Taekwondo

Writer: Scott Nickel

Bear Essentials

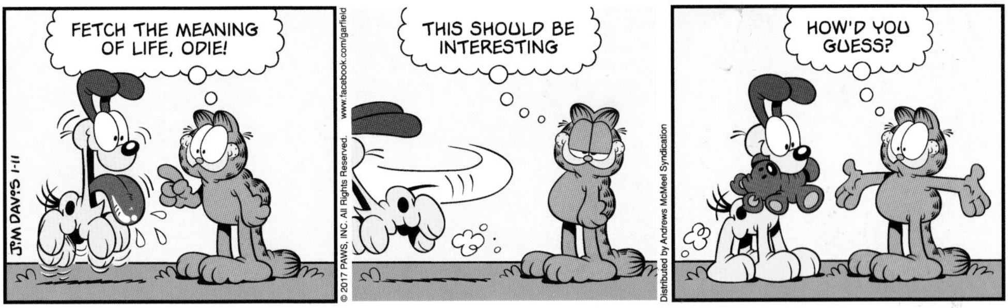
FETCH THE MEANING OF LIFE, ODIE!
JIM DAVIS 1-11
© 2017 PAWS, INC. All Rights Reserved. www.facebook.com/garfield
THIS SHOULD BE INTERESTING
Distributed by Andrews McMeel Syndication
HOW'D YOU GUESS?

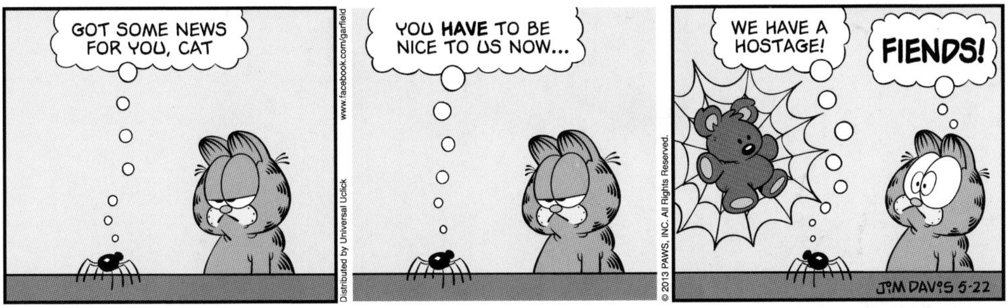
GOT SOME NEWS FOR YOU, CAT
Distributed by Universal Uclick www.facebook.com/garfield
YOU **HAVE** TO BE NICE TO US NOW...
© 2013 PAWS, INC. All Rights Reserved.
WE HAVE A HOSTAGE!
FIENDS!
JIM DAVIS 5-22

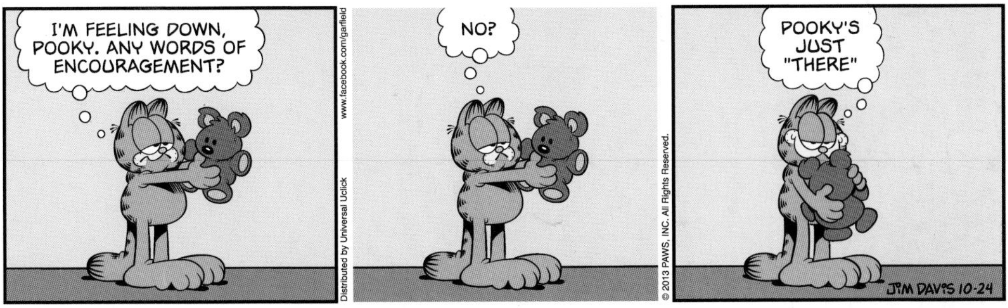
I'M FEELING DOWN, POOKY. ANY WORDS OF ENCOURAGEMENT?
Distributed by Universal Uclick www.facebook.com/garfield
NO?
© 2013 PAWS, INC. All Rights Reserved.
POOKY'S JUST "THERE"
JIM DAVIS 10-24

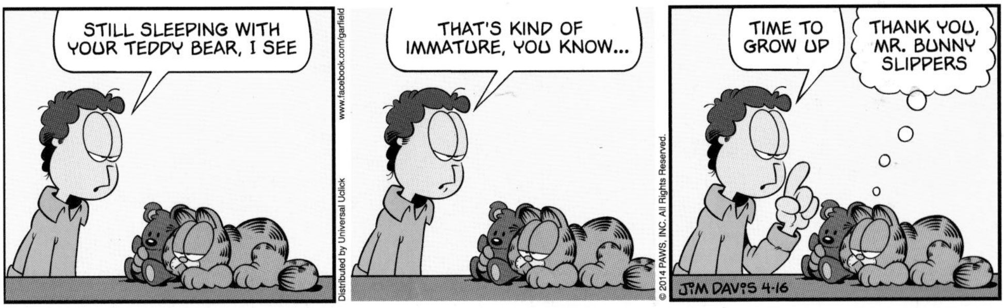
STILL SLEEPING WITH YOUR TEDDY BEAR, I SEE
Distributed by Universal Uclick www.facebook.com/garfield
THAT'S KIND OF IMMATURE, YOU KNOW...
© 2014 PAWS, INC. All Rights Reserved.
TIME TO GROW UP
THANK YOU, MR. BUNNY SLIPPERS
JIM DAVIS 4-16

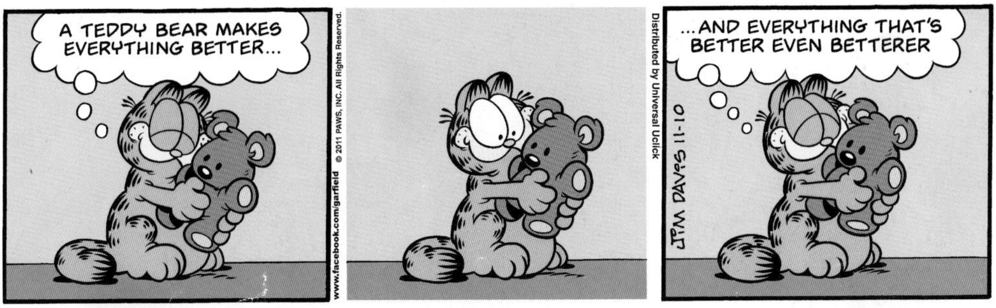
A TEDDY BEAR MAKES EVERYTHING BETTER...
www.facebook.com/garfield © 2011 PAWS, INC. All Rights Reserved.
Distributed by Universal Uclick
...AND EVERYTHING THAT'S BETTER EVEN BETTERER
JIM DAVIS 11-10

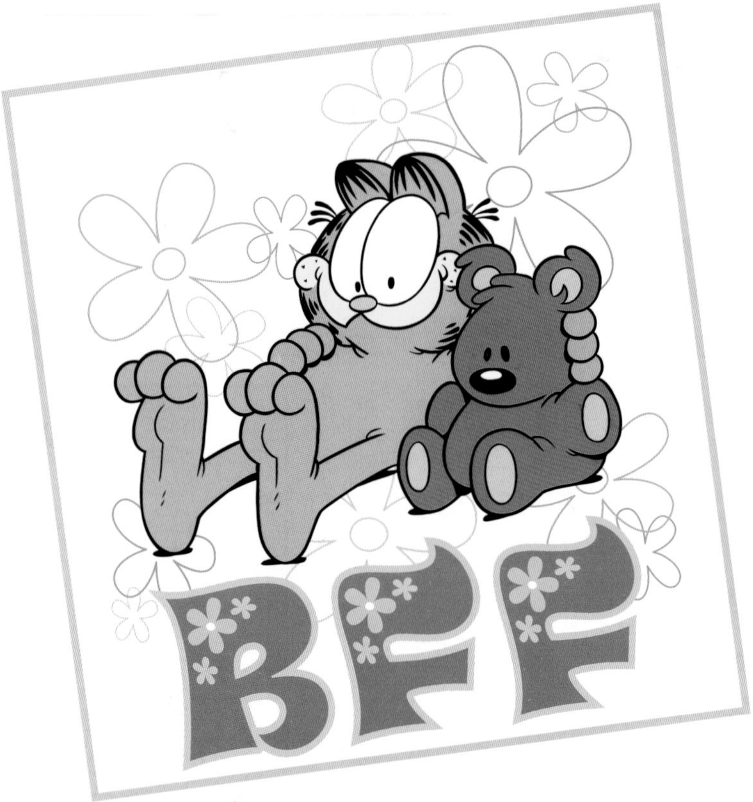
BFF

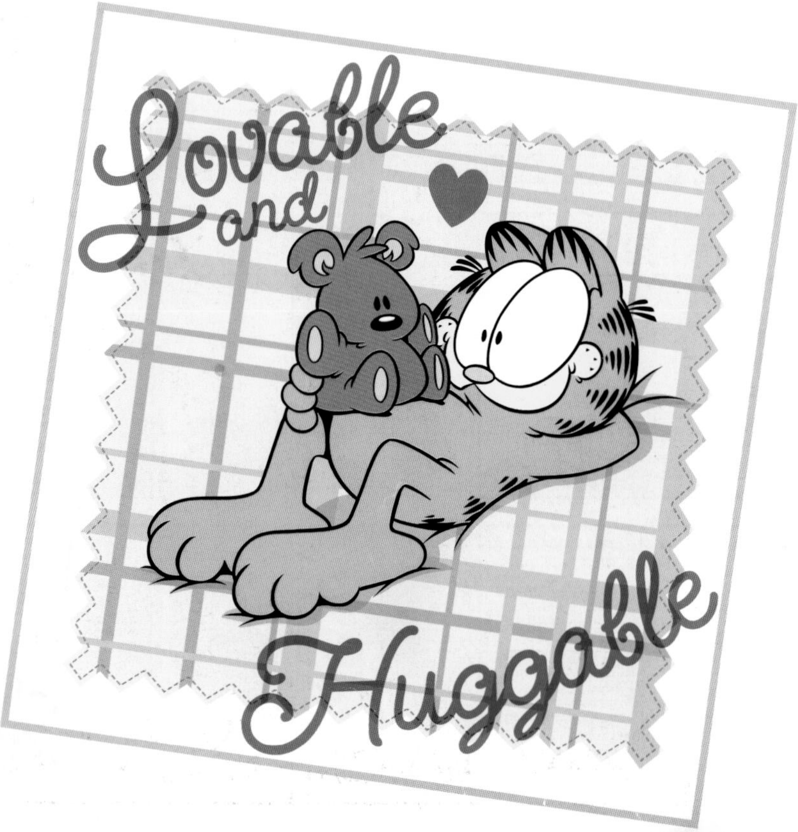
Lovable and Huggable

classic cat classic cat
classic cat classic cat

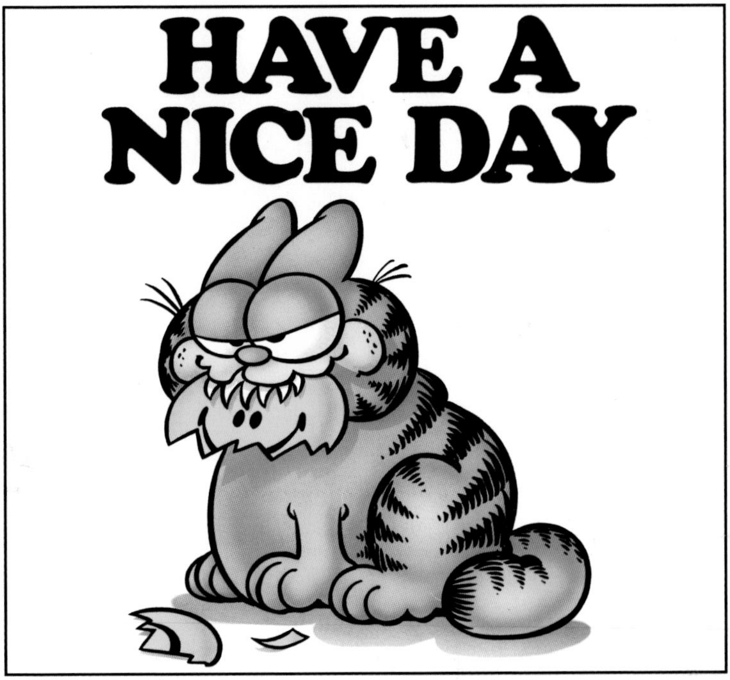
HAVE A
NICE DAY

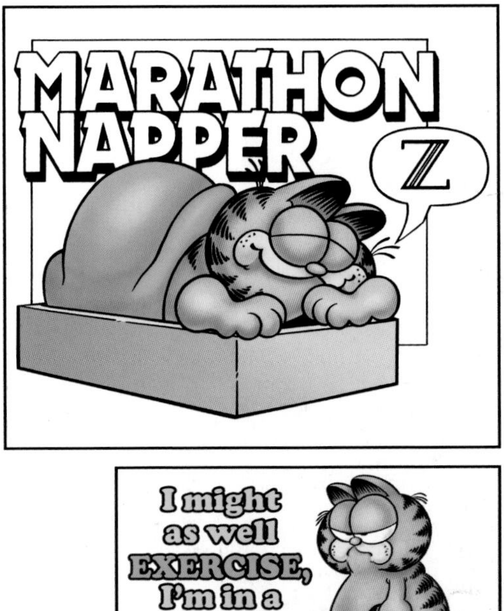
MARATHON
NAPPER
Z

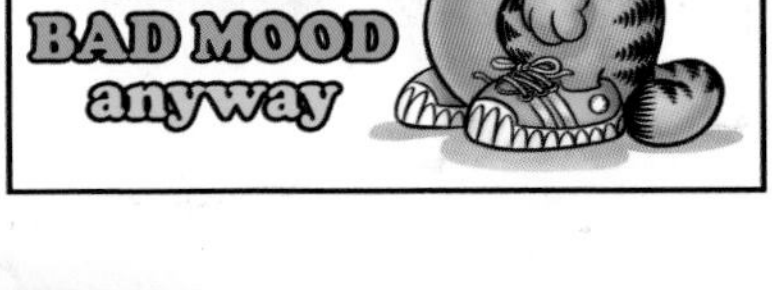
I might
as well
EXERCISE,
I'm in a
BAD MOOD
anyway

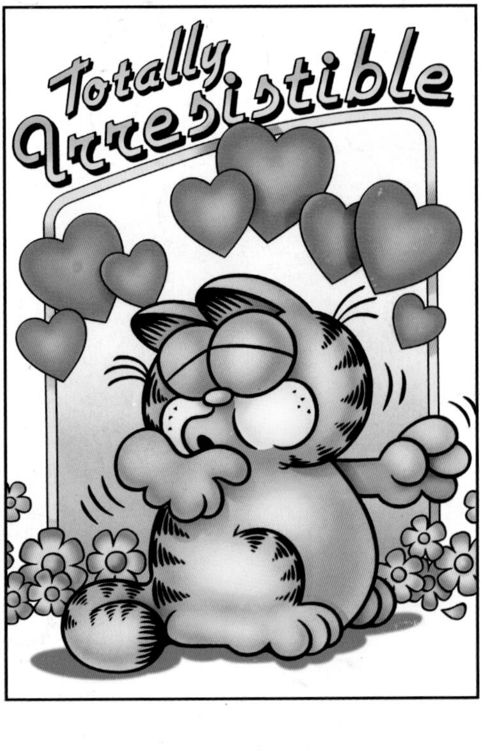
Totally
Irresistible

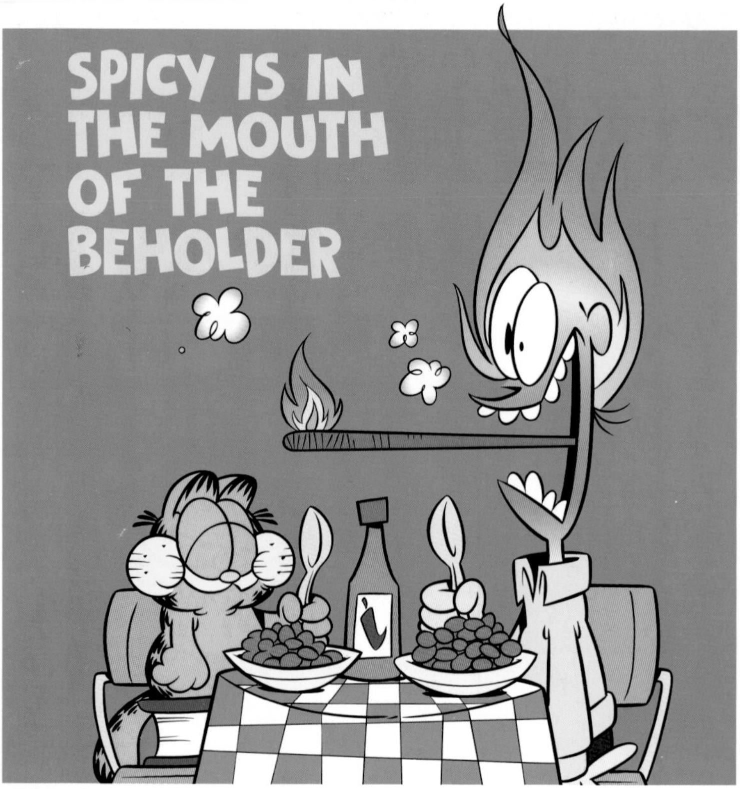
SPICY IS IN THE MOUTH OF THE BEHOLDER

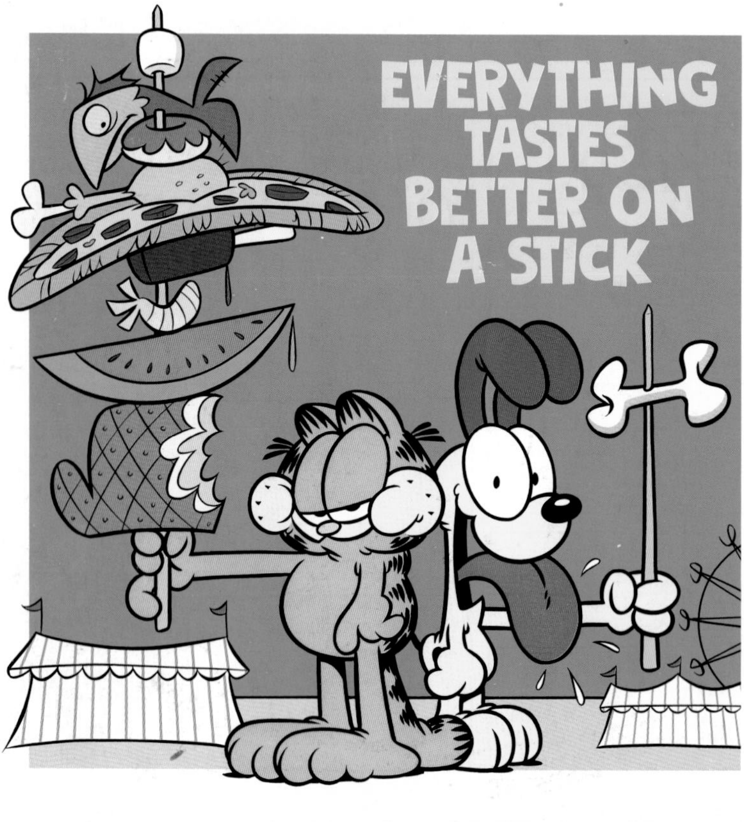
EVERYTHING TASTES BETTER ON A STICK

Writer: Mark Acey

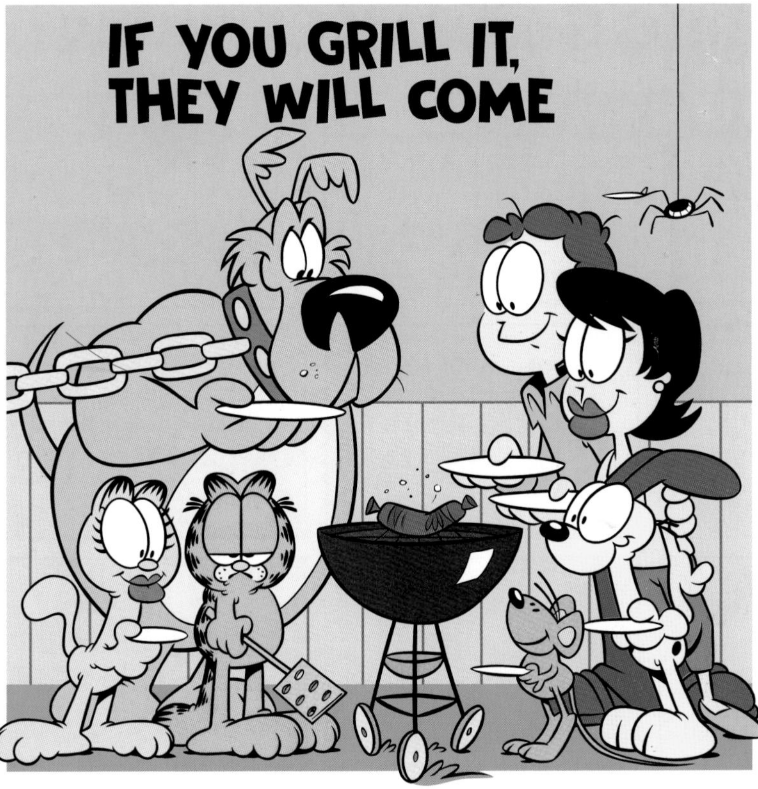
IF YOU GRILL IT, THEY WILL COME

Writer: Mark Acey

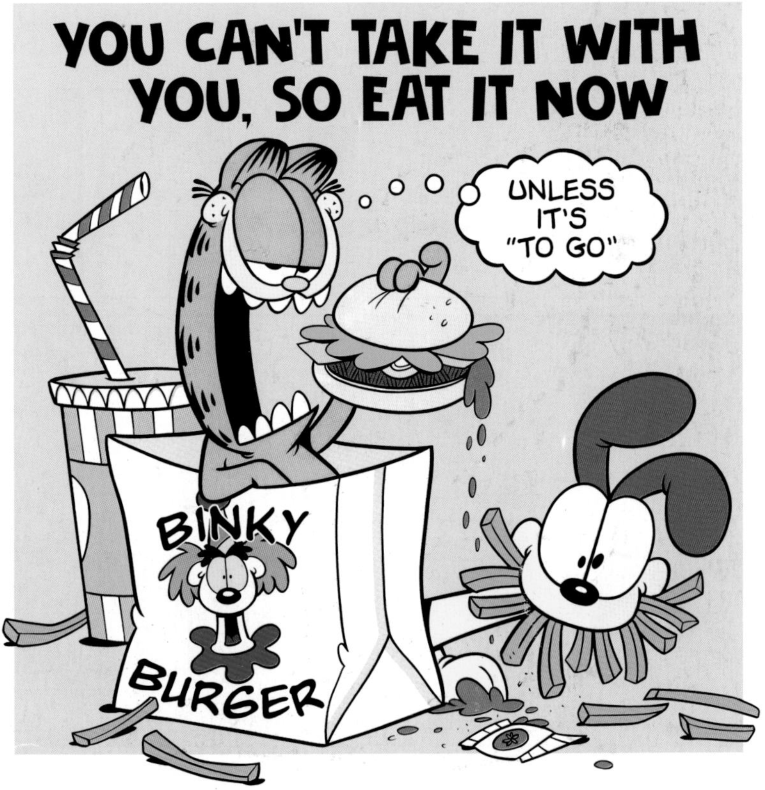
YOU CAN'T TAKE IT WITH YOU, SO EAT IT NOW
UNLESS IT'S "TO GO"
BINKY BURGER

Garfield Sunday Classics

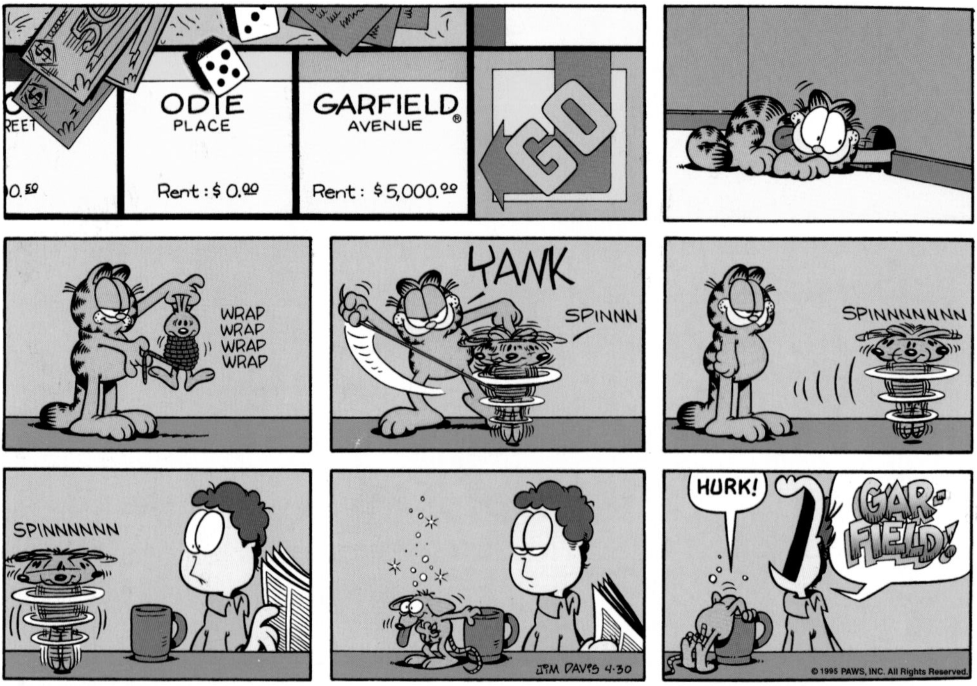
ODIE
PLACE
Rent : $ 0.00
GARFIELD
AVENUE
Rent : $ 5,000.00
GO
WRAP
WRAP
WRAP
WRAP
YANK
SPINNN
SPINNNNNNNN
SPINNNNNNN
HURK!
GAR-FIELD!
JIM DAVIS 4-30
© 1995 PAWS, INC. All Rights Reserved.

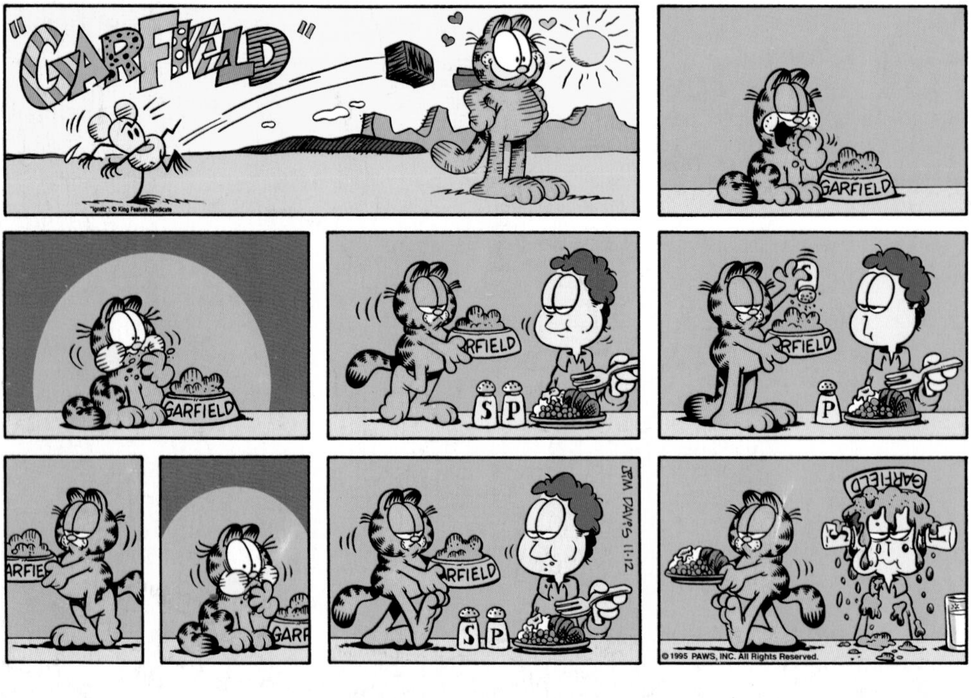
"GARFIELD"
"Ignatz": © King Feature Syndicate
GARFIELD
GARFIELD
RFIELD
S
P
RFIELD
S
P
ARFIE
GARF
JIM DAVIS 11-12
RFIELD
S
P
GARFIELD
© 1995 PAWS, INC. All Rights Reserved.

DISCOVER
EXPLOSIVE NEW WORLDS

ADVENTURE TIME

The AMAZING WORLD OF
GUMBALL

STEVEN UNIVERSE
VOLUME ONE

OVER THE GARDEN WALL

Garfield
BY JIM DAVIS

Charles M. Schulz
PEANUTS

kaboom!

AVAILABLE AT YOUR LOCAL COMICS SHOP AND BOOKSTORE

To find a comics shop in your area, call 1-888-266-4226

WWW.**BOOM-STUDIOS**.COM

Adventure Time
Pendleton Ward and Others

Volume 1
ISBN: 978-1-60886-280-1 | $9.99

Volume 2
ISBN: 978-1-60886-323-5 | $14.99 US

Adventure Time: Islands
ISBN: 978-1-60886-972-5 | $9.99

Regular Show
J.G. Quintel and Others

Volume 1
ISBN: 978-1-60886-362-4 | $14.99

Volume 2
ISBN: 978-1-60886-426-3 | $14.99

Regular Show: Hydration
ISBN: 978-1-60886-339-6 | $12.99

The Amazing World of Gumball
Ben Bocquelet and Others

Volume 1
ISBN: 978-1-60886-488-1 | $14.99

Volume 2
ISBN: 978-1-60886-793-6 | $14.99

Over the Garden Wall
Patrick McHale, Jim Campbell and Others

Volume 1
ISBN: 978-1-60886-940-4 | $14.99

Volume 2
ISBN: 978-1-68415-006-9 | $14.99

Steven Universe
Rebecca Sugar and Others

Volume 1
ISBN: 978-1-60886-706-6 | $14.99

Volume 2
ISBN: 978-1-60886-796-7 | $14.99

Steven Universe & The Crystal Gems
ISBN: 978-1-60886-921-3 | $14.99

Steven Universe: Too Cool for School
ISBN: 978-1-60886-771-4 | $14.99

Peanuts
Charles Schultz and Others

Volume 1
ISBN: 978-1-60886-260-3 | $13.99

Garfield
Jim Davis and Others

Volume 1
ISBN: 978-1-60886-287-0 | $13.99

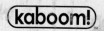